$1

D0933550

FitSkiing

FitSkiing

YOUR GUIDE FOR PEAK SKIING FITNESS

ANDREW HOOGE
CERTIFIED STRENGTH AND CONDITIONING SPECIALIST

Connecting the World with Health and Fitness

Active Media titles may be purchased for business and promotional use or for special sales. For information, please write to:
Active Media, LLC.,
PO Box 1302, Crested Butte, CO 81224.

Visit our web site at www.actvmedia.com

Library of Congress Cataloging-in-Publication Data

Hooge, Andrew, 1973-
FitSkiing®: Your Guide for Peak Skiing Fitness
By Andrew Hooge-1st ed.

ISBN 0-9745138-0-6

1. Skiing 2. Exercise 3. Physical Fitness I. Title

Library of Congress Control Number: 2003111421

Printed in the United States of America

10 9 8 7 6 5 4 3 2 1

First Edition

Photographs by Tom Stillo
Illustrations by Peter Stallard

"ENDEAVOR TO PERSEVERE"

-LITTLE BIG MAN

"WE ARE SO OFTEN CAUGHT UP IN OUR DESTINATION THAT WE FORGET TO APPRECIATE THE JOURNEY, ESPECIALLY THE GOODNESS OF THE PEOPLE WE MEET ON THE WAY. APPRECIATION IS A WONDERFUL FEELING; DON'T OVERLOOK IT"

-ANONYMOUS

ACKNOWLEDGEMENTS

I would like to thank all of the individuals who helped produce this book. Thank you to Tom Stillo and Peter Stallard for their contributions to the visual images that have assisted in bringing life to this book. I would like to thank *The Gym* in Crested Butte for allowing us to shoot many of the exercises in their facility.

Thank you to my friends who have encouraged me over the years to pursue my true passion, writing. I would also like to thank Michelle and Kasha for performing many of the exercises throughout the book.

Finally, I would like to thank my parents, for their incredible support and help through the production of this book. Thank you both for being such wonderful parents, and for always encouraging me to pursue my dreams.

A WORD OF CAUTION

The FitSkiing® Program is intended for healthy adults age 18 and over. This book is only for informational and educational purposes and is not medical advice. Please consult a doctor or health care professional before you begin any new exercise, nutrition, or supplementation program or if you have questions regarding your health. The individuals featured in this book are professionals and have had years of training experience. As individuals differ, their results will also, even when using the same program.

Many people ski themselves into shape when the season begins, and can barely make it down the mountain without gasping for air. Others risk injury, while many wander aimlessly wondering what exercises will get them in better shape when they hit the snow. FitSkiing® has taken the guess work out of your ski conditioning program.

This book was written because there is a lack of comprehensive strength and conditioning resources for skiers. Some magazines have produced helpful articles on getting into shape for skiing, however skiers lack one solid conditioning resource for their time off the slopes.

CONTENTS

CONTENTS

INTRODUCTION

Would you like to improve your skiing without ever setting foot on the slopes? Do you dream of looking good in the latest ski fashions? Wouldn't it be nice to ski the mountain from top to bottom without gasping for air?

If that sounds inviting, then this book is required reading. The strength and conditioning program outlined here will show you how to radically improve your skiing during the off season as well as when you are on the slopes.

What is strength and conditioning? It incorporates aerobic (with oxygen) and anaerobic (without oxygen) training to improve overall body strength, balance, and endurance. Aerobic activities include running longer distances, cycling, and even fast walking. Lifting weights is a good example of an anaerobic activity. Skiing is a sport that incorporates anaerobic and aerobic components.

FitSkiing will teach you how to get in shape before your skis ever touch the snow. You might find that you fit into clothes you haven't tried on in years. *FitSkiing* is the first book to truly focus on the strength and conditioning aspects of training for skiers.

I've been on skis since I was old enough to walk. My dad began skiing backwards while holding me up at a local ski area in Ohio. My coordination has never been anything to brag about. It took me 2 years before I could stand on my own two skis. Nothing pertaining to exercise or sport has come easy for me. That is one of the major factors that contributed to my interest in exercise.

For the past decade I've devoted my time to studying the science of exercise. From my earliest years lifting weights to studying human movement and physiology in college, I've been investigating how people react uniquely to exercise. Although I've worked with athletes ranging from football players to triathletes, my passion has always been with skiing. The FitSkiing program will take you to the peak of your skiing abilities and beyond.

Before you dive into this program, here are some tips to make the FitSkiing program work for you.

- **Determine your level of fitness.** This is important, because you will need to know where to start your conditioning program. It is also vital because it might help you prevent future injuries. The FitSkiing fitness scale ranges from 1 to 5. 1 being sedentary and 5 being that of an individual who exercises regularly and intensely. *FitSkiing* will assist you in determining your fitness level later in this book.
- **Figure out your daily schedule.** Do you have time to spend an hour a day at the gym? Is most of your time spent outside your home? Or do you work from home? Whether you are a corporate vice president or a stay-at-home mom or dad, FitSkiing can assist you in scheduling your workout to fit your day and lifestyle.
- **Set goals.** Write your goals and post them where you can see them every day. Maybe you simply want to look good in your ski outfit. Although that is not the primary goal of this book, it will help get you there. Maybe you are turning 50 this year and you want to ski the entire mountain. Whatever your goals are write them down and read them everyday. FitSkiing will help you achieve them.
- **Track your eating habits.** By figuring out what you eat now, you will be better prepared to figure out the nutrition plan that is best for you. Do you eat one meal a day? Are you starving yourself to lose weight? Or do you adhere to the current trend of six meals a day, all of it protein and fat? Whatever your eating habits are, FitSkiing will help you determine what to eat to lose body fat, gain muscle and, provide ample energy for a day on the slopes.
- **Above all else, remember to have fun.**

Although some of the changes you make might be a challenge, you should enjoy yourself. Remember that the results you feel when you are skiing and in everyday life will make those challenges worth it.

As a certified strength and conditioning coach, I am responsible for getting elite athletes in the best condition possible. My mission is now to empower everyone to become the athlete of his or her dreams. I have discovered that FitSkiing benefits elite athletes as well as the weekend warrior or the individual who simply wants to feel and look good. I want to be your personal coach, to guide you through a ski-conditioning program that will get you in to the best shape of your life on and off the mountain. As a result, you're going to ski better and be more fit than you've ever dreamed possible.

"LIVE YOUR LIFE EACH DAY AS YOU WOULD CLIMB A MOUNTAIN. AN OCCASIONAL GLANCE TOWARDS THE SUMMIT KEEPS THE GOAL IN MIND, BUT MANY BEAUTIFUL SCENES ARE TO BE OBSERVED FROM EACH NEW VANTAGE POINT."

-HAROLD B. MELCHART

CHAPTER ONE

DEFINING FITSKIING

What Is FitSkiing?

You are about to embark on a fitness journey that will take you to a new level of skiing. FitSkiing is a 12-week strength and conditioning program that will enable you to obtain almost any fitness goal. The following is a list of things you will accomplish over the next 12 weeks and beyond.

- Determining your baseline fitness level.
- Defining your skiing goals and reaching them.
- Proper preparation for the ski season.
- What to feed your body before and after a day on the slopes.
- What and when to eat to provide the most efficient fat loss and strength gain.
- Understanding how to workout for your fitness level and goals.
- Preparing your children properly for the snow if you have them.
- Prevention and rehabilitation of sports injuries.
- Developing your own FitSkiing gym.
- Getting in to the best shape of your life in only 12 weeks.

For years I have been looking for a good resource on ski conditioning. Most of the information I have found about ski conditioning is either outdated or it is a single article in a magazine. Many of my clients have asked me for good books on getting in shape for the ski season, but I simply haven't found one I can recommend. That is how the book *FitSkiing* was born. I wanted to give people a comprehensive guide on how to prepare for skiing.

What Makes *FitSkiing* Different From Other How-To-Ski Books?

FitSkiing sets itself apart by being the only book devoted solely to the strength and conditioning of skiers. It incorporates close to 70 exercises that are ski specific. Most of the skiing books that are published today explain how to turn the ski, how to ski steeps, or how to become an expert skier. Unfortunately, one fundamental aspect of skiing is missing from many of these books: the strength and conditioning level required to be able to turn the ski. It is easier for Olympic racers such as Picabo Street to maneuver the ski and also to recover when she gets in trouble. This would not be possible were it not for her tireless effort in the gym. Racers like Herman Meier (The Hermenator) are known for their strength and power, as well as their signature leg development. You might not have aspirations of achieving this level of conditioning, but being stronger and more balanced off the slopes results in being a better skier on the slopes.

How Much Does FitSkiing Cost?

With the popularity of fit balls (those large, round beach balls that look more like toys than fitness equipment), medicine balls, and other strength and balancing tools, the average person now can develop his or her home gym for less than $250. One of the best pieces of equipment for skiers to date is something called the Bosu Ball (see Chapter 11). This modified fit ball enables you to gain strength and endurance in your muscles and increase your proprioception and balance. *Proprioception* is a fancy word that basically means "one's awareness of space". An example of proprioception in use is walking down a set of stairs in the middle of the night. You might not see the next stair, but somehow your foot finds it. If you missed the step, your proprioceptive abilities would help you keep your balance. Similarly, proprioception becomes important when you catch an edge or lose your balance. FitSkiing works on this area to promote more stability while skiing. Do you think you have good proprioceptive abilities? Try standing on one foot with your eyes closed and balancing. Can you do it? If you can, try squatting down on one leg. If you can't, or even if you can, after 12 weeks of the FitSkiing program, your body will be able to respond automatically to an unbalanced situation.

Although $250 will sound like very little to some, and a lot to others, whatever your income the FitSkiing program can accommodate anyone. In Chapter 11 you will learn how to set up your own gym for as little as $100 or as much as $7,000. For those who do not have access to a gym, and are a little short on cash, FitSkiing also incorporates outdoor alternatives.

That is the beauty of the FitSkiing program. It works for everyone. Young, old, rich, or not so rich, this book has a plan to get you in shape and keep you injury free. If the illustrations and pictures in this book don't seem to be enough, then log onto www.fitskiing.com and view the FitSkiing workout. At the Web site exercises incorporated in the book are demonstrated (December 2003). You can also get the FitSkiing training log (available in December 2003). It incorporates many of the strength training exercises, but you also will get a handy training tool to track your progress. This is the most complete conditioning resource for any skier.

"OUR GOALS CAN ONLY BE REACHED THROUGH A VEHICLE OF A PLAN. IN WHICH WE MUST FERVENTLY BELIEVE, AND UPON WHICH WE MUST VIGOROUSLY ACT. THERE IS NO OTHER ROUTE TO SUCCESS."

-STEPHEN A. BRENNAN

CHAPTER TWO

DETERMINING YOUR FITNESS LEVEL

One of the most common questions I receive regarding fitness programs is "Where do I start?" The answer isn't always easy. Everyone is different. Many of you may have played sports when you were young. Studies have shown that those who are introduced to sports at a young age develop better coordination and athletic abilities as adults. I was lucky to have had parents who encouraged me to get involved with many different types of sports. I also consider myself privileged to have a father who spent countless hours teaching me how to hit or kick a ball, as well as having the patience to not get frustrated when it took hours to teach me.

I was not a gifted athlete. My brother is the type of person who can simply watch somebody perform and then miraculously imitate that performance. This made the transition from local ski racer on the icy hills of Ohio to becoming a top ski racer relatively easy. I always have appreciated watching the best athletes perform. Those who have the talent and the determination to train harder than anyone else. The benefit that many of these athletes have is that they, like my brother, were born with a gift that most of us can only dream about. So when someone asks me where to start with a conditioning program my answer is always the same. As with anything, we must look at history to help us decide the future.

How long have you been training? How intensely do you train? How many hours each week do you devote to your workouts? Have you trained with weights before? These are common questions that you should ask yourself. The FitSkiing program starts here: how to determine your fitness level.

Determining your baseline fitness level can be difficult; however, FitSkiing has taken the long hours of guesswork out of it for you. Four major components define your baseline fitness level: duration, intensity, frequency and experience. Here is a brief description of each and an explanation of how they will help you figure out your baseline fitness level

Frequency: How often you train
Duration: How long you train
Intensity: How hard you train
Experience: Number of months or years you have trained in a gym related environment

The FitSkiing fitness scale ranges from 1 to 5. Next you will find a simple description of how to rate your FitSkiing baseline fitness level.

1 to 1.5
Frequency: Less than 2 days/week
Duration: Less than 15 minutes/session
Intensity: Little work with weights or sporadic aerobic activity
Experience: Little to none

2 to 2.5
Frequency: 3 days/week
Duration: 15- to 30 minutes/session
Intensity: Light weights/Moderate reps/session; easy breathing during aerobic work
Experience: Less than 6 months

3 to 3.5
Frequency: 4 days/week

Duration: 30 to 45 minutes/session
Intensity: Moderate weights/Moderate repetitions/Breathing during aerobic activity becomes more difficult
Experience: 6 months to 1 year

4 to 4.5
Frequency: 5 days/week
Duration: 45 minutes to 1 hour/session
Intensity: Moderate to heavy weights and low repetitions/Difficult to maintain conversation while performing aerobic work
Experience: 1 to 2 years
5.0
Frequency: 5+ days/week
Duration: 1 hour +/session
Intensity: Heavy weight and moderate repetitions/Can not speak while performing aerobic activity (sprinting at maximal effort)
Experience: 2 years +

If your like me, you probably want more specific information before you calculate your baseline FitSkiing fitness level. If you scored a 1 it means you've basically been a couch potato for the last 6 months to a year. A 2 is defined by a low level of workout frequency as well as duration and intensity. As stated earlier, frequency refers to the number of days per week that you train. Duration concerns itself with the amount of time you spend during each training session. Intensity is defined as how hard you are working. Experience simply means the number of months or years you have been frequenting the gym. Each one of these components is key to figuring out where to start and your baseline fitness level.

Frequency

Let's start with frequency. If you work out fewer than 2 days per week, you would be considered a 1 on the FitSkiing fitness scale. Working out 2 to 3 days per week would give you a 2; 3 to 4 days per week, a 3 and 4 to 5 days a week a 4. Five days of training per week or more would be considered a 5.

Duration

Next, figure out your duration. Remember, duration is the amount of time each workout consumes. Anything less than 15 minutes is considered a 1. Fifteen minutes to 30 minutes is a 2, 30 to 45 minutes a 3, 45 minutes to 1 hour a 4, and anything over 1 hour is a 5.

Intensity

Finally, you need to figure out your intensity. Intensity is the hardest to define. One person might consider his or her intensity a 5 and someone else doing the exact same workout might consider it only a 2. If you are able to talk comfortably while walking or running, then you should give yourself a 2. Similarly, if you take long rest periods between sets and use light weight when you are resistance training give yourself a 2. Only give yourself a 1 if you do not workout at all. If you are breathing harder but can still talk to your training partner when doing aerobic activity, give yourself a 3. If you take less than 2 minutes between sets during weight training and train with moderate weights, give yourself a 3. A 4 is given if you are breathing hard yet can still maintain a conversation with some effort. If you are using moderate to heavy weights and take a minute between sets, you also score a 4. If your aerobic activity consists of vigorous training such as spinning where you don't even want to think about talking, give yourself a five. With regards to weight training a 5 is given if you train with heavy weights (5 to 8 repetitions) and rest periods last no longer than 1 minute. I score someone a 5 only on rare occasions. Olympic athletes, professional football players, elite triathletes, etc.. What if you only lift weights or if you only perform aerobic activity? If you only resistance train, subtract 1 point. Similarly, if you only run or bike and don't involve weights in your training, take 1 point away. Both are important in preparing for the slopes.

Experience

Does experience count for anything? Of course, it does. You can be a novice at training and still score a 4 on any of the scales however, that does not necessarily mean you are ready for an advanced workout. The more you train the more adaptive your neuromuscular system becomes. The longer you work out the more efficiently your body works. You will find that it is easier to learn new exercises, or you might find that your strength and balance improve more rapidly. If you have been training for less than 6 months give yourself a 2. If you don't currently have a training program, then you have a lot to look forward to. However, you should only score yourself a 1. If you have trained for 6 months to a year, give yourself a 3, 1 to 2 years a 4 and 2 or more years a 5. Remember, this means consistent training. If you trained for 2 months and then took 2 months off, that does not count. To score yourself properly, base it on the number of years you have consistently trained.

How can you use this information to figure out your baseline fitness level? Next, you will find a simple, step-by-step method of figuring out where you belong.

1. Figure out your score from the frequency scale.
2. Figure out your score from the duration scale.
3. Add your aerobic intensity score and weight training intensity score together.
4. Divide by 2; that is your intensity score.
5. Subtract a point if you don't weight train.
6. Subtract a point if you don't perform aerobic activity.
7. Figure out your score from the experience scale.
8. Add your scores and divide by 4
9. Your answer is your FitSkiing baseline fitness level.

Let's figure out my baseline fitness level as an example. If I go a day without doing some sort of activity, I turn into Mr. Hyde. A typical week consists of 6 to 7 workout days. I score a 5. As far as duration goes, my typical workout consists of 40 to 50 minutes of weights and 20 to 30 minutes of jogging, Nordic skiing, etc.. I would give myself a 5 for duration. As far as intensity goes, I consider myself intense when I work out however, according to the scale, I would only score a 3. Why? Although I score a 4 for weight training intensity, I only scored a 2 for aerobic intensity. I have work to do, too. Finally, I give myself a 5 for experience. I have been working out for more than 10 years consistently. Of course it is my job, so that makes it a little easier.

Let's take a look at my fitness-scoring breakdown.

Frequency: 5
Duration: 5
Intensity: 3
Experience: 5
Total: 18
Fitness Score: 184 = 4.5

What does that mean? Your baseline fitness score will help you decide which FitSkiing program is right for you. Should you start with the General Conditioning program? Maybe the Basic FitSkiing workout is for you. Or maybe you are up for the Advanced FitSkiing challenge. The great thing about this program is that it is progressive over 12 weeks. You can add some of the advanced exercises to the basic program or vice versa. Always remember to train smart though. Which FitSkiing program do you fall into? Next is a simple list to help you decide.

Score 1 to 1.5: You have been sedentary and need a good conditioning program to get you ready for FitSkiing. Start with the General Conditioning program and then move to the Basic Program.

Score 2 to 3: You work out regularly but need a little fine-tuning. FitSkiing's Basic program is the perfect way to get in shape for skiing the terrain you've always dreamed about.

Score 3.5 to 4.5: You are well accustomed to weights and taxing your aerobic system. Try the FitSkiing Advanced program. If you find it is a little too difficult, start with the Basic program for a month and then progress to the Advanced program.

Score 5: Do you really need this book? Of course, you do. The FitSkiing Advanced program can give you new ideas and a workout plan that will enable you to ski Mount Everest.

There you have it. Figure out your baseline fitness level and determine which program is right for you. Now move on to the next chapter We have work to do.

CHAPTER THREE

DEFINING YOUR GOALS

It wasn't long ago that I graduated from college, and began training people. I learned that the biggest roadblock for many of my clients in reaching their goals was not a lack of knowledge, nor was it a lack of motivation. Most of my clients were motivated to lose weight, get stronger, and improve their health. Many of them also came to me with a vast array of information on fitness. Some of them had worked with numerous trainers, and for others I was their first. I found my job was devoted to about 25 percent assessment, 25 percent program design, and 50 percent motivation. Much of what I learned in college did not prepare me to help my clients with motivation. I gained some experience in sports psychology while working with athletes; however, those individuals are already rather motivated to succeed. It wasn't until I trained one of my first clients that I understood how to motivate people other than athletes to reach their goals. My client was a recreational skier who wanted to improve not only his skiing, but more importantly his health. He came to me and explained his goals. It occurred to me that something that requires little common sense could make a huge impact on one's results. Goals!

"I want to improve my skiing."

"I need to lose some weight."

"I want to have more time to myself."

"I want to ski Everest" (I don't hear this one too often; however, these are all things many of you might think about).

I began having my clients break down their goals into segments. I would tell them to pick one thing and focus on it. Some of you might be multitaskers, but I still recommend starting with only one goal at a time. Let's use my client as an example. His goal was to "get healthy and lose some weight." I asked him to go home and break down his statement into smaller, more specific goals. The next day, he faxed them to me. This is what he wrote:

Lose 35 *pounds.*
Get off a blood pressure medication.
Ski a mountain non-stop.
Take more time for myself.

After reviewing his goals, I sat down with him and discussed how he would attain them. Although his goals were now more specific, they were still too general. "Lose 35 pounds of body fat", would have been better, and "devoting an hour per day to myself" is a little more specific and easier to understand.

Our brain works in groups of seven to ten. For example, it is not nearly as difficult to remember a seven-digit phone number as it is to remember a 20-digit serial number. That is how I approach setting goals and getting people to meet them; I break them down into smaller, more easily attainable goals.

Remember, that earlier in this chapter I said to focus on one goal at a time. My client had four goals. It is not impossible to focus on all of them, but I suggested that we start with one goal and focus on it for 3 months until it became a pattern. Studies have shown that patterns can form in as little as 2 weeks, but my personal experience has been that it takes at least 1 month and normally 2 or 3. My client started with losing 35 pounds of body fat. First, we had to find a baseline. Just as you rated your FitSkiing baseline fitness level in the last chapter, my client and I rated his. One of the most important assessments was weight and body fat. His beginning body fat was 35 percent at a weight of 200 pounds. After doing the calculations, I figured he had about 70 pounds of body fat. To get rid of half of that, we needed a plan. The great thing about FitSkiing is that I have designed the plan for you. However, setting your own personal goals will assist you in staying on track and keeping motivated. I like to break goals down into five segments. Although our brain works well in chunks of seven, I have found that blocks of five work better. The following is a list that will help you attain your goals.

The FitSkiing Five

1. Creating a Well-Formed Goal Statement

A goal statement forms your entire process so make sure it is clear and accurate. I utilize the S M A R T. acronym used by many experts in goal setting. It represents:

Specific
Measurable
Action Oriented
Realistic
Time and Resources Constrained

The goal should be **specific** enough that you know exactly what you are striving for, **measurable** so you can tell exactly when the goal has been reached, **action oriented** to indicate an activity that will produce results, **realistic** as in practical and achievable and **time and resources constrained** meaning it has a definite deadline for completion and realizes limited availability of resources. The goal statement "I will be able to ski Vail from top to bottom without stopping yet not sacrifice injury or exhaustion" is an example that follows these rules. The question is How do you accomplish this?

2. Breaking Down Goals Into Manageable Steps

Once you have a well-formed goal statement, you need some direction to follow to achieve this goal. The creation of goal steps will give you a list of the important things that need to be done to achieve the goal; an action plan; and also allows you to track your progress toward the goal. Although the goal "I will be able to ski Vail from top to bottom without stopping yet not sacrifice injury or exhaustion" is a good goal statement, it is a huge task that needs to be broken down into smaller, detailed steps.

3. Motivation and Commitment

Motivation and commitment are what make you strive to achieve. They give you the push, desire, and resolve to complete all of the other steps in the goal process. This motivation can be obtained by developing a statement that creates a high level of emotion and energy which guarantees achievement. Commitment is what sets us on a direct course to reach our goals.

4. Reminders and Keeping on Track

Reaching your goals requires persistence and regular attention; you need some sort of system to keep you focused and accountable. Some people might use a trainer or coach and others use a simple Palm Pilot that beeps to remind them to train or eat. It might sound pathetic, but many of us are so busy that we need someone or something to keep us on track. If some accountability system is not used then we are likely to lose sight and fail.

5. Frequent Review and Reassessment

Goal setting is definitely an ongoing process that is accomplished over time. When you first sit down and start to define goals, it can seem like a difficult and daunting task, but over time it begins to get easier. Patience is required. All goals due in the next year should be reviewed at least once a week and daily if possible. The great thing about frequent review is that it forces you to make big decisions and determine priorities in your life. You should watch for goals that aren't being achieved on time.

Let's take a look at my client and apply the FitSkiing Five to his goal of losing 35 pounds of body fat. The following is a breakdown of how he will accomplish his goals.

1. Creating a Well-Formed Goal Statement

"I will lose 35 pounds of body fat in the next year, without sacrificing time with my family and friends." This is a healthy goal statement. My client has successfully used the SMART program. His goal is specific (lose 35 pounds of body fat). It is measurable (over the next year). The goal is action oriented (I will lose 35 pounds of body fat). It is realistic (35 pounds of body fat is ambitious but can still be accomplished in 1 year with hard work and dedication). Finally, his goal statement is time and resource constrained (in the next year without sacrificing my time with family and friends).

2. Breaking Down Goals Into Manageable Steps

Let's take apart my clients goal.

- Lose 35 pounds of fat
- 1 year
- Without sacrificing time with family and friends

Just as I broke down each section for my client, I also have broken down your program, assuming that your goal is to get in shape by the ski season.

Basically, I broke my client's goal down like this:

- 35 pounds of body fat/12 months = 3 pounds per month.
- Months 1 to 3: Lose 15 pounds of body fat and gain 5 pounds of muscle. Ambitious, but remember to always set your goals high. That way you can always be assured of working hard to reach them. I set up a fitness program for my client to follow. Three days a week my client was to meet with me and he was to train 3 days a week on his own. I also included a nutrition program for him to follow.
- Months 4 to 6: Lose 12 pounds of body fat and gain 3 pounds of muscle mass.

Notice how the goals have changed a little. This is because the body does not respond as quickly after about the first 3 months or so. I changed my client's routine a little as I have changed the FitSkiing program every so often, as well. This helps the body (namely the neuromuscular system) stay fresh so the results remain constant.

3. Motivation and Commitment

My client maintained his motivation and commitment by doing a number of things.

- Seeing results was probably one of the most important factors in my client's success. By keeping a record of body fat lost and muscle mass gained, my client saw results and was motivated to train even harder. He also saw his blood pressure reduced, which kept him committed to the program.
- Positive reinforcement from family and peers also helped with motivation. Make sure you surround yourself with individuals who compliment you when you attain results. Negative reinforcement has its place, but for most goals to be reached, positive reinforcement works

much better.

- Having someone to guide my client also created motivation. Many times you have other issues in your life that are frustrating. Having a trainer or training partner can provide an external motivation on days when you don't feel like pushing quite as hard.

4. Reminders and Keeping on Track:

Reminders can take any number of forms. Sticky notes, your Palm Pilot/ organizer, or a trainer can give you reminders of when to train, eat, and so on. Reading your goals first thing in the morning and before bed-time also embeds them in your subconscious. The following are some of the things that assisted my client in keeping on track.

•Reviewing his daily, weekly, and monthly goals first thing in the morning and before bed-time

•Setting his cell phone to beep at him when it was time to eat. This might sound a little extreme but it worked.

•Consistently asking me questions regarding why we were doing a certain exercise or why I had him eating a specific food. This created a thought process that reminded him to eat certain foods as opposed to others because he knew why he was consuming them. It also reminded him of which exercises to do when we were not working together.

5. Frequent Review and Reassessment:

Were we reaching my client's short-term and long-term goals? Did my client still have time to spend with family and friends? These are some of the questions my client and I addressed each month. I suggest you do the same.

•At the end of each month, my client filled out a questionnaire about how he felt his progress was going in all areas of the goal.

•Some months my client would exceed his goals; other months he would be a little behind. As long as you stay focused and motivated, you eventually will reach your goal.

•My client met his goal. It did take an extra few months, but he accomplished it. many times, we sat down together to reassess the program. What was working? What wasn't working? It was helpful for both of us to keep a training log listing weight, sets/reps, what was eaten that day, and my client's overall mood. Based on this information we could figure out where we were in relation to his goals and how to progress.

Follow the FitSkiing Five and you will have a clear path for reaching your goals. Next is a list of tools I have found useful for clients and me over the years. Pick and choose the ones that will assist you the most.

Trainer: I am a little biased on this issue. Trainers can motivate you and provide you with a program to work from. For me, designing a Web site was somewhat overwhelming. Designing a fitness program can be the same for many of you. I hired a professional to design my Web site; you should think about doing the same for your fitness program.

Be aware, however, that not all trainers are the same. As in any profession, there are good trainers and bad trainers. In Chapter 11, I will briefly discuss how to choose a trainer.
Price: $30 to $150/hour

PDA (Personal Digital Assistant): A PDA is useful for keeping track of your workouts, goals and so on. I have found mine helpful in tracking my workouts, accomplishments, and everything in between.
Price: $100 to $500

Training and Nutrition Software: At the end of this book, I have given you some workout and nutrition logs, which will help you continue moving forward. However, a company called Healthetech has a great software program that you can download onto your Palm. It will give you a way to track your meals and workouts, and it also gives you caloric goals. It has worked wonderfully for many of my clients, most of whom say it is easy to use. The Web site is www.healthetech.com.
Price: $50 to $150 depending on software

A Reliable Training Partner: This might sound kind of silly, but a good training partner can help push you to your goals. You can motivate each other and help one another make it through the training session. When someone is counting on us, we are more likely to accomplish goals.
Price: Free

CHAPTER FOUR

FITSKIING FACTS AND FICTION

Many of you might be wondering why this chapter is included in FitSkiing. Over the years, a great deal of confusion has developed regarding what to do to get into shape for skiing and to attain general fitness, as well. Some information says to do three sets of moderate weight and moderate reps. Others say to do one set of maximal weight. With the battery of options out there, what to eat becomes even more confusing. To top it off, we are bombarded by misleading infomercials that claim their machine will get you into the best shape of your life in a short period of time. No magic pills exist for getting into shape for skiing.

Conditioning for skiing is similar in many ways to training for anything else; however, it is also different. Don't let yourself fall into the trap of the following myths. The FitSkiing program might not work overnight, but in the long run you will gain more strength and endurance, and you'll be in better health.

Fiction

Skiing yourself into shape is the best way to prepare for the ski season.

Remember when you were in high school and waited too long to read Shakespeare? Did you go to the local bookstore and purchase the Cliff Notes to help you with the essay portion of the final exam? Unless you had a lenient professor or were good at pulling the wool over the instructor's eyes then you probably ended up with a C at best. Skiing yourself into shape is similar to reading Cliff Notes to prepare for an exam; just like getting a mediocre grade on your essay, you also might end up in mediocre condition for the first part of the season. More importantly, you also risk injury.

Fact

Preparing for 3 months before the season with weights and aerobic intervals will condition the body properly for skiing.

Just as reading the actual book results in an improved grade, your performance on skis will improve if you prepare for the slopes early. By incorporating weight training, aerobic conditioning, and interval training (short bursts of maximal effort followed by longer bursts of less intense work) into your preseason skiing regime you will enjoy significantly improved strength and stamina when your skis touch the snow and also lessen your risk of injury.

Fiction

Running, biking, and so on are the best ways to condition your body for the slopes.

Although running and biking are good ways of conditioning your body for skiing, they are only part of the equation. If you read only fashion magazines, chances are you will have limited knowledge of other areas like art and politics. Similarly, if you run only long distances and neglect weights and balance-related training, your body will be only partially prepared for the season.

Fact

Weight training, as well as running, biking, and other conditioning activities, creates a well-rounded skier.

By adding strength and balance training to your current aerobic training schedule your body will become more responsive to varying terrain. You also will have more stability and power when traversing the mountain.

Fiction

Women who weight train will get bulky muscles.

This has been one of the most common myths people have been drawn into for decades. Remember when ski racers were told not to lift weights because it would make them inflexible? If you take a look at any of the top racers, they train with weights because it makes them stronger and gives them more stability on the snow. Another myth was that women couldn't run the marathon because their bodies couldn't handle it. Some of the fastest runners in the world are women.

Fact

Women who lift weights build stronger, leaner bodies.

By resistance training, women increase muscle mass, which elevates levels of hormones like thyroid and growth hormone in turn increases one's metabolism. So if you want your body to be an efficient furnace, train with weights. Getting stronger also means more strength and stability on skis, so when you catch an edge or lose your balance, your body immediately picks up the slack.

Fiction

Skiing the whole day means I burned enough calories to drink a case of beer and eat a pizza.

I enjoy a good beer or glass of wine as much as the next person after a hard day of skiing; however, it is not the best way to refuel your body after a tough workout. When you ski and exert energy, your body dehydrates, leaving your cells craving fluid. By drinking alcohol and eating sodium-rich foods like pizza, you are increasing dehydration and setting yourself up for a not-so-enjoyable morning. If you are migrating from sea level to the mountains, you also increase your risk for altitude sickness and even heart attack.

Fact

By drinking plenty of water and fluid-replacement drinks like Gatorade, coupled with quality protein like chicken or fish you will recover faster from a tough day on the slopes.

In Chapter 5 on fueling your body, you will find out what to eat while conditioning before the season begins, as well as what to eat before, during and after you ski.

Fiction

A general overall bodybuilding or fitness program is the best way to get in shape for the ski season.

Although a general, cookie-cutter fitness program might be better than nothing, skiing requires a much more specific type of training. FitSkiing does incorporate some basic strength exercises like the squat, but it modifies many of the exercises to fit skier's specific training needs. For example, a typical exercise for the abdominals is the crunch, but this exercise only works the "six-pack" muscles and not efficiently (although it is included). The FitSkiing program incorporates more than 15 different core exercises to strengthen the midsection as well as the lower back and your deep pelvic-floor muscles, which help your stability when skiing.

Fact

A ski-specific conditioning program will assist you in getting in the best possible shape before the ski season begins.

By incorporating the FitSkiing program into your daily routine, you will find that you have more strength, stability, and endurance when your skis hit the snow. Single-leg bosu ball squats and medicine ball rotation with twist are just a couple of the exercises that will assist you in preparing for the slopes. In Chapter 8 you will be introduced to all the FitSkiing exercises.

Fiction

Only younger skiers should incorporate strength training into their conditioning program.

Many people believe that training with free weights can be dangerous and cause injury. Some still believe in the myth that they will lose flexibility. As we age, our hormones like testosterone, growth hormone, and estrogen decrease. Unfortunately, this leads to a loss of muscle mass and consequently metabolism slows down and strength decreases. This process can begin as early as the mid 20's for some, and can lead to increased body fat leaving you more prone to injuries.

Fact

Individuals of all ages should utilize strength training to promote a stronger, more stable body.

Recent studies have shown increases in growth hormone and testosterone when older individuals (60+) trained with weights. This led to an increase in strength and muscle as well as a decrease in body fat. By properly training with weights your strength and metabolism increase and performance on skis improves. Another added benefit of incorporating weight training into your program is increased bone density and muscle, which helps the body resist injury.

CHAPTER FIVE

SKIING FUEL

Beer, pizza, ribs and the list of après ski foods continues. These are the foods you should fuel your body with for skiing, right? If it were only that easy. In reality it is not as difficult as you might think to eat properly to prepare for the ski season.

In this chapter, you will learn how to fuel your body for strength gains and fat loss. You also will learn what to eat prior to your day on the slopes, as well as how to refuel your muscles after a long day of skiing. Imagine how good it will feel in just 12 weeks to be able to fit into the ski outfit you've always dreamed of, or how you will be able to feed your body the proper nutrients so you can have the energy you need to ski all day, every day. At the end of this chapter, you will know how to refuel your body properly so you can recover quickly and ski just as hard the next day. However, first I will briefly discuss macronutrients, commonly known as carbohydrates, proteins, and fats.

As much as we all enjoy a good rack of ribs or an ice-cold beer after a long day of work, those foods are not recommended while on the FitSkiing program. The nutrition plan outlined in this chapter is nothing new and certainly not rocket science. As a matter of fact it is probably the same thing you've heard over the last few years. The basic concept is to minimize the amount of carbohydrates you consume while at the same time properly fueling your muscles so you still have energy to train, work, and play with your children if you have them. I am not an advocate of the high-protein and extremely low-carbohydrate fad diets; however, I do believe that too many carbohydrates can lead to excess fat storage. It all depends on how your body handles sugar, or what is commonly called insulin sensitivity in the medical world. I will break down what insulin sensitivity is and how it relates to your body's ability to handle sugar a little later.

Macronutrient Breakdown

Carbohydrates

What is a carbohydrate? Carbohydrates are compounds made up of carbon, hydrogen, and oxygen. The most basic carbohydrates are simple sugars. They include table sugar, soda drinks, fruits, and juices. A common simple sugar called glucose is found in foods like fruits, honey, and some vegetables. It is also a substance, that is measured in blood and is otherwise known as blood glucose (sometimes referred to as blood sugar). As the name implies, carbohydrates are fairly simple in their chemical structure. When many of these sugars are grouped or linked together, they form a more complicated structure known as a complex carbohydrate.

Plants are made up of complex carbohydrates and are known as starches. Complex carbohydrates are found in foods like grains, vegetables, and breads. Whether you consume a lot of candy or some cereal, they are considered carbohydrates.

Understanding Sugar

When you consume a carbohydrate-rich food like oatmeal, your body increases the amount of sugar circulating in the blood. The pancreas responds by secreting a hormone called insulin, which in turn (if you have normal sugar or insulin regulation) pulls the sugar into muscles. If the muscles are already full of glycogen (the stored form of glucose), then the sugar is diverted to fat. The carbohydrates in oatmeal are released fairly slowly so the body utilizes them more efficiently. Therefore, more sugar is used for energy and less is stored as fat. On the other hand, if you eat something like cornflakes, your body will rapidly increase the amount of sugar in your blood-stream, thereby releasing large amounts of insulin, consequently converting more sugar into fat if the muscles can't utilize it. Different forms of sugar respond differently in the body. The following is a common example of utilizing the same food in different circumstances.

High Sugar Consumption Scenario 1

1. Your muscles are starving for sugar because they have been depleted from exercise.
2. You eat cornflakes immediately after your workout.
3. Your blood sugar level increases.
4. Your body responds by releasing a significant amount of insulin.
5. Because your muscles are depleted of glycogen, the insulin pulls the sugar into your muscles to help replenish energy stores.
6. Carbohydrates are utilized for mostly restoring energy.

High Sugar Consumption Scenario 2

1. It is late in the evening and you have had three solid carbohydrate-filled meals already.
2. You decide to eat a bowl of cornflakes because you are hungry.
3. Your blood sugar level increases.
4. Your body responds by releasing a significant amount of insulin.
5. Because your muscles are already full of glycogen, the sugar is diverted into fat stores, thus making you fatter.
6. Carbohydrates are not utilized efficiently.
   A better suggestion for scenario 2 would be to have some protein instead of the cornflakes. The body utilizes a protein better. Some peanut butter or a small piece of cheese late in the evening would be better choices.

Glycemic Index of Selected Foods

Foods	Glycemic Rating
Glucose	100
Corn Flakes	84
All Bran	42
White Bread	70
Mixed Grain	30-45
Jelly beans	80
Chocolate Bar	49
Baked Beans	48
Soybeans	18
Watermelon	72
Apple	38
Ice Cream	61
Skim Milk	32
Gatorade	78
Soda	68

How Much?

How much is too much, and what is too little? This seems to be an area of controversy in the nutrition world. The FitSkiing nutrition plan has varying carbohydrates for different phases of the training program. Later I will discuss specific carbohydrate percentages and when to consume them. Just to give you an idea, however, carbohydrates will account for 20 percent to 50 percent of your food intake depending on which phase of the training program you are in.

Protein

What Is a Protein?

Proteins are not found only in food. Your organs, tendons, muscles, and many other important parts of your body are made up of proteins. Proteins are comprised of carbon, hydrogen, oxygen, and nitrogen. They are distinct because of this last element. Nitrogen separates proteins from carbohydrates and fats.

Proteins can be broken down into smaller parts called amino acids. Amino acids are often referred to as the building blocks of protein. Twenty different amino acids exist. The way they are put together determines their function. As my anatomy and physiology professor always told me, "Form fits function." You can think of amino acids like the alphabet, but there are 20 amino acids instead of twenty-six. As the letters in the alphabet create words, amino acids can be put together too. The only difference is that it is protein language, not the English language. For example, proteins that make up hormones are totally different from those that comprise enzymes.

Out of the 20 amino acids, 11 can be manufactured by your body. That leaves nine that need to be taken in from outside sources. Your body cannot function without all 20 amino acids. The nine amino acids your body can't produce are called "essential."

Complete Versus Incomplete Proteins

Complete proteins contain all essential amino acids. Incomplete proteins, like the name implies, do not. Animal proteins like fish, chicken and eggs are considered complete because they have ample amounts of the essential amino acids. Vegetable proteins like grains, nuts and other vegetables are considered incomplete because they lack one or more of the amino acids. This is why many vegetarians have a difficult time getting complete proteins in their diet. The solution is to combine certain vegetable proteins like beans and rice so you get all the essential amino acids. If you want a list of foods that you can combine to get all the essential amino acids, log on to the American Dietetics Association Web site at www.ada.org. This site lists good sources of incomplete proteins that you can combine with other foods to make a complete protein.

Building Blocks Equal Building Muscle

Let's get rid of one myth right now. Taking in excessive amounts of protein doesn't mean you will build muscle like a pro linebacker. That being said, different people need different amounts of protein. For example, suppose you have two individuals of the same height, weight, sex, and body fat percentage. Subject one works at a desk all day and exercises sporadically. Subject two is a ski instructor who works out 5 days per week with weights. Subject two expends more energy and breaks down muscle by weight training. Subject one does not. According to the Recommended Daily Allowances, both subjects should eat a maximum of about 0.6 gram per pound of body weight. Assume that both individuals weigh 180 pounds. That means they should take in a maximum of 100 grams of protein per day.

Let's backtrack just a little. The first thing your body uses amino acids (the building blocks of protein) for is to help the immune system and other organs function properly. One of the last things amino acids are used for is to repair muscle tissue. If you are like subject one, 90 grams of protein is probably enough. However, if you are breaking down muscle like subject two, you might need more to help repair muscle tissue.

According to nutrition expert Lonnie Lowery, some athletes or individuals can consume up to

1.5 grams per pound of body weight without any problems. These individuals work out intensely with weights, and they frequent the cardio machines. Whether you're sedentary or score a 5 on the FitSkiing fitness scale, in the next section you will find out how much protein you need to take in to gain muscle mass, lose fat and above all have enough fuel for a day on the slopes.

How Much?

Skiing isn't any different than any other sport when it comes to protein consumption. Specifics regarding exactly how much and what kinds of protein you should consume will be addressed later in this chapter. Just to give you an idea though, you should consume somewhere between 1 and 1.5 grams per pound of body weight depending on the amount and intensity of exercise you engage in that day. As far as percentages go, FitSkiing recommends that you take in anywhere between 30 percent to 50 percent of total calories from protein, depending on what phase of the program you are in. The more you exercise, the more you break down your body. Therefore, the more protein you need to repair your muscles.

1. Body weight x 1-1.5 Grams of Protein=Total Daily Protein Intake
2. Total Daily Protein Intake/5-6 Meals per Day=Amount of Protein per Meal

Example

1. 180 pound skier x 1-1.5 Grams of Protein=180-270 grams of protein
2. 180-270 grams/5-6 Meals=35-55 Grams per Meal

Soy Protein

Why do I include soy protein in this section when I don't include any other types of protein? Because soy protein, as opposed to other proteins, can have positive and negative effects on the body. Let's discuss the positive effects first.

Science has shown that soy's phytoestrogen components, namely genistein have the ability to act similarly to female estrogen hormones like estradiol. This has certain benefits such as increasing estrogen levels in women who need it. In addition, soy is a complete protein, and it is available in many products like tofu. Soy is the only vegetable-related protein that has all nine essential amino acids, which makes it a complete protein.

Unfortunately, soy also has its downsides. For the same reason soy's estrogen-related benefits are positive for some, they can be potentially detrimental to others. For example, in one study plasma testosterone and androstenedione levels were significantly lower in the animals fed a phytoestrogen rich diet compared with animals fed phytoestrogen-free diet. What does this mean? Basically, it shows that testosterone (a major male hormone that contributes to many male characteristics) levels might decrease when too much soy is consumed. In another study of Japanese men, total and free testosterone concentrations were inversely correlated with soy product intake. Finally, in a study that might correlate more strongly with weight-training athletes, diets that consist of soy may increase protein breakdown in skeletal muscle. Pigs were fed diets based on soybean protein isolate or casein for 15 weeks. A transient rise in the level of cortisol was shown to occur in the soybean group.

All this technical jabber basically means that soy protein may decrease testosterone and increase cortisol (a stress hormone that breaks down muscle) levels. However, you have to weigh the positives and negatives yourself.

Fats

What Are Fats?

Technically, fats are carbon atoms attached on a long chain. The longer the chain is, the more difficult it is for the body to process it. Fat comes in a compendium of packages, some more detrimental than others. Let's take a look at some of the positive aspects of fat first.

- Fat provides humans with energy.
- Fat assists in the growth of children.
- Fat is an insulator that helps keep you warm and helps you stay afloat in water.
- Fat enables the body to absorb fat-soluble vitamins like D, E, and K.
- Fat assists in keeping hair and skin healthy.
- Fat produces hormones including, testosterone and estrogen.

Fat is not only positive in many ways, it is also a necessity. Before we move on, you may need to know some important fat-related terminology. Here is a list of the different types of fats and how they apply to your body.

Triglycerides: This is a very general term for the fat found in food. The chemical structure of a triglyceride is commonly called a glycerol, or a chain of carbon atoms linked together. Triglycerides are categorized into four different types: monounsaturated fats, polyunsaturated fats, saturated fats and trans fatty acids.

Monounsaturated fats: Olive oils, peanut oils, avocados, and canola oils are high in this type of fat. According to studies, these fats might help lower cholesterol.

Polyunsaturated fats: Corn oils, sunflower oils, mayonnaise, and soybean oils are considered polyunsaturated. Most types of fatty fish also contain polyunsaturated fats. These are called omega-3 fatty acids. These fats have been shown to reduce the risk of heart disease.

Saturated fats: When most people think of fat, this is the type they think of. These are the fats that increase cholesterol levels and contribute to heart disease. Most saturated fats are found in animals. Dairy products, chicken, and red meat contain saturated fat. Most vegetables do not contain saturated fats. Try to keep your intake of saturated fats to a minimum.

Trans-fatty acids: This fat does not occur naturally, but is produced when unsaturated fats are hydrogenized; that is when a semisoft fat is converted into a more solid form. Trans-fatty acids are harmful because they're similar to saturated fats when ingested. Unfortunately, these fats are not regulated by the government and therefore are not listed on nutrition labels. You can not do a whole lot about this, and it is almost impossible to avoid them in your diet. By reducing your total fat intake, you can mitigate some of the trans-fatty acids from clogging your arteries.

Common Foods and Their Predominant Fats

Saturated	Monounsaturated	Polyunsaturated
Beef Fat	Avocados	Sunflower Oil
Cheese	Olive Oil	Fish Oils
Palm Oil	Many Nuts	Soft Margarine
Butter	Peanut Oil	Mayonnaise
Whole Milk	Canola Oil	Flaxseed Oil
Coconut Oil	Sesame Oil	Soybean Oil

Good Fat vs. Bad Fat

How do you know which fats are good to eat and which fats are not so good to eat? Later in this chapter, I will discuss specifically which fats are suggested in the FitSkiing program and which fats are discouraged. It is important to remember that fat is a necessity for survival. Without fat your body eventually would stop producing hormones, and you would have little protection from outside elements like the cold. It also could cause damage to your organs. Next, you will find the American Heart Association's (AHA) percent recommendations for fat and cholesterol consumption.

• Consume between 25 and 35 percent of each day's calories from fat.
• Consume less than 7 to 10 percent of each day's calories from saturated fat.
• Consume less than 200 milligrams of cholesterol per day.

TYPES OF GOOD FAT SUPPLEMENTATION

1. Flaxseed Oil: One to Six Tablespoons Daily
2. Omega-3 and Omega-6 Fatty Acids: 1000 to 2000 mg. Daily
3. Medium Chain Triglycerides: Start With Small Amounts and Progressively Increase to One to Two Tablespoons Twice a Day
Note: Medium Chain Triglycerides May Upset Your Stomach for the First Few Days. If Irritation Does Not subside Within the First Week, Discontinue Use.

How Much?

I agree with the AHA's statements regarding fat consumption. However, I would like to add that the lower your carbohydrate intake is, the higher your fat intake should be. For example, if you reduce your carbohydrate intake by 10 percent you should consume 5 percent more fat and 5 percent more protein in your diet to compensate. I also recommend taking in those fats from flaxseed oil added to your protein shakes. This is an easy, convenient way to increase your protein and fat intake.

Cholesterol exists in two basic forms: high-density lipoproteins (HDLs) and low density lipoproteins (LDLs). HDLs are what health professionals consider healthy fats; LDLs are considered bad cholesterol. A simple way to remember this is the *H* in HDL stands for *healthy* and the *L* in LDLs stands for *loser* cholesterol. In short, HDLs get rid of the cholesterol in your blood. A level of cholesterol above 60 milligrams per deciliter is a good number to shoot for. LDLs on the other hand, cause the buildup of cholesterol in the arterial walls and increase your risk for heart disease. A good number to shoot for is below 100 milligrams per deciliter. To reiterate, you should consume between 25 percent and 35 percent of your daily calories from fat, with no more than 10 percent coming from saturated fat. Your total cholesterol should be below 200 milligrams per deciliter, with HDLs at 60 milligrams per deciliter and LDLs below 100 milligrams per deciliter.

Hangover Helpers

You might find it odd that I have included this section in a health and fitness-related book. However, this book is written primarily for skiers, and they tend to enjoy their après-ski as much as their time on the slopes. FitSkiing covers all the basics of skiing, fitness, and health, and that includes mitigating hangovers.

On the following page you will find an article I wrote on how to cure or at least dull a hangover.

Hangover Helper
Andrew Hooge
Certified Strength and Conditioning Specialist

You may notice after a hard day on the slopes and a long night of beer binging that your hangover seems a little worse than usual. This is not an illusion. After an enduring day on the slopes your body dehydrates leaving your cells craving fluid. Dehydration can lead to headaches, and an overall feeling of exhaustion. After ingesting alcohol, your body breaks it down into acetaldehyde before converting it into less harmful substances. Acetaldehyde affects the normal function of the brain, while at the same time depleted minerals are short circulating your nervous system. This is in addition to low blood sugar and the classic headache and dry mouth symptoms caused by dehydration. The result: nausea, twitchy nerves, unpleasantness, and a world left spinning. Simply put, a hangover is the dehydration of your body, coupled with the by-products of alcohol (namely acetaldehyde) which causes the reaction you feel during a hangover.

Many of you may head straight for the pub and then worse the hot tub or jacuzzi after an extended day on the slopes. What!!!! You might ask. I thought pouring back a pint and boiling over with members of the opposite sex was what apres ski was all about. Well, maybe, but if you want to mitigate many of these next day poundings (and I don't mean the moguls), then you might want to try these hangover helpers. Compiled by some of Crested Butte ski areas brightest bartenders, your body will be sure to puree the powder after a hard night at the bar as opposed to enduring a pounding headache.

According to Princess Wine Bar Manager, Ruta Martell, it's best to be proactive. "If you take steps to prevent the hangover then you will be better off the morning after a long night at the bar."

Martell suggests that drinking plenty of water during your day on the slopes as well as before your night out is the best way to prevent a hangover. "Because we are at such a high altitude it always seems to affect people more, and lots of water seems to always help."

Veteran Crested Butte Bartender, Mike Keith agrees, "The more water one drinks the less chance they have of becoming dehydrated which is one of the major causes of a hangover."

Martell also says that a beer the morning after has worked for many she has talked to. "I don't know why, but it always seems to help." She warns that although it might make you feel good, it can also increase dehydration. Not necessarily an advantage if you plan to have a good powder day.

Keith explains that sugar is what primarily breaks down alcohol. "Try drinking some fluid replacement drinks that contain electrolytes and carbohydrates (sugar)." By breaking down the alcohol, many of the hangover symptoms can be diminished.

"Be wary of cheap liquor though," Keith explains, "The cheaper the alcohol the worse the hangover." This is probably due to the fact that cheaper alcohol's have more by-products and fillers that can cause the nausea and other side effects of a hangover.

Working out also seems to help according to Keith. "I always feel so much better after a hard work out when I used to get hangovers".

Always remember to be aware and courteous of your fellow skiers if you do plan to make tracks the day after a hard night of drinking. According to Gary Huresky, seven year veteran of the Crested Butte Ski Patrol, there can be many risks to skiing with a hangover.

"Dizziness, impaired vision, slowed reaction time, and shortness of breath are all problems I have seen associated with skiers who have hangovers."

Huresky recommends taking at least half a day off after a night of drinking before returning to the slopes. "Although fresh air and exercise are good for a hangover, taking a half a day off before you hit the slopes is a good precaution."

Below is a sure fire way to cure what ails you after a hard night of pounding beers, so that you can pound the bumps just as easily.

Hangover Helpers

Preparing for the night out:
1. Water, water, and more water!
2. Eat something! Food helps absorb alcohol

During the evening:
1. Choose your Alcohol with Care!
-Darker drinks, such as bourbon, scotch, and red wine have more congeners (chemicals that make you go blah) than lighter beverages like white wine and vodka.
-Take special care with cheap red wine. It contains an extra hangover inducer called tyramine.
2. Ingest less than one drink per hour!
-Your liver can break down about one drink per hour, enough said.
3. Drink Fruit Juice or Gatorade between alcoholic drinks!
-These beverages have electrolytes and carbohydrates which will help with hydration.

When you get Home:
1. More Water!
-Probably not the first thing on your mind, but it may save you an unneeded headache in the morning.
2. No Headache Medicine!
-You might think this is a good preventative measure, however aspirin may upset your stomach and aggravate symptoms of a headache.
-Take a B vitamin, it might replenish some of what you lost during your bathroom breaks.

The Morning After:
1. Go Back to bed!
-Call in sick, seriously. You are actually sick. Probably best to tell your boss that you feel nauseated and have an upset stomach as opposed to saying you have a hangover though.
2. No More Alcohol!
-Contrary to popular belief more alcohol actually dehydrates the body further. Leaving you with the possibility of worsening your hangover.
3. Coffee.
-Ok, many of us love coffee, including myself, but caffeine is a diuretic, which again dehydrates the body. Remember dehydration is one of the main causes of a hangover.

If All Else Fails: The Ultimate Hangover Solution

Remember to always consult your physician if you feel you may have had too much to drink.
Consult a doctor before ingesting any of the above remedies.

FitSkiing Grocery List

The following is a list of foods that you can use when shopping at your local grocery store. For each macronutrient (protein, fats, carbohydrates), you will find foods that are recommended for the FitSkiing program. You also will find foods that you should eat sparingly and foods you should consume only on rare occasions. Remember that you don't have to use these foods, but it will speed up your results on and off the slopes.

Recommended: Foods that are recommended are ones that carry the highest nutritional value for fit skiers. You can eat them anytime, but that doesn't mean you should overconsume. For example, don't use a whole bottle of olive oil a day. Have an apple or two a day, but not a whole bag.

Use Sparingly: These are foods you should consume very little of, meaning no more than two servings per day. For example, you might choose to have a carrot late in the morning and a serving of brown rice with dinner.

Rare Occasions: Eat these foods rarely. You might treat yourself to a bowl of ice cream or a couple slices of pizza once a week.

Note: This is an abbreviated list of foods that are available to you. Just because your favorite sugar cereal is not on the list doesn't mean you can have all you want. At the same time, you might want to indulge in a certain fish that is not listed in the FitSkiing grocery list but is perfectly okay to eat all the time. Use your best judgment when it comes to these types of questions.

What Is a Serving? A typical serving is the size of a deck of cards or the size of the palm of your hand. Typically, 3 to 4 ounces of meat is considered a serving. For example a 4-oz. piece of chicken is about the size of a deck of cards. A serving of nuts is typically a handful. A serving of an apple or other fruit or vegetable is usually a whole piece. For example, one serving of grapefruit is a whole grapefruit.

FitSkiing Grocery List

CARBOHYDRATES
Recommended (Eat Anytime)
Apples
Avocados
Bananas
Blueberries
Cantaloupe
Grapefruits
Oranges
Asparagus
Bell Peppers
Broccoli
Romaine Lettuce
Spinach
Tomatoes
Oatmeal (slow cooked regular)
Yams

Use Sparingly (Limit to No More Than Two Servings Per Day)
Carrots
Squash
Black Beans
Any Breads
Pizza Crust
Rice Cakes
Granola
Kashi
Pasta
Brown Rice
Popcorn
Potato Chips (light)
Rare Occasions (No More Than One Serving Twice Weekly)
Cookies
Cake
Potato Chips
Ice Cream
Non-Diet Soda
Granola Bars
Breakfast Bars
Candy
Maple Syrup
Honey
Catsup
Beer
Wine
Mixed Drinks
Sweetened Coffee

PROTEIN
Recommended (Eat Anytime)
Ground Sirloin
Filet Mignon
Roasted Lamb
Pork Tenderloin
Chicken Breasts
Ground Turkey
Buffalo
Bass
Cod
Halibut
Salmon
Tuna
Protein Shakes

Use Sparingly (Limit to No More Than Two Servings Per Day)
Corned Beef
Ground Chuck Beef
Ribs
Pork Chops
Chicken Dark Meat
Fried Fish
Cheese
Soy (Any)
Rare Occasions (No More Than One Serving Twice Weekly)
Sandwich Meats
Prime Rib
Hot Dogs
Bacon
Sausage
Fried Chicken

FATS
Recommended (Eat Anytime)
Medium Chain Triglycerides (MCTs)
Flax Seed Oil
Olive Oil
Use Sparingly (Limit to No More Than Two Servings Per Day)
Nuts
Corn Oil
Vegetable Oils
Rare Occasions (No More Than One Serving Twice Weekly)
Butter

The FitSkiing Meal Planner

The FitSkiing meal planner is your guide to what to eat, when to eat, and how much to eat. Detailed in the next few pages is how to create a daily meal plan based on your daily schedule and the FitSkiing workout program. Just as the FitSkiing workout has different stages, the FitSkiing Nutritional Planner has different stages too. The following is a list of what you will know by the end of this chapter.

•*What foods you will eat and when to eat them.*
•*A different meal plan for each phase of the FitSkiing Program.*
•*Your own sample weekly meal planner.*
•*Your "Day on the Slopes Diet."*

Your current weight, lifestyle (type of job, children and so on), and what phase of the FitSkiing workout you are in will define how much food you should consume. The following are general guidelines for every phase of the FitSkiing meal planner.

•**Eat five to six small meals daily:** Eating five to six meals per day helps keep your blood sugar stable, which means less insulin is circulating in your bloodstream. In short, you will be utilizing more of your food for energy and less will be stored as fat. Food contains calories, and calories produce heat. By eating often, you keep your furnace fueled so your metabolism increases. If you starve your body, it will react by decreasing your metabolism as a safety mechanism to survive. This means more fat storage and reduced performance on the slopes. Finally, eating more frequently teaches the body to use its food more efficiently, which translates to better fuel efficiency while skiing.

•**Consume eight to ten cups of water per day:** Your body is made up of 60 percent to 70 percent water, which means that your cells won't function properly without it. If you have a hard time consuming enough water, put a gallon of water in your refrigerator and make sure it is gone by the end of the day. You don't want to end up looking and performing like a raisin as opposed to a grape.

•**Keep It Simple:** If you keep things simple, you will have an easier time succeeding. We fail when we become overwhelmed. Follow the FitSkiing guidelines, and you will find it easy to get the results you want on and off the slopes.

Phase 1: Improving Strength and Overall Condition

Weeks 1 to 4

Phase 1 is designed to improve your overall conditioning level and strength. It eases you into the FitSkiing program. During this phase, you will probably consume more protein than you have before. In turn, you will find yourself craving carbohydrates less (protein helps stabilize blood sugar, which helps curb your desire for sugar), and you will experience an increase in energy. You also will see substantial improvements in your overall strength and body composition.

During the first phase, you will consume 1 gram of protein per pound of body weight every day. If you weigh 180 pounds, you should consume 180 grams of protein. Remember that every gram of protein has 4 calories. Eat the recommended proteins whenever possible. Because consuming this much protein might be difficult at first, you may want to stock up on protein powder for the first week.

The recommended carbohydrates should be eaten freely throughout the day. You will increase the amount of vegetables and fruits substantially in this phase. During the first phase, you should not consume a lot of the carbohydrates under the "use sparingly" category. Overall, you should consume no more than 2 grams of carbohydrates per pound of body weight. The same 180-pound person mentioned listed previously, would consume a maximum of 360 grams of carbohydrates per day. Remember that each gram of a carbohydrate has 4 calories.

Fat should be eaten at a rate of about 0.25 gram per pound of body weight. Remember that fat has 9 calories per gram. That means a 180-pound individual should consume 45 grams, or 405 calories per day in fat. Use the recommended fats in protein shakes and on salads. Stay free of the fats that are in the "use sparingly" or "rare occasions" categories.

On the following pages, you will find charts that will help you determine your carbohydrate, protein, and fat intake.

Macronutrient	Calories per Gram
Carbohydrate	4
Protein	4
Fat	9

FitSkiing Meal Planner

Stage 1: Improving Strength and Overall Condition

Macronutrient	Daily Recommendations
Protein	**1 gram per pound of body weight** ›Recommended Protein: Most foods should come from this category. ›Use Sparingly: Like it says; consume no more than two servings daily. ›Rare Occasions: No more than two servings per week.
Carbohydrates	**2 grams per pound of body weight** ›Recommended Protein: Most foods should come from this category. ›Use Sparingly: Like it says. Consume no more than two servings daily. ›Rare Occasions: No more than two servings per week.
Fat	0.25 grams per pound of body weight

Menu

Day 1 Example

Phase 1: Improving Strength and Overall Condition

Meal	Meal
1. 1 serving oatmeal with fruit/protein shake/ coffee/water	4. Protein bar
2. Apple with regular peanut butter/water	5. Turkey breast sandwich/water
3. 1 serving chicken breast/salad with low-fat dressing/water	6. 1 serving salmon/brown rice/fruit/water

Menu

Day 2 Example

Phase 1: Improving Strength and Overall Condition

Meal	Meal
1. 3 egg whites/1 whole egg/fruit/water	4. Protein shake
2. Grapefruit/water	5. Barbecued Chicken Salad
3. 1 serving halibut/salad with low fat dressing/ water	6. 1 serving ground sirloin with stir fried vegetables/fruit/water

Menu
Day 3 Example
Phase 1: Improving Strength and Overall Condition

Meal	Meal
1. Protein Shake	4. 1 can tuna w lemon/steamed asparagus/water
2. Chicken breast sandwhich/fruit/water	5. Protein shake
3. Protein bar	6. 1 serving salmon with stir fried vegetables/fruit/ water

Menu
Day 4 Example
Phase 1: Improving Strength and Overall Condition

Meal	Meal
1. 4 Scrambled eggs with vegetables/whole wheat toast/water	4. Protein shake
2. Grapefruit/water	5. 1 can salmon/steamed vegetables/water
3. 1 serving chicken breast/salad with low fat dressing/water	6. 1 serving cod/spinach/water

Menu
Day 5 Example
Phase 1: Improving Strength and Overall Condition

Meal	Meal
1. Low fat cottage cheese/oatmeal/water/coffee	4. Protein bar
2. 1 apple with peanut butter	5. 1 serving chicken breast with steamed vegetables/water
3. Protein shake	6. 1 serving ribs/water/1 beer

Menu
Day 6 Example
Phase 1: Improving Strength and Overall Condition

Meal	Meal
1. Protein shake	4. Protein shake
2. Fresh fruit/oatmeal/cottage cheese/water	5. 1 can tuna/steamed vegetables/water
3. 1 serving salmon/salad with low fat dressing/ water	6. 1 serving ground turkey breast with steamed vegetables/fruit/water

Menu
Day 7 Example
Phase 1: Improving Strength and Overall Condition

Meal	Meal
1. 4 Scrambled eggs/oatmeal/water	4. 1 can tuna w lemon/steamed asparagus/water
2. Turkey breast sandwich/fruit/water	5. Protein shake
3. Protein bar	6. 1 serving halibut with stir fried vegetables/fruit/ water/1 glass of wine

Phase 2: Improve Muscular and Aerobic Endurance

Weeks 5 to 8

During phase 2, you will be focusing more on getting your muscles and lungs in gear for the ski season. By improving muscular and aerobic endurance, you also will be better able to handle phase 3. You should maintain protein intake at 1 gram per pound of body weight. Again make most of your selections from the recommended proteins in the FitSkiing grocery list. Reduce your occasional proteins to one serving per day and your rare proteins to once a week.

The recommended carbohydrates remain unlimited in phase 2; however, you need to reduce your total carbohydrate intake to 1.5 grams per pound of body weight. This will enable you to burn more fat because you will be utilizing your stored body fat for fuel. By reducing excess body fat, you will be lighter and therefore less impact will be placed on your joints. If you are already lean (less than 8 percent body fat for men and less than 12 percent body fat for women), maintain your carbohydrate intake at 2 grams per pound of body weight.

Fat should remain at .25 grams per pound of body weight.

FitSkiing Meal Planner
Stage 2: Improve Muscular and Aerobic Endurance

Macronutrient	Daily Recommendations
Protein	**1 gram per pound of body weight** ›Recommended Protein: Most foods should come from this category. ›Use Sparingly: Like it says; consume no more than 1 serving daily. ›Rare Occasions: No more than 1 serving per week.
Carbohydrates	**1.5 grams per pound of body weight** ›Recommended Protein: Most foods should come from this category. ›Use Sparingly: Like it says; consume no more than 1 serving daily. ›Rare Occasions: No more than 1 serving per week.
Fat	0.25 grams per pound of body weight

Menu
Day 1 Example
Phase 2: Improve Muscular and Aerobic Endurance

Meal	Meal
1. Scrambled eggs with shredded chicken/water	4. 1 can tuna w lemon/steamed asparagus/water
2. Protein shake/water	5. Protein shake
3. Protein bar/fresh fruit/water	6. 1 serving halibut with stir fried vegetables/fruit/water

Menu
Day 2 Example
Phase 2: Improve Muscular and Aerobic Endurance

Meal	Meal
1. Low fat cottage cheese/fruit/water	4. 1 can salmon w lemon/steamed vegetables/water
2. Protein Bar/water	5. Protein shake
3. Chicken breast sandwich/spinach salad/water	6. 1 serving ground sirloin/ with stir fried vegetables/fruit/water

Menu
Day 3 Example
Phase 2: Improve Muscular and Aerobic Endurance

Meal	Meal
1. Protein shake/fruit/water	4. 1 serving chicken breast/salad/water
2. Tuna salad/water	5. 1 serving salmon/steamed vegetables/water
3. Protein bar	6. Protein shake

Menu
Day 4 Example
Phase 2: Improve Muscular and Aerobic Endurance

Meal	Meal
1. 4 Scrambled Eggs/oatmeal/water	4. 1 can tuna w lemon/steamed asparagus/water
2. Turkey breast sandwhich/fruit/water	5. Protein shake/fruit
3. Protein bar	6. 1 serving halibut with stir fried vegetables/fruit/water

Menu
Day 5 Example
Phase 2: Improve Muscular and Aerobic Endurance

Meal	Meal
1. 3 egg omelet/fruit/coffee/water	4. 1 can tuna w lemon/steamed asparagus/water
2. Protein shake	5. Protein bar/bar/water
3. 1 chicken breast/steamed vegetables/water	6. 1 serving salmon/salad/water

Menu
Day 6 Example
Phase 2: Improve Muscular and Aerobic Endurance

Meal	Meal
1. 4 Scrambled Eggs/oatmeal/water	4. 1 can tuna w lemon/steamed asparagus/water
2. Turkey breast sandwhich/fruit/water	5. Protein shake/fruit
3. Protein bar	6. 1 serving cod with stir fried vegetables/fruit/water

Menu
Day 7 Example
Phase 2: Improve Muscular and Aerobic Endurance

Meal	Meal
1. Protein shake/fruit/coffee/water	4. Cottage cheese/fruit/water
2. Grilled turkey burger/garden salad/water	5. Protein shake/fruit
3. Protein bar/water	6. 1 serving salmon with steamed broccoli/fruit/water

Stage 3: Improve Power Endurance, Speed, and Balance

Weeks 9 to 12

During phase 3 you should be about a month from your first days of skiing. You will increase your ability to power through turns quickly and explosively for long periods of time. Balance and proprioceptive abilities will improve, as well as help prevent injury and increase stability on the slopes. Because of the increase in the large explosive muscles used, as well as an increase in overall workout intensity, your protein intake will increase to 1.25 grams per pound of body weight. During this phase, you should consume only the recommended proteins. Eliminate all proteins in the "use sparingly" category, as well as those in the "rare occasions" category.

The recommended carbohydrates remain unlimited in phase 3; however, you want to reduce your total carbohydrate intake to 1 gram per pound of body weight. By reducing carbohydrates further, you will do two things. First, your body will learn to use less carbohydrates for fuel, enabling you to ski longer without sugar. Second, it will help reduce body fat further. During phase 3; your body does not need as many carbohydrates. Although the intensity of the workout increases, the duration decreases. If you are already lean (less than 8 percent body fat for men and less than 12 percent body fat for women), maintain your carbohydrate intake at 1.5 grams per pound of body weight.

Increase fat intake to 0.5 gram per pound of body weight during phase 3. Because of the decrease in carbohydrates, a 0.25-gram increase is needed to keep the metabolism running efficiently. If you drop too many calories, your body's metabolism eventually will go into starvation mode and slow down.

FitSkiing Meal Planner

Stage 3: Improve Power Endurance, Speed, and Balance

Macronutrient	Daily Recommendations
Protein	**1.25 grams per pound of body weight** ›Recommended Protein: All foods come from this category. ›Use Sparingly: None. ›Rare: None.
Carbohydrates	**1 to 1.5 grams per pound of body weight** ›Recommended Protein: Most foods should come from this category. ›Use Sparingly: Like it says; consume no more than one serving daily. ›Rare Occasions: No more than one serving per week.
Fat	**0.5 gram per pound of body weight**

Menu

Day 1 Example

Phase 3: Improve Power Endurance, Speed, and Balance

Meal	Meal
1. Protein shake/fruit/water	4. 1.5 serving chicken breast/steamed vegetables
2. Cottage cheese/water	5. Protein shake/water
3. Protein bar/water	6. 1.5 serving halibut with stir fried vegetables/ fruit/water

Menu
Day 2 Example
Phase 3: Improve Power Endurance, Speed, and Balance

Meal	Meal
1. 4 Scrambled Eggs with ham and cheese/water	4. 1 can tuna w lemon/steamed asparagus/water
2. Protein Shake/fruit/water	5. Protein shake/fruit/water
3. Turkey burger/salad/water	6. 1.5 serving salmon/with stir fried vegetables/ fruit/water

Menu
Day 3 Example
Phase 3: Improve Power Endurance, Speed and Balance

Meal	Meal
1. Protein bar/fruit/water	4. 1 chicken breast sandwich/spinach salad/water
2. 4 whole eggs/chesse/water	5. Protein shake/fruit/water
3. Protein bar/steamed vegetables/water	6. 1.5 servings chicken breast/with stir fried vegetables/fruit/water

Menu
Day 4 Example
Phase 3: Improve Power Endurance, Speed and Balance

Meal	Meal
1. Protein shake/oatmeal/water	4. 1 can salmon w lemon/steamed vegetables/ water
2. Cottage cheese/fruit/water	5. Protein shake/fruit/water
3. Protein bar/water	6. 2 slices chicken pizza/water

Menu
Day 5 Example
Phase 3: Improve Power Endurance, Speed, and Balance

Meal	Meal
1. Protein bar/fruit/water	4. Chicken breast sandwich/salad/water
2. 4 whole eggs/cheese/water	5. Protein shake/fruit/water
3. Protein bar/water	6. 1.5 serving halibut with stir fried vegetables/ fruit/water

Menu
Day 6 Example
Phase 3: Improve Power Endurance, Speed, and Balance

Meal	Meal
1. Scrambled Eggs with shredded chicken/water	4. 1 can tuna w lemon/steamed asparagus/water
2. Protein Shake/water	5. Protein shake/water
3. Protein bar/fruit/water	6. 1.5 servings ground sirloin with stir fried vegetables/fruit/water

Menu
Day 7 Example
Phase 3: Improve Power Endurance, Speed, and Balance

Meal	Meal
1. Protein shake/oatmeal/water	4. 1 can salmon w lemon/steamed vegetables/ water
2. Cottage cheese/fruit/water	5. Protein shake/fruit/water
3. Turkey breast sandwich	6. 1.5 servings chicken breast/salad/water

Pre and Post Skiing

During Your Day on the Slopes

Give yourself a pat on the back! You've made it through the FitSkiing program. You should now be prepared to do battle with the slopes. However, that does not mean the FitSkiing nutrition program ends here. It is important to follow the following guidelines so you can maintain your newfound fitness and have ample energy for your night on the town.

In my years of training, I have found that most people like their weekends to be times when they can consume food freely. This phase of the nutrition program will focus on what you should eat before and after your day on the snow. Before you hit the slopes you should consume between 30 and 50 grams of protein, depending on your weight. For example, a male weighing 180 pounds might consume 40 grams of protein, and a female weighing 130 pounds might consume 30 grams of protein. You also should eat ample carbohydrates before strapping on your boots. Plan to eat between 80 and 100 grams of carbohydrates before you head to the lifts. Don't forget the fat. Fat is essential for energy, hormone production, and insulation. Try to get between 10 and 15 grams before you head out the door. An easy way to accomplish this is simply to add one or two tablespoons of flax-seed oil to your protein shake. In the following section, you will find a sample of what your meal plan should look like for a day.

Menu
Typical Ski Day
Maintain Ample Energy Both On and Off the Slopes

Meal	Meal
Pre Ski: 3 egg omelet/fruit/2 slices whole wheat toast/16 oz of water	Post Ski: Protein shake/1 tablespoon flax seed oil/fruit/water
Snack: Protein Bar/16 oz water	Snack: Protein bar/16 oz water/beer
Lunch: Chicken breast sandwich/fries/16 oz water	Dinner: 1.5 servings salmon/brown rice/salad/2 glasses wine/16 oz water

Supplements

Over the past decade, sports supplementation has become one of the most talked about subjects in the exercise and nutrition world. Supplements have gone mainstream garnering enough controversy to land segments on shows ranging from 60 Minutes to Oprah. The following is a list of commonly asked questions I receive regarding supplements.

•Which ones should I use and when?
•How much should I take?
•Are supplements dangerous?
•Can I give them to my kids?
•What types of results will I see?

I am going to answer these questions with regards to skiing performance only. Hundreds of supplements are available and I could write a whole book just on that. If you would like more information, refer to the Recommended Reading section in the appendices

Which ones should I consume?

That depends on your fitness level and goals. If you are new to exercising or coming back from a long layoff, food and exercise are plenty. If, however, you have been working out for longer than a year, some supplements might benefit you. I am going to discuss three supplements I believe can assist in improving your results in the gym and on the slopes: creatine, meal replacements, and myostatin.

How much should I take?

This typically depends on your weight and exercise intensity level. For example, a 180-pound male skier would consume 10 to 15 grams of creatine a day, and a 130-pound female skier would consume only 5 to 10 grams per day. On days you don't exercise, you might consume only half that amount. The following will explain daily amounts to consume.

Are supplements dangerous?

As with anything else, if you overdo them, supplements can be dangerous. If you drink two pots of coffee a day, that also could be considered dangerous. The one supplement that I have used and that I don't recommend is ephedrine. Although ephedrine works well to aid in increasing metabolism and stimulating fat loss, it also speeds up the heart rate and can have an effect on your emotional state. Because it affects the adrenal glands, it causes a rapid increase in heart rate. Some people can tolerate the jitters and others can't. There have been many cases that have tried to link ephedrine to deaths, but none have been substantiated. Although I have used ephedrine with success, I do not recommend it, nor do I use it anymore.

Can I give supplements to my children?

No, no, no, and no. Children should enjoy their childhood. Teach your children good nutrition, but wait until they ask about supplements or until they are old enough to make their own decisions. Let children be children.

What types of results will I see?

Results can vary depending on the person. One person might gain 10 pounds of muscle in 6 months while using creatine, and a different person might gain only 5 to 7 pounds. A lot of it depends on your current fitness level, the amount of lean muscle, and so on. A person who has a significant amount of muscle already probably will see less gain than someone who doesn't. This is because it is more difficult to put on muscle mass if you are already nearing your genetic potential. Almost anyone will see gains with the supplements I discuss next.

Supplement	What it Does	Suggested Amount	What you Might See
Creatine	Amino acid which improves strength and power.	Days 1 to 5: 20 grams/day After that: 5 grams/day Cycle off after 12 weeks.	Can improve strength by as much as 10 percent.
Meal Replacements	Quick and easy way to get a meal and meet your protein requirements.	1 to 3 shakes daily. Try to get meal replacements that have at least 30 grams of protein and have less than 25 grams of carbohydrates.	Increases in muscle as well as energy. Possible decrease in body fat due to a better nutrition program.
Myostatin	Binds to certain receptors to block myostatin which impedes muscle growth. This may improve lean muscle mass.	As recommended on supplement label.	Increases in lean muscle after 60-90 days of use. Must use continuously to see results.

Ten Tips for Eating Out

Tip One	If there is butter or excess sauce on the meal then ask for it on the side.
Tip Two	Most restaurants now offer a healthy side to their menu. Try to make choices from there.
Tip Three	Order chicken or fish whenever possible.
Tip Four	Lots of water. Many times restaurants over salt their food. Extra water will help flush the excess sodium from your system.
Tip Five	When drinking alcohol stick to the lighter variety. Darker liquors tend to have more calories.
Tip Six	Eat slowly. This actually goes for anytime however, you are more likely to consume more food when you are out. By eating slower you will give your body a chance to register the food and you will have a feeling of fullness.
Tip Seven	Whenever possible order steamed vegetables in place of french fries or other high fat foods.
Tip Eight	When eating breakfast, ask for Egg Beaters in place of regular eggs.
Tip Nine	Ask for fruit instead of hash browns or toast.
Tip Ten	Dine in whenever possible. It allows you more control over what you eat and it's cheaper so you can spend more money on your skiing.

So there you have it: 12 weeks of nutrition information to get you to your ultimate goal; becoming a fit skier. Remember to always consult a physician or a licensed nutritionist before you begin any nutrition program.

"IF YOU CAN DREAM IT, YOU CAN DO IT."

-WALT DISNEY

CHAPTER SIX

FITSKIING OVERVIEW

Now that you have the tools to eat for a FitSkiing body, you need to train to complete your conditioning. Over the 20 or so years that I have put skis to snow, I have struggled and prevailed to ski some of the toughest terrain available. As I plodded along the first 15 or so years, I simply was going through the motions not really aware of why my ski turned or what my muscles and brain were doing. But after coaching ski racers for a year, I became more aware of how the muscles and biomechanics worked to improve performance. I began watching the best skiers in the world. At the time, Alberto Tomba was at the top of his game and was by far one of the strongest skiers I had ever seen race. You may never have any interest in being as strong or as powerful as Alberto Tomba, but you can utilize many of his conditioning practices (après-ski aside) to improve your skiing

The FitSkiing workout provides a specific strength-training and conditioning program that will prepare you for the ski season and beyond. If you follow this program, you will improve your strength and endurance and lose body fat. As mentioned earlier in the book, skiing requires aerobic and anaerobic energy systems. As a result, you will be performing endurance activities such as running or biking at a moderate pace, as well as strength training and anaerobic activities such as sprinting. Although I believe that working on aerobic endurance is important, skiing is a sport that requires more lactate buffering (remember, lactic acid builds up when your body can no longer produce enough oxygen to clear the lactate from your muscles) than oxygen uptake. To improve lactate buffering, a combination of interval training (short, maximal bursts of energy, followed by longer, lower-intensity exercise), aerobic endurance, and muscular endurance training will be performed.

One of the keys to a successful training program is planning. Before each session, you will plan which exercises to do, as well as the number of sets and repetitions to perform. You also will have a general idea of exactly how much time you should block for your workouts. In the FitSkiing program, you will never workout without a plan. At the end of this book, you will find workout and nutrition logs to record your progress. Use these progress reports to record what you have completed and as a guide on how to progress. By tracking your training and nutrition information, you can find out what is working and reasons for not improving. For example, maybe you are following the FitSkiing nutrition plan to perfection, but your intensity levels in the gym aren't high enough.

Rating of Perceived Exertion

The FitSkiing program uses a common practice to rate your level of intensity. This should not be confused with the intensity scale described in Chapter 2 to figure out your FitSkiing fitness level. The rating of perceived exertion scale (commonly called RPE) ranges from 1 to 10. On the lower end, a 1 would be indicative of sitting on the couch or barely lifting any weight. Level 2 might be standing; level 3, walking; level 4, climbing stairs; and level 5 might be a brisk walk. As the scale increases, so does the intensity. A 10 is an all-out, 100 percent maximal effort.

This makes the FitSkiing program individual. Any person, no matter what his or her age or level of conditioning, can participate in this program. For example, you might be a beginner, squatting 95 pounds for 10 repetitions, and that is your 10 on the RPE scale. Another person with 5 years of training might consider squatting 405 pounds for 10 repetitions his or her RPE of 10. Your RPE is unique to you. As you progress, so does the FitSkiing program. This is why you can continue year after year performing the same workout with only minor changes and still see results.

You probably won't reach a 10 every time you work out. That would be like Picabo Street winning every single race she competed in. Reaching a 10 is never easy. Throughout the FitSkiing program, there will be specific times when I tell you to go all out and try to reach an RPE of 10.

The following chart defines what constitutes each level of RPE for weight training and aerobic training.

Rating of Perceived Exertion Scale	
RPE	Level of Intensity Aerobic/Weight Training
1	Sitting on the couch/Very light amount of weight lifted
2	Slow walking/light amount of weight lifted
3	Normal walking speed/Begin to feel some tension in the muscles being worked
4	Fast walk or walking up hill/May start to feel the muscles at the end of the set
5	Jogging or walking fast up hill/typical warm up weight, should feel the muscles begin to work at the end of the set, only about half of your maximal effort
6	Running at moderated speed, breathing noticeably increases/Moderate weight, muscles begin to burn towards the end of the set
7	Running up hill, breathing hard but can still talk to the person next to you/Should feel a burn in the muscles at about three quarters of the way through your set
8	Running at a fast pace, breathing harder and difficult to talk to the person next to you/ Moderately heavy weight, muscles start to fatigue at the end of the set, you might have two or three more repetitions left
9	Moderate Sprint, breathing rapidly and cannot talk to the person next to you/Heavy weight, could perform one more repetition at the end of the set
10	Sprinting at maximal speed/100% of maximum weight lifted, no more reps can be completed without assistance

Picking a Weight

During each separate stage of the FitSkiing training program, you will be using a variety of different weights. For each stage, you should start with a light weight. If you can perform the recommended number of repetitions with a particular weight easily, then you should increase the weight by 10 percent to 20 percent depending on how light the first selection was. For example, in the general conditioning program, it is recommended that you do 12 to 15 repetitions. If you can complete 15 repetitions easily with a certain weight, then you need to increase it on the following sets until you reach a point where you can barely get to 12 to 15 repetitions. On the flip side, if you can complete only eight repetitions then you should decrease the weight until you find a weight where you can complete 12 to 15 repetitions. The final set should always be the toughest. You should be toward the lower end of the repetitions for the final set. For example, in the General Conditioning stage, you should find that you can perform only 12 to 14 repetitions for the second work set. If you can perform 15, repetitions then you need to increase the weight by 10 percent for the next workout.

Picking a Mode of Aerobic Activity

Deciding on a form of aerobic activity might sound easy. However, sometimes throwing on a pair of shorts and a T-shirt and going for a run will not be the best choice. On the following pages, you will find the recommended types of aerobic activities for each program and phase. For example, in the

General Conditioning program, you can choose from a variety of activities, including walking, jogging, biking, and hiking. Basically, anything that gets your heart rate elevated counts. During the power endurance phase of the Advanced program, however, you might choose to do a plyometric box jump workout consisting of 30-second work intervals followed by 1-minute rest intervals. It all depends on what phase and program you are in. Always remember to be smart about your training though. If you have knee problems, then performing plyometrics might not be a good choice. Hitting the stationary bike for 30-second intervals might be a better idea.

General Conditioning Program

The General Conditioning program is geared for the person who scored between a 1 and a 2 on the FitSkiing baseline fitness level. If you have forgotten your baseline fitness level, refer to Chapter 2. This program is geared toward the person who has had a long layoff (3 months or more) from training or has never trained. The following are general guidelines for the program.

General Conditioning
6 weeks/2 days weight training per week/3 days aerobic training per week
• 1 warm up set (50% of work set) • 2 work sets • 12-15 repetitions each set • Increase weight by 10% when you can complete the fifteenth repetition in the second set • Weight training RPE: 8 • 2 minutes between sets • 10-30 minutes of aerobic activity per week • Begin with 10 minutes the first week and add five minutes per week until 30 minutes are reached • Aerobic RPE: 6-7

Basic Program

The Basic program is designed for the person who scored between 2 and 3.5 on the FitSkiing baseline fitness scale, although some may choose to start with this program even if you scored a 4 on the FitSkiing baseline fitness scale. Remember that the basic program is for those who have been training for at least 6 months or more and have some experience working with weights and different types of aerobic training. The following are general guidelines for the program.

Stage 1: Improving Strength and Overall Condition
4 Weeks/3 days weight training per week/3 days aerobic training per week
• 1 warm up set (50% of work set) • 3 work sets • 5-8 repetitions per set • Weight training RPE: 9-10 • Rest 2 minutes between sets • Interval Training • Begin with 5 intervals and increase to 8 intervals by week 4 • Interval training RPE: 9

Stage 2: Improve Muscular and Aerobic Endurance
4 Weeks/6 days/week
• 1 warm up set (50% of work set) • 3 work sets • 15-20 repetitions per set or 1-5 minutes per set • Weight training RPE: 8 • Rest 30 seconds between sets • Aerobic Training: 30-60 minutes • Begin with 30 minutes and increase 10 minutes per week until 60 minutes are reached • Aerobic endurance RPE: 7

Stage 3: Improve Power Endurance Speed, and Balance
4 Weeks/6 days/week
• 1 warm up set (50% of work set) • 3 work sets • 30 seconds to 1 minute per set • Weight training RPE: 7 • Rest 2 minutes between sets • Plyometric and Interval Training • Begin with 30 second intervals increasing to two minutes by week four • Plyometric and interval RPE: 9

Advanced Program

The Advanced program is similar to the Basic rogram with a few minor differences. If you scored between 4 and 5 on the FitSkiing baseline fitness scale, then this is the program you should be participating in. You will find in the next chapter that your workout mainly consists of the advanced exercises in Chapter 8. However, that does not mean you can't alternate some of the basic exercises to your routine. Remember, the Advanced program is for individuals who have been training more than 1 year and have a good grasp of weight training and aerobic training.

The Advanced program is a little more intense and a little longer than the Basic program. If you find yourself too exhausted after the first week, you should consider doing the Basic program for a couple of weeks. You will be utilizing more plyometrics as well during the Advanced training program.

Stage 1: Improve Overall Strength and Conditioning
4 Weeks/3 days weight training per week/3 days aerobic training per week
• 1 warm up set (50% of work set) • 4 work sets • 5-8 repetitions per set • Weight training RPE: 9 • Rest 1.5 minutes • Interval Training • Begin with 7 intervals increasing to 10 intervals by week four • Interval training RPE: 8

Stage 2: Improve Muscular and Aerobic Endurance
4 Weeks/6 days/week
• 1 warm up set (50% of work set) • 4 work sets • 15-20 repetitions per set or 1-5 minutes per set • Weight training RPE: 8 • Rest 30 seconds between sets • 30-60 minutes of aerobic activity • Begin with 30 minutes and increase 10 minutes per week until 60 minutes are reached • Aerobic endurance RPE: 7

Stage Three: Improve Power Endurance Speed, and Balance
4 Weeks/6 days/week
• 1 warm up set (50% of work set) • 5 work sets • 30 seconds to 1 minute per set or 3-5 repetitions • Weight training RPE: 5 • Rest 2-4 minutes between sets • Plyometric and Interval Training • Begin with 30 second intervals increasing to two minutes by week four • Plyometric and interval RPE: 9

A Typical Training Day

Now that you have a better understanding of how to train for FitSkiing, I am going to share one of my typical training days to get in shape for skiing. I prepare for my workout the previous day. I might look at my schedule for that day and decide when to work out so I have plenty of time to focus on my training. Never schedule your workout session when you know you have a meeting 30 minutes after your training. You will be thinking about your meeting and not your workout. I begin my workout at 8 a.m. This gives me ample time to eat and go over my schedule for the day. You might want to schedule yours for 7 a.m or at lunch. It only takes about 5 to 10 minutes to plan your workout, and it is well worth the time.so take the time.

I start with the improving strength and overall conditioning stage of the Advanced workout. I work my lower body on Monday, my upper body on Tuesday, and my lower body again on Friday. This might sound like a lot, but this is the Advanced program, and I have been training consistently for more than 10 years. I start with the largest muscle group, the legs. The Bosu Ball squat is my first exercise because it gets my neuromuscular system warmed up to do regular squats. I do ten repetitions with no weight for a warm-up set. Then I do two sets holding 25-pound dumbbells at my sides. After that, I complete two more sets holding 35-pound dumbbells. I rest 1.5 minutes between each set. Next I move to the barbell squat. I perform one set with 135 pounds (about a 5 on the RPE scale for me) for ten repetitions. I then complete four more sets with 275 to 365 pounds for 5 to 8 repetitions. Again I rest 1.5 minutes between sets. After squats, I move to the leg curl. I complete one warm-up set with 50 pounds for ten repetitions. After a 1.5 minutes I do four more sets with weights of 70 to 100 pounds for 5 to 8 repetitions. Next I move to the reverse calf raise to strengthen my shins. I do four sets with a 20-pound dumbbell for 5 to 8 repetitions.

After legs, I move to my core training. I complete one warm-up set of ski crunches on the fit ball for ten repetitions. I do four more sets of ten repetitions. I then move to rope crunches. I perform ten repetitions with 50 pounds. I complete four more sets with 100 pounds for 8 to 10 repetitions. After exhausting my abdominal muscles, I move to my lower back. I perform four sets of back extensions at ten repetitions per set.

After my weight training,I stretch my lower body to remove some of the lactic acid build-up. Remember, lactic acid is the chemical that builds up in the muscles when there is not enough oxygen to clear it from the muscles. It is the substance that makes your muscles burn and fatigue. I complete a quadriceps, hamstring, and hip stretch, doing two sets on each side. I hold each stretch for 30 seconds to 1 minute.

It takes me about 30 minutes to complete the first half of my workout. The next half of my workout is the aerobic portion. During this part, I do interval-style training (more about this in Chapter 7). I jog on the treadmill for 2 minutes at a speed of 5.5 m.p.h. to get my body warmed up. I then increase the speed to 7 m.p.h. for 1 minute, which would be and RPE of about 7 for me. After that I reduce the speed to 5.5 m.p.h. to recover for 2 minutes. I then move up to 8 m.p.h. (RPE of 8) for 1 minute. I return to 5.5 m.p.h. for 2 minutes. Then I increase the speed to 8 m.p.h. again for 1 minute. I repeat this sequence two more times. I then reduce the speed to 3 m.p.h. for 2 minutes to cool down. I complete five intervals.

After my workout, I have two glasses of water and relax for a while. About a half hour after my workout, I have another protein shake.

On Wednesday, I have my upper body workout. Each time I work out I switch the exercises. For example, on my next leg day, I might do the leg press, single leg squat, and stiff leg deadlift. It is always good to switch exercises so you work all the muscles as opposed to the same muscles every time. This provides more strength and stability on the slopes. It also gives the neuromuscular system changing stimuli, which your body responds to by getting stronger and more efficient.

In Chapter 7, you will get the specific details for each program and each phase within that program. Now move on; we have work to do!

CHAPTER SIX

"TODAY IS THE FIRST DAY OF MY LIFE"

-LANCE ARMSTRONG

CHAPTER SEVEN
TWELVE WEEKS TO FITSKIING

Now that you know how to eat for FitSkiing and have a basic idea of the different training programs, you can advance to the actual workout. The first thing to focus on is which program you should do. Remember back in Chapter 2 when you figured out your FitSkiing baseline fitness level? Now you are going to put it to work. The following is a brief summary of fitness levels and their corresponding training program.

Score 1 to 1.5: You have been sedentary and need a good conditioning program to get you ready for FitSkiing. Start with the general conditioning program, and then move to the basic program.

Score 2 to 2.5: You workout regularly, but need a little fine-tuning. FitSkiing's basic program is the perfect way to get in shape for skiing the terrain you've always dreamed.

Score 3.0 to 3.5: You are well accustomed to weights and taxing your aerobic system. Try the FitSkiing advanced program. If you find it is a little too much, then start with the basic program for a month and then progress to thc Advanccd program.

Score 4.0 to 5: The FitSkiing advanced program can give you new ideas and a workout plan that will enable you to ski Mount Everest (ok maybe not Everest).

General Conditioning Program

The General Conditioning program is designed to last 6 weeks and is for individuals who need a little tune-up before they get into the FitSkiing basic program. The program is to be performed 2 days per week with 72 hours between workouts. The following are general guidelines to follow for this program.

What is a set?

A set is a group of repetitions (lifting and lowering a weight) of an exercise after which you take a brief rest period. For example, if you complete 12 repetitions, set the weight down, complete 10 more repetitions, set the weight down again and complete 8 to 10 more repetitions, you have competed three sets of that exercise.

Warm-up set: A warm-up set is the first set in the sequence of sets. It helps get blood flowing to the muscles and gets your body prepared for the exercise.

Work set: A work set is the sets that follow the warm-up set. These sets usually are the ones which stress the muscles and help them grow and get stronger.

General Conditioning
Phase Instructions (See Exercises Descibed and Illustrated in Chapter 8)
• 1 warm up set (50% of work set) • 2 work sets • 12-15 repetitions each set • Increase weight by 10% when you can complete the fifteenth repetition in the second set • Weight training RPE: 8 • Rest 2 minutes between sets • 10-30 minutes of aerobic activity per week • Begin with 10 minutes the first week and add five minutes per week until 30 minutes are reached • Aerobic RPE: 6-7

General Conditioning/Weight Training Workout 1
1 Warm-Up Set/2 Work Sets/12 to 15 Repetitions Per Set For Exercises Listed Below
Single Leg Extension
Single Leg Curl
Lat Pull-down
Bench Press
Dumbbell Shoulder Press
Seated Dumbbell Curl
Triceps Press-down
Crunches
Downward Dog
Chest Stretch
Hamstring Stretch
Quadriceps Stretch

General Conditioning/Weight Training Workout 2
1 Warm-Up Set/2 Work Sets/12 to 15 Repetitions Per Set For Exercises Listed Below
Dumbbell Squats
Standing Leg Curl
Seated Row
Incline Dumbbell Press
Lateral Raise
Barbell Curl
Triceps Extension
Crunches
Overhead Stretch
Hip Stretch
Low Back/Hip Stretch
Latisimus Stretch

The aerobic portion of the General Conditioning program is to be performed 3 days per week on nonweight-training days. Remember to increase your duration by 5 minutes per week until you reach 30 minutes per session. The following is what a typical training week might look like.

Day	Weight Training	Aerobic Training
Monday	Workout One	None
Tuesday	None	10 Minutes Fast Walk
Wednesday	None	10 Minutes Stepper
Thursday	Workout Two	None
Friday	None	10 Minutes Recumbent Bike
Saturday	None	None
Sunday	None	None

A Typical Training Week

Now that you have a better idea of how to train for the General Conditioning program, I am going to provide you with a detailed sample training week. We will use the name Joe to denote the person who is training.

Joe starts his week on Sunday night when he prepares for Monday morning's training session. He writes down what exercises he will perform, as well as how many sets and repetitions he will be shooting for. because this is his first week of training, Joe does not have a workout log to look back on. If he did, he would look to see how much weight he used, as well as the number of repetitions and sets he performed.

Monday: Joe gets up at 7:30 A.M. and prepares for his day. He makes it to the gym around 8:30 A.M. and performs workout 1 in the General Conditioning program. He performs one warm up set with 10 pounds for the single leg extension exercise. After 2 minutes of rest, he completes another set with 20 pounds. Feeling that the first work set was a little light, he decides to add 10 pounds and completes 12 repetitions with 30 pounds. He completes the rest of the exercises in similar fashion.

Tuesday: It's an aerobic training day, so Joe decides to get out early and walk fast for 10 minutes. At 7:30 A.M., Joe is off to work and done with his training for the day.

Wednesday: Joe feels some soreness in his muscles from Monday's workout and remembers that it is normal to feel that way during the first month. He gets out and goes on another 10-minute walk. He is breathing a little harder than normal but can still carry on a conversation.

Thursday: Weight training workout 2 is scheduled for today, but Joe feels a little tired. He pulls himself together and heads to the gym. After he is there, he feels a little more energized and begins his workout. He starts with dumbbell squats with no weight for 15 repetitions. He rests for about 2 minutes and then completes a set, holding 20-pound dumbbells at his sides. After 2 more minutes, he completes 15 more repetitions with 20-pound dumbbells and decides he needs to increase the weight next week. He then moves to the standing leg curl and finds that it is much more difficult than the lying leg curl. He puts 10 pounds on the machine and completes 12 repetitions. Feeling that this was enough, he completes two more sets with the same weight. Joe finishes the rest of the exercises in a similar fashion.

Friday: It's Friday, and Joe is looking forward to spending the weekend with his children. He gets up early and walks for 15 minutes instead of 10. He feels a little tight from the previous day's workout, so he stretches for about 10 minutes after his walk. This helps remove some more of the lactic acid from his muscles, thereby minimizing his soreness the next day.

Saturday: Joe has an active day with his family.

Sunday: Joe relaxes on the couch, and reads the newspaper. He prepares for Mondays workout.

So there you have it. Now get training so you can move on to the Basic program!

Before You Begin the Basic or Advanced Training Program

The FitSkiing program is to be performed in three 4-week stages. Each stage is designed to improve a certain aspect of your skiing. The first stage is to help improve your strength and overall condition for skiing. The second stage is designed to improve muscular and aerobic endurance. The final phase helps improve power endurance, speed, and balance. Why are these components used in each stage? In the following section you will find what is included in each stage and what each stage is designed to do.

Stage 1: Improve Overall Strength and Conditioning

This stage is designed to get your body prepared for the more ski-specific stages. Stage 1 will help you become accustomed to the different exercises and intensities you will be experiencing in the following 8 weeks. You will be performing compound movements (utilizing more than one muscle group or joint) that improve total body strength. This stage requires maximal effort on the work sets. In other words, you probably will need someone to spot you.

This stage also was created to help improve your lactate-buffering ability. It will help your body remove the lactic acid that builds up during long bouts of intense aerobic work like skiing. Lactic acid, as explained earlier in the book, causes that burning sensation in your muscles when your body does not have enough oxygenated blood to circulate. To help buffer the lactic acid, you will be performing five to eight intervals of 1 to 2 minutes, 3 days per week after your weight training session. A detailed interval training schedule is outlined later in this chapter.

Stage 2: Improve Muscular and Aerobic Endurance

In stage 2, you will be working on improving your muscles' ability to withstand long bouts of anaerobic (without oxygen) and aerobic (with oxygen) work. When you are skiing, your muscles might feel strong at the beginning of the day, but by the end of the day they might feel like JellO. Most people's muscles are not accustomed to being used repetitively for hours at a time. We typically use them for a couple of seconds, not hours. *Muscular endurance* is defined as "how long you can use the strength in your muscles as opposed to how much force they can provide." Some athletes, like rock climbers, need significantly more muscular endurance because of how long they might be hanging in a certain spot. if you don't believe me, try holding on to a pull up-bar for 1 minute or more. These athletes are using their muscles for hours on end with little rest. Although skiing isn't as taxing as rock climbing, it still requires a considerable amount of muscular endurance. In this stage, you will be performing a lot of repetitions, as well as holding certain skiing-related positions for long periods of time.

You also will be performing longer aerobic training sessions in stage 2. Again, this is to help improve the length of time your body can stay on the slopes and to minimize injury. Your goal is to reach 60 minutes of consistent aerobic training by the end of stage 2.

Stage 3: Improve Power Endurance, Speed, and Balance

This is the final stage of the program before you head off to make some tracks. Improving your power endurance is one of the most ski-specific types of training you will perform. It comprises the bulk of an elite ski racer's training.

What is power endurance? It basically comprises performing repetitions quickly for a long period of time with enough stimulus to cause fatigue. *Power* is defined as the "amount of load (weight) being used, multiplied by the distance moved and the time it takes to move it." *Endurance* is defined as "how long the body can handle a certain stimulus such as running a marathon or skiing a certain number of runs before it begins to fatigue." Putting the two together defines *power endurance*. For example, squatting 250 pounds two or three times in less than 5 seconds would be a good indicator of power. Running a personal best in a 5-k race would concern itself more with overall endurance. Skiing 4,000 feet of vertical in 20 to 30 minutes would incorporate power and endurance; hence the term, *power endurance*. Because you are repetitively squatting up and down quickly, you need to recruit more fast-twitch fibers (larger white fibers that help produce more power). However, because you are utilizing your legs and core over a long period of time you also need a considerable amount of muscular and aerobic endurance. Making more than 100 turns in 10 minutes is a good example of power endurance.

Reaction time or speed is also an important component in skiing. In stage 3 you will incorporate more plyometric exercises to recruit more type II B fibers (power fibers) and improve the speed at which your neuromuscular system reacts (reaction time).

Finally, stage 3 will incorporate exercises to improve your balance and proprioception. These exercises will help you maintain stability on your skis if you begin to fall or catch an edge. Stage 3 is positioned during the last 4 weeks because it incorporates the most ski specific-training.

BASIC PROGRAM

The Basic program is for individuals who scored between 2 and 3.5 on the FitSkiing baseline fitness scale. It incorporates the three stages explained earlier and lasts 12 weeks. You might want to start with the General Conditioning program for a couple of weeks to get used to the FitSkiing program and nutritional plan. If you have questions regarding which program you should be performing, turn to Chapter 2 and determine your FitSkiing baseline fitness level. At the end of this chapter, you will find a visual guide to your workouts. It gives a quick reference to the exercise, as well as their sequence. The following are general guidelines for stage 1 of the Basic program.

Stage 1: Improving Strength and Overall Condition
4 Weeks/3 days/week
• 1 warm up set (50% of work set) • 3 work sets • 5-8 repetitions per set • Weight training RPE: 9-10 • Core Training: As many repetitions as possible • Rest 2 minutes between sets • Interval Training • Begin with 5 intervals and increase to 8 intervals by week 4 • Interval training RPE: 9

Stage 1 Workout

Stage 1 workouts should be performed 3 days per week with 48 hours between workouts. The following are the weight-training workouts. Remember to check out the visual outline of the workouts at the end of this chapter for another view of how to organize your training.

Basic Program
Workout 1
Single Leg Extension (pp. 118) Dumbbell Squat (pp. 128) Lunge (pp. 112) Single Leg Curl (pp. 116) Reverse Calf Raise (pp.122) Crunch* (pp. 184) Downward Dog (pp. 224) Overhead Stretch (pp. 235) Quadriceps Stretch (pp. 233) Hamstring Stretch (pp. 228) *As many repetitions as possible

Basic Program
Workout 2
Internal Rotation (8-12 repetitions) (pp. 164)
External Rotation (8-12 repetitions) (pp. 162)
Dumbell Bench Press (pp. 154)
Bosu Ball Push Up (pp. 156)
Dumbbell Shoulder Press (pp. 160)
Lateral Raise (pp. 166)
Reverse Crunch* (pp. 200)
Latisimus Stretch (pp. 231)
Chest Stretch (pp. 227)
Triceps Stretch (pp. 234)
Low Back Relaxation (pp. 232)
*As many repetitions as possible

Basic Program
Workout 3
Lat Pull-down (pp. 144)
Scapular Retraction (pp. 150)
Shrug (pp. 146)
Seated Dumbbell Curl (pp. 172)
Triceps Press-down (pp. 176)
Crunches* (pp. 184)
Latisimus Stretch (pp. 231)
Chest Stretch (pp. 227)
Triceps Stretch (pp. 234)
Overhead Stretch (pp. 235)
*As many repetitions as possible

A Word About Stretching

Stretching is a great way to aid the body in recovery after a tough workout. It helps remove lactic acid (which causes soreness and fatigue) from the muscles and increases the amount of blood circulation so you will be more flexible the following day. Perform two sets of 30 seconds to 1 minute for the stretches listed in the FitSkiing program.

Interval Training

The interval component to the Basic FitSkiing program is to be performed after your weight-training workout. The entire workout should last less than 90 minutes. As explained earlier, you should begin with five intervals the first week and increase to eight intervals by week 4. The instructions also indicate that you should perform each interval in 1 to 2 minutes at close to maximal effort. You can choose cycling or running as your mode for the intervals. Remember to choose something that involves the legs because they are what you primarily use while skiing. The elliptical machine is also a great way to perform your intervals. See the following chart which provides a detailed description of how to progress each week.

Week	Number of Intervals	Duration of Intervals	Rest Between Intervals
1	5	60 seconds	2 minutes
2	6	75 seconds	2.5 minutes
3	7	90 seconds	3 minutes
4	8	120 seconds	4 minutes

This chart is not set in stone. Always remember to train by how you feel. If you are totally exhausted after your weight training, you might choose to do four intervals instead of five. Just remember, the closer you stay to the guidelines, the faster you will progress. For those of you who can't afford 90 minutes of continuous time during the day, you can split the workouts in half. You might choose to perform the weight training in the morning and the intervals in the evening or the other way around. If you are totally exhausted by the end of your weight training you might choose to do your intervals the following day.

FitSkiing recommends that you perform the weight training first and the intervals immediately after because of the added fat-burning benefit. When you train with weights, you burn off most of the glycogen (stored form of carbohydrates) in your muscles. Therefore you are primarily running on fat during your intervals. You also have the added benefit of building more lactic acid in the muscles. How is this a benefit? It might not feel like a benefit at the time, but your body will learn to buffer lactic acid faster and more efficiently. Then when you hit the slopes, your muscles will not fatigue as quickly. Studies also have shown that when lactic acid increases in the muscles the body releases more growth hormone as a response to the stress. Growth hormone has been shown to increase anabolism (building muscle) and decrease body fat. The following is a weekly guide to help keep you on track.

Day	Weight Training	Interval Work
Monday	Workout One	5-8 Intervals
Tuesday	None	None
Wednesday	Workout Two	5-8 Intervals
Thursday	None	None
Friday	Workout Three	5-8 Intervals
Saturday	None	None
Sunday	None	None

Alternative for Weekly Training

Day	Weight Training	Interval Work
Monday	Workout One	None
Tuesday	None	5-8 Intervals
Wednesday	Workout Two	None
Thursday	None	5-8 Intervals
Friday	Workout Three	None
Saturday	None	5-8 Intervals
Sunday	None	None

Stage 2 Workout

Stage 2 is designed to improve muscular and aerobic endurance. For a more in-depth discussion of this stage, refer to page 72 earlier in this chapter. The following are the guidelines for stage 2 of the Basic program.

Stage 2: Improve Muscular and Aerobic Endurance
4 Weeks/6 Days Per Week
• 1 warm up set (50% of work set) • 3 work sets • 15-20 repetitions or 1-5 minutes per set • When 20 repetitions are reached on the third set, increase weight by 10% • Weight training RPE: 8 • Rest 30 seconds between sets • Aerobic Training: 30-60 minutes • Begin with 30 minutes and increase 10 minutes per week until 60 minutes are reached • Aerobic endurance RPE: 7

Stage 2 training comprises 6 days per week with 48 hours between weight training and aerobic workouts. Three days per week you will train with weights, and 3 days per week you will walk, run, bike, hike, or perform any other mode of aerobic exercise that appeals to you. Remember that a Rating of Perceived Exertion level of 7 means you are breathing hard but can still maintain a conversation with the person next to you.

For some of the exercises, you will perform a certain number of repetitions; with others, you will be shooting for time. For example, during the squat you will perform between 15 and 20 repetitionss; however, the wall sit requires 1 to 5 minutes per set. The following are detailed charts that describe your weekly exercise and training schedule.

Basic Program
Weight Training Workout One
Dumbbell or Barbell Squat (pp. 128) Wall Sit* (pp. 132) Lat Pull-down (pp. 144) Straight Arm Pull-down (no bosu ball)* (pp. 148) Dumbbell Bench Press (pp. 154) Dumbbell Shoulder Press (pp. 160) Lateral Raise (pp. 166) Biceps Curl (pp. 172) Triceps Press-down (pp. 176) Back Extension (pp.180) Fit Ball Oblique Crunch* (pp. 186) Downward Dog (pp. 224) Hamstring Stretch (pp. 228) Quadriceps Stretch (pp. 233) Latisimus Stretch (pp. 231) **Indicates that you should train for time rather than repetitions*

Basic Program
Weight Training Workout Two
Lateral Lunge (pp. 114)
Ski Tuck* (pp. 126)
Reverse Calf Raise (pp. 122)
Scapular Retraction (pp. 150)
Shrug (pp. 146)
Internal Rotation (pp. 164)
External Rotation (pp. 162)
Bosu Ball Push Up (pp. 156)
Triceps Extension (pp. 174)
Bridge* (pp. 182)
Fit Ball Reverse Crunch* (pp. 200)
Transverse Abdominal Hold (pp. 202)
Overhead Stretch (pp. 235)
Hip Stretch (pp. 229)
Chest Stretch (pp. 227)
**Indicates that you should train for time rather than repetitions*

Basic Program
Weight Training Workout Three
Single Leg Press (pp. 120)
Single Leg Extension (pp. 118)
Single Leg Squat (pp. 124)
Lat Pull-down (pp. 144)
Straight Arm Pull-down (no bosu ball)* (pp. 148)
Dumbbell Bench Press (pp. 154)
Dumbbell Shoulder Press (pp. 160)
Lateral Raise* (pp. 166)
Biceps Curl (pp. 172)
Triceps Press-down (pp. 176)
Opposing Arm/Leg Extension* (pp. 188)
Crunch* (pp. 184)
Downward Dog (pp. 224)
Quadriceps Stretch (pp. 233)
Hamstring Stretch (pp. 228)
Overhead Stretch (pp. 235)
**Indicates that you should train for time rather than repetitions*

Determining Time for Exercises with an Asterisk

Building muscular endurance is an important component to improving your skiing. However, determining the duration for the exercise may be a little confusing at first. Any exercise denoted with an asterisk should be performed in 1 to 5 minutes as opposed to repetitions. How do you know how long to shoot for? Remember that your weight training RPE is an 8, so you should be working close to maximal effort. If you begin to feel a burn during the last quarter of the exercise, you have chosen a good duration. If you feel very little toward the end of the set, you should increase your duration by 15-second increments until you feel a slight burn in the muscles during the last quarter of the set.

For example, if you were performing the crunch, then you might start with 1 minute for the first two sets. If you can barely make it to 1 minute, you might choose to complete 45 seconds on the next set. On the other hand, if you feel very little you might choose to shoot for 1.5 minutes on the last set. Remember that the more endurance your muscles can provide the longer you will be able to ski. You also will find you are at less risk of injury and are more stabile on your skis.

Try to increase your duration by 15 seconds for each exercise every week. If you begin doing crunches for 1 minute in week 1, by week 4 you should be doing crunches for 2 minutes or more.

Aerobic Training

The aerobic training component during the second 4 weeks of your training begins with 30 minutes on nonweight-training days. You should increase your duration by 10 minutes each week until you reach 60 minutes. You will be increasing the amount of lactic acid during your weight training workouts so running, biking, hiking, or any other form of exercise the following day will help remove the acid from your muscles. This will aid in your recovery.

If you find that 30 minutes is too much in the beginning, simply start with 15 or 20 minutes and increase to 45 or 50 minutes by week 4. Although following the FitSkiing program as closely as possible is important to achieve the best conditioning, do not overtrain your body. In Chapter 12 I answer some commonly asked questions, including how to know if you are overtraining and what to do about it.

The following training guiide will help you with scheduling your week.

Weekly Training Chart

Day	Weight Training	Aerobic Training
Monday	Workout One	None
Tuesday	None	Aerobic Training
Wednesday	Workout Two	None
Thursday	None	Aerobic Training
Friday	Workout Three	None
Saturday	None	Aerobic Training
Sunday	None	None

Stage 3 Workout

Stage 3 is designed to improve your power endurance, speed and balance. For a more in-depth discussion of this stage, refer to page 72 earlier in this chapter. The following guidelines are for stage 3 of the Basic program.

Stage Three: Improve Power Endurance, Speed and Balance
4 Weeks/6 Days Per Week
• 1 warm up set (50% of work set) • 3 work sets • 30 seconds to 1 minute • When 60 repetitions are reached in 1 minute increase weight by 10% • Weight training RPE: 7 • Rest 2 minutes between sets • Plyometric Training • Begin with 30 second intervals increasing to two minutes by week four • Interval Training • Begin with 5 x 40 meter sprints, increasing to 10 x 40 meter sprints by week 12 • Plyometric and Interval Training RPE: 9

During the final 4 weeks of the FitSkiing program, you will be working on improving your power and speed between turns, as well as your reaction time and balance. Your weight training will include sets that last from 30 seconds to 1 minute. How do you decide what amount of weight to use? You are trying to recruit fast-twitch fibers, which produce power while at the same time lengthening the amount of time you can utilize that power. To do this, you should try to complete one repetition per second. Use a weight such that you can complete 30 repetitions in 30 seconds to start. Every week, you should increase your repetitions by ten until you reach 60 repetitions in 1 minute. If you reach 60 repetitions in 1 minute before week 4, then increase the weight by 10 percent.

You will notice that some of the exercises are denoted with an asterisk. When you see this, simply revert back to the stage 1 strength-training program. You should do as many repetitions as you can until you reach an RPE of 8 to 9 and occasionally a 10. For exmple, if you are performing the Transverse Abdominal Exercise, you might be able to perform ten repetitions, but on the decline sit up, you might be able to complete 50 repetitions or more. Always remember to focus on the muscles you are working. The following are the charts of exercises for weeks 9 through 12.

Basic Program
Weight Training Workout One
Transverse Abdominal Hold* (pp. 202) Single Leg Bosu Ball Stability (pp. 140) Leg Press (pp. 120) Dumbbell or Barbell Squat (pp. 128) Reverse Calf Raise (pp. 122) Lateral Hop (pp. 217) Four Square Plyometric (pp. 216) Decline Sit Up* (pp. 208) Fit Ball Oblique Crunch* (pp. 186) Back Extension* (pp. 180) Downward Dog (pp. 235) Low Back Hip Stretch (pp. 229) Quadriceps Stretch (pp. 234) Hamstring Stretch (pp. 228) *Denotes using stage one's repetition and intensity

Basic Program
Weight Training Workout Two
Transverse Abdominal Hold* (pp. 202)
Dumbbell Bench Press (pp. 154)
Lat Pull-down (pp. 144)
Bosu Ball Push Up (pp. 156)
Shrugs (pp. 146)
Dumbbell Shoulder Press (pp. 160)
Lateral Raise (pp. 166)
Barbell Curl (pp. 172)
Triceps Extension (pp. 174)
Bridge* (pp. 182)
Latisimus Stretch (pp. 231)
Chest Stretch (pp. 227)
Triceps Stretch (pp. 234)
Overhead Stretch (pp. 235)
*Denotes using stage one's repetition and intensity

Basic Program
Weight Training Workout Three
Transverse Abdominal Hold* (pp. 202)
Leg Extension (pp. 118)
Lunge (pp. 112)
Lateral Lunge (pp. 114)
Single Leg Hamstring Curl (pp. 116)
Step Up (pp. 130)
Reverse Calf Raise (pp. 122)
Lateral Hop (pp. 217)
Four Square Plyometric (pp. 216)
Crunch* (pp. 184)
Fit Ball Oblique Crunch* (pp. 1860
Back Extension* (pp. 180)
Downward Dog (pp. 224)
Overhead Stretch (pp. 235)
Quadriceps Stretch (pp. 234)
Hamstring Stretch (pp. 228)
*Denotes using stage one's repetition and intensity

Plyometric Training

In stage 3 you will be including some plyometrics in your program. In Chapter 8 you will find a full description of what plyometrics are, what they do, and how they will improve your skiing. Start with 30 seconds for each set during week 1 and increase by 30 seconds each week until you reach 2 minutes per set. Your RPE should be at a 9, but I recommend that you start slowly and then increase the speed of the repetitions until you feel comfortable with the exercise. Plyometrics are not necessarily the easiest type of exercise to learn. When I first started performing them about 8 years ago, I was falling all over the place, and I thought I was an accomplished athlete. I learned to take each exercise in steps and to learn them slowly. After I felt comfortable with the plyometric exercise, I increased my speed until I was moving explosively through each repetition.

Interval Training

Stage 3's interval program focuses more on speed than endurance or lactate buffering. You will be performing three speed workouts per week, each lasting 20 to 30 minutes. Begin with a 5-minute warm up (this is important because it will help get the blood circulating and assist in preventing injuries), and then move into the intervals. Your warm-up should be a light jog around a field or track. After your initial warm-up perform four or five of the lower-body stretches from Chapter Eight. This will help keep the muscles warm so you can ease into your intervals.

Start with five 40-meter intervals at close to maximal or maximal speed, or an RPE of 10. Your rest intervals will be about 2 minutes. Increase by two intervals per week until you reach 10 intervals in week 12. The final week, you will increase by only one interval. It is best to perform your intervals on a track. You should see marks for the start and 100-meter finish on the track. If you don't, you can count 40 meters by taking 40 normal steps (rough guideline). If you do not have a track close by, then you can use a football or soccer field. Apply the same principle to measure 40 meters. A good time to shoot for is 5 to 8 seconds.

A full recovery between sets is important. Remember, you are not trying to improve your endurance; you are improving your speed. A good gauge of full recovery is to take your resting heart rate before you warm up. Most people range between 60 and 85 beats per minute (BPM). **If you are above 90 BPM prior to warming up you should consult a physician.** Take your heart rate after each interval until it reaches your pre-workout level. For example, if you start your workout at 75 BPM, then you should wait until your heart rate comes within 10 BPM of this before you start the next interval. It might take 1 minute to reach close to your baseline level after your first interval but by your fifth interval it might take as long as 4 or 5 minutes, depending on the kind of condition you were in when you started. The following is the interval schedule for the final 4 weeks of training.

Week	Number of Intervals	Length of Intervals	Rest Between Intervals
1	5	40 meters	2 minutes
2	7	40 meters	2 minutes
3	9	40 meters	2 minutes
4	10	40 meters	2 minutes

The final stage of the Basic program is the most ski-specific type of training you will perform during the course of the program. You can perform the speed workouts after your weight training, or on nonweigh-training days. Remember to always gauge your workouts by how you feel. If you have taxed your body physically by moving furniture on Monday, you might want to wait an extra day before your next hard workout.

That is the Basic FitSkiing program. Now get started so you can be ready to make some tracks when the snow starts falling. Your weekly schedule for stage 3 follows.

Day	Weight Training/Plyometrics	Speed Training
Monday	Workout One	None
Tuesday	None	Speed Intervals
Wednesday	Workout Two	None
Thursday	None	Speed Intervals
Friday	Workout Three	None
Saturday	None	Speed Intervals
Sunday	None	None

ADVANCED PROGRAM

If you have chosen to start with the Advanced program, then you are in good shape to begin with. You should have fallen between 4 and 5 on the FitSkiing fitness scale. The Advanced program is not that much different than the Basic program, but it incorporates some changes. First, the intensity is about one and a half to two times as high as that of the Basic program. The duration (time of workouts) is also longer. More plyometrics and weight-training exercises are involved as well. If you find the Advanced program too taxing at first, try going to the basic program to start and then when you feel ready, move to the Advanced program. Without further interruption, here is the Advanced program.

Stage 1 Workout

As in the Basic workout you will be improving your overall strength and conditioning level. The following are the general guidelines for stage 1.

Stage 1: Improve Overall Strength and Conditioning
4 Weeks/3 days/week
• 1 warm up set (50% of work set) • 4 work sets • 5-8 repetitions per set • Weight training RPE: 9-10 • Rest 1.5 minutes • Core Training: As many repetitions as possible • Interval Training • Begin with 7 intervals increasing to 10 intervals by week four • Interval training RPE: 8

Phase 1 workouts should be performed 3 days per week with 48 hours between workouts. The following are the weight-training workouts. Check out the visual outline of the workouts at the end of this chapter for another view of how to organize your training.

Advanced Program
Workout 1
Single Leg Extension (pp. 118) Barbell Squat (pp. 128) Lunge (pp. 112) Single Leg Curl (pp. 116) Fit Ball Hamstring Curl (pp. 138) Reverse Calf Raise (pp. 122) Medicine Ball Crunch (as many repetitions as you can) (pp. 212) Fit Ball Rotation (as many repetitions as you can) (pp. 210) Back Extension (pp. 180) Downward Dog (pp. 224) Overhead Stretch (pp. 235) Quadriceps Stretch (pp. 234) Hamstring Stretch (pp. 228)

Advanced Program
Workout 2
Internal Rotation (8-12 repetitions) (pp. 164)
External Rotation (8-12 repetitions) (pp. 166)
Bench Press (pp. 154)
Bosu Ball Push Up (pp. 156)
Dumbbell Shoulder Press (160)
Lateral Raise (168)
Reverse Crunch (as many repetitions as you can) (pp. 190)
Opposing Arm/Leg Extension (as many repetitions as you can) (pp. 188)
Latisimus Stretch (pp. 231)
Chest Stretch (pp. 227)
Triceps Stretch (pp. 234)
Low Back Relaxation (pp. 232)

Advanced Program
Workout 3
Lat Pull-down (pp. 144)
Scapular Retraction (pp. 150)
Shrug (pp. 146)
Dumbbell Curl (pp. 172)
Triceps Press-down (pp. 176)
Medicine Ball Crunches (as many repetitions as you can) (pp. 212)
Back Extension (as many repetitions as you can) (pp. 180)
Latisimus Stretch (pp. 231)
Chest Stretch (pp. 227)
Triceps Stretch (pp. 234)
Overhead Stretch (pp. 235)

Interval Training

The Advanced program requires seven intervals of 2 minutes during the first week, increasing to ten intervals for 2 minutes by week 4. The instructions also indicate that you should perform each interval at close to maximal effort. As with the Basic program, you can choose cycling or running as your mode for the intervals, but choose something that involves the legs because that is what you are primarily using while skiing. The elliptical machine is also a great way to perform your intervals. The following chart provides a detailed description of how to progress each week.

Week	Number of Intervals	Duration of Intervals	Rest Between Intervals
1	7	120 seconds	4 minutes
2	8	120 seconds	4 minutes
3	9	120 seconds	4 minutes
4	10	120 seconds	4 minutes

This chart is not set in stone. Always train by how you feel. If you are totally exhausted after your weight training you might choose to do six intervals instead of seven. The closer you stay to the guideline, the faster you will progress. For those of you who can't afford 90 minutes of continuous time during the day, you can split the workouts in half. You might choose to perform the weight training in the morning and the intervals in the evening or the other way around. If you are totally exhausted by the end of your weight training, you might decide to do your intervals the following day.

FitSkiing recommends that you perform the weight training first and the intervals immediately afterwards because of the added fat-burning benefit. When you train with weights, you burn off most of the glycogen (stored form of carbohydrates) in your muscles. Therefore you are running primarily on fat during your intervals. You also have the added benefit of building more lactic acid in the muscles. This might not feel like a benefit at the time, but your body will learn to buffer lactic acid faster and more efficiently, so when you hit the slopes, your muscles will not fatigue as quickly. Studies also have shown that when lactic acid increases in the muscles the body releases more growth hormone as a response to the stress. Growth hormone has been shown to increase anabolism (building muscle) and decrease body fat. The following weekly guide will help keep you on track.

Day	Weight Training	Interval Work
Monday	Workout One	7-10 Intervals
Tuesday	None	None
Wednesday	Workout Two	7-10 Intervals
Thursday	None	None
Friday	Workout Three	7-10 Intervals
Saturday	None	None
Sunday	None	None

Alternative for Weekly Training

Day	Weight Training	Interval Work
Monday	Workout One	None
Tuesday	None	7-10 Intervals
Wednesday	Workout Two	None
Thursday	None	7-10 Intervals
Friday	Workout Three	None
Saturday	None	7-10 Intervals
Sunday	None	None

Stage 2 Workout

Stage 2 is designed to improve your muscular and aerobic endurance. For a more in-depth discussion of this stage, refer to page 72 earlier in this chapter. The following guidelines are for stage 2 of the Advanced program.

Stage 2: Improve Muscular and Aerobic Endurance
4 Weeks/6 Days Per Week
• 1 warm up set (50% of work set) • 4 work sets • 15-20 repetitions per set or 2-5 minutes per set • When 20 repetitions are reached on the third set, increase weight by 10% • Weight training RPE: 9 • Rest 30 seconds between sets • Aerobic Training: 30-60 minutes • Begin with 30 minutes and increase 10 minutes per week until 60 minutes are reached • Aerobic endurance RPE: 8

Stage 2 training comprises 6 days per week with 48 hours between weight training and aerobic workouts. Three days per week you will train with weights, and 3 days per week you will walk, run, bike, hike, or perform any other mode of aerobic exercise that appeals to you. Bear in mind that a Rating of Perceived Exertion level of 8 means you are breathing hard but can still have a conversation although you don't want to.

For some of the exercises, you will perform a certain number of repetitions; for other, you will be shooting for minutes instead. For example, during the squat you will perform between 15 and 20 repetitions, but the Bosu Ball ski tuck requires 2 to 5 minutes per set. The following pages provide detailed charts that describe your weekly exercise and training schedule.

Advanced Program
Weight Training Workout 1
Barbell Squat (pp. 128) Bosu Ball Ski Tuck* (pp. 126) Lat Pull-down (pp. 144) Straight Arm Pull-down (with bosu ball)* (pp. 148) Dumbbell Bench Press (pp. 150) Dumbbell Shoulder Press (pp. 160) Lateral Raise (pp. 168) Biceps Curl (pp. 172) Triceps Press-down (pp, 176) Back Extension (pp. 112) Fit Ball Rotation* (pp. 210) Plank* (pp. 206) Downward Dog (pp. 224) Hamstring Stretch (pp. 228) Quadriceps Stretch (pp. 234) Latisimus Stretch (pp. 231) **Indicates that you should train for time rather than repetitions*

Advanced Program
Weight Training Workout 2
Transverse Abdominal Hold (pp. 202)
Lateral Lunge (pp. 114)
Single Leg Squat* (pp. 124)
Reverse Calf Raise (pp. 122)
Scapular Retraction (pp. 150)
Shrug (pp. 146)
Internal Rotation (pp. 164)
External Rotation (pp. 162)
Bosu Ball Push Up* (pp. 156)
Triceps Extension (pp. 174)
Bridge* (pp. 180)
Fit Ball Ski Crunch* (pp. 218)
Overhead Stretch (pp. 235)
Hip Stretch (pp. 229)
Chest Stretch (pp. 227)
**Indicates that you should train for time rather than repetitions*

Advanced Program
Weight Training Workout 3
Single Leg Press (pp. 120)
Single Leg Extension (pp. 118)
Single Leg Bosu Ball Squat* (pp. 136)
Lat Pull-down (pp. 144)
Straight Arm Pull-down (no bosu ball)* (pp. 148)
Dumbbell Bench Press (pp. 152)
Dumbbell Shoulder Press (pp. 160)
Lateral Raise* (pp. 168)
Biceps Curl (pp. 172)
Triceps Press-down (pp. 176)
Medicine Ball Rotation* (pp. 222)
Side Plank* (pp. 214)
Downward Dog (pp. 224)
Quadriceps Stretch (pp. 233)
Hamstring Stretch (pp. 228)
Overhead Stretch (pp. 235)
**Indicates that you should train for time rather than repetitions*

Determining Time for Exercises with an Asterisk

Building muscular endurance is an important component to improving your skiing. However, determining the duration for the exercise can be a little confusing at first. Any exercise denoted with ansterisk should be performed in 2 to 5 minutes. How do you know how long to shoot for? Your weight training RPE is 9 to 10, so you should be working close to maximal effort. If you begin to feel a burn during the last quarter of the exercise, you know you have chosen a good duration. If you feel very little toward the end of the set you should increase the duration by 15-second increments until you feel a slight burn in the muscles during the last quarter of the set.

For example, if you were performing the plank, then you might start with 2 minutes for the first few sets. If you can barely make it to 2 minutes, you might decide to go 1 minute and 45 seconds on the last set. On the other hand, if you feel very little, you might decide to shoot for 2.5 minutes on the last set. The more muscular endurance your muscles have, the longer you will be able to ski. You also will find you are at less risk of injury and are more stable on your skis.

Try to increase your duration by 30 seconds for each exercise every week. For example, if you begin doing the plank for 2 minutes, by week 4 you should be doing the exercise for 3.5 minutes or more.

Aerobic Training

The aerobic training component during the second 4 weeks of your training begins with 30 minutes on nonweight-training days. You should increase your duration by 10 minutes each week until you reach 60 minutes. You will be increasing the amount of lactic acid during your weight-training workouts, so running, biking, hiking, or any other form of aerobic exercise the following day will help remove the acid from your muscles. This will aid in your recovery.

In Chapter 12, I answer some commonly asked questions, including how to know if you are overtraining and what to do about it. The following training guide will help you schedule your week.

Weekly Training Chart

Day	Weight Training	Aerobic Training
Monday	Workout One	None
Tuesday	None	Aerobic Training
Wednesday	Workout Two	None
Thursday	None	Aerobic Training
Friday	Workout Three	None
Saturday	None	Aerobic Training
Sunday	None	None

Stage 3 Workout

Stage 3 is designed to improve your power endurance, speed, and balance. For a more in-depth discussion of this stage, refer to page 72 earlier in this chapter. The following guidelines are for stage 3 of the Advanced program.

Stage 3: Improve Power Endurance, Speed, and Balance
4 Weeks/6 Days Per Week
• 1 warm up set (50% of work set) • 4 work sets • 30 seconds to 1 minute • When 60 repetitions are reached in 1 minute increase weight by 10% • Weight training RPE: 7 • Rest 2 minutes between sets • Plyometric Training • Begin with 30 second intervals increasing to two minutes by week four • Interval Training • Begin with 5 x 40 meter sprints, increasing to 20 x 40 meter sprints by week 12 • Plyometric and Interval Training RPE: 9-10

During the final 4 weeks of the FitSkiing program, you will be working on improving your power and speed between turns, as well as your reaction time and balance. Your weight training will include sets that last from 30 seconds to 1 minute. How do you decide what amount of weight to use? You are trying to recruit fast-twitch fibers, which produce power while at the same time lengthening the amount of time you can utilize that power. To do this, you should try to complete one repetition per second. Use a weight such that you can complete 30 repetitions in 30 seconds to start. Every week, increase the number of repetitions by ten until you reach 60 repetitions in 1 minute. If you reach 60 repetitions in 1 minute before week 4, then increase the weight by 10 percent. You are not trying to totally exhaust your muscles. Use a weight that you can move explosively. If you can complete only ten repetitions in 30 seconds, then the weight you are using is too heavy.

Plyometric Training

In stage 3 you will add some plyometrics to your program. In Chapter 8, you will find a full description of what plyometrics are, what they do, and how they will improve your skiing. Start with 30 seconds for each set during week 1 and increase by a 30 seconds each week until you reach 2 minutes per set. Your RPE should be at a 9, but I recommend that you start slowly and then increase the speed of the repetitions until you feel comfortable with the exercise. Plyometrics are not necessarily the easiest type of exercise to learn. When I first started performing them about 8 years ago, I was falling all over the place, and I thought I was an accomplished athlete. I learned to take each exercise in steps and to learn them slowly. After I felt comfortable with the plyometric exercise, I increased my speed until I was moving explosively through each repetition.

You will notice that some of the exercises are denoted with an asterisk. When you see this, simply revert back to stage 1's strength-training program. You should do as many repetitions as you can until you reach an RPE of 9 and occasionally a 10. For example, if you are performing the Transverse Abdominal Exercise, you might be able to perform ten repetitions, and on the decline sit up you might be able to complete 50 repetitions or more. Always remember to focus on the muscles you are working.

Advanced Program
Weight Training Workout 1
Transverse Abdominal Hold* (pp. 202)
Single Leg Bosu Ball Stability (140)
Bosu Ball Squat (pp. 136)
Barbell Squat (pp. 128)
Fit Ball Hamstring Curl (pp. 138)
Reverse Calf Raise (pp. 122)
Decline Sit Up* (pp. 208)
Medicine Ball Rotation* (pp. 222)
Back Extension* (pp. 180)
Hill Bounding (pp. 218)
Jump Lunge (pp. 219)
Downward Dog (pp. 224)
Low Back Hip Stretch (pp. 229)
Quadriceps Stretch (pp. 233)
Hamstring Stretch (pp. 228)
*Denotes using stage one's repetition and intensity

Advanced Program
Workout 2
Internal Rotation (8-12 repetitions) (pp. 164)
External Rotation (8-12 repetitions) (pp. 162)
Dumbbell Bench Press (pp. 152)
Bosu Ball Push Up (pp. 154)
Straight Arm Pull-down (pp. 148)
Shrug (pp. 146)
Dumbbell Shoulder Press (pp. 160)
Lateral Raise (pp. 168)
Bosu Ball Abdominal Stability (as many repetitions as you can) (pp. 204)
Opposing Arm/Leg Extension (as many repetitions as you can) (pp. 200)
Medicine Ball Side Toss (pp. 220)
Medicine Ball Overhead Toss (pp. 222)
Latisimus Stretch (pp. 231)
Chest Stretch (pp. 227)
Triceps Stretch (pp. 234)
Low Back Relaxation (pp. 232)

Advanced Program
Weight Training Workout 3
Transverse Abdominal Hold* (pp. 202)
Single Leg Extension (pp. 118)
Lateral Lunge (pp. 214)
Medicine Ball Reach and Squat (pp. 235)
Single Leg Hamstring Curl (pp. 238)
Step Up (pp. 230)
Reverse Calf Raise (pp. 122)
Decline Sit Up* (pp. 208)
Fit Ball Rotation* (pp. 210)
Back Extension* (pp. 180)
Stair Jumps (pp. 223)
Medicine Ball Sit Up and Toss (pp. 220)
Downward Dog (pp. 224)
Overhead Stretch (pp. 235)
Quadriceps Stretch (pp. 233)
Hamstring Stretch (pp.228)
*Denotes using stage one's repetition and intensity

Interval Training

Stage 3's interval program focuses on speed rather than endurance or lactate buffering. You will be performing three speed workouts per week, each lasting 20 to 30 minutes. Begin with a 5-minute warm-up (this is important because it will help get the blood circulating and assist in preventing injuries) and then move into the intervals. Your warm-up should be a light jog around a field or track. After your initial warm-up, perform four or five of the lower-body stretches from Chapter 8. This also will help keep the muscles warm so you can ease into your intervals.

Start with five 40-meter intervals at close to maximal speed, or an RPE of 10. Your rest intervals will be about 2 minutes. Increase by five intervals per week until you reach 20 intervals in week 12. The best place to perform your intervals is on a track. You should see marks for the start and the 40-meter finish on the track. If you don't, you can count 40 meters by taking 40 normal steps (rough guideline). If you do not have a track close by, then you can use a football or soccer field. Apply the same principle to measure 40 meters. A good time to shoot for is 5 to 8 seconds.

A full recovery between sets is important. You are not trying to improve your endurance; you are working on your speed. A good gauge of full recovery is to take your resting heart rate before you warm up. Most people range between 60 and 85 beats per minute (BPM). **If you are above 90 BPM prior to warming up you should consult a physician.** Take your heart rate after each interval until it reaches your pre-workout level. For example, if you start your workout at 75 BPM, then you should wait until your heart rate comes within 10 BPM of this before you start the next interval. It might take 1 minute to reach your baseline level after your first interval, but after your fifth interval it might take as much as 4 or 5 minutes, depending on the kind of condition you were in when you started. See the interval schedule for the final 4 weeks of training.

Week	Number of Intervals	Length of Intervals	Rest Between Intervals
1	5	40 meters	2 minutes
2	10	40 meters	2 minutes
3	15	40 meters	2 minutes
4	20	40 meters	2 minutes

The final stage of the Advanced program is the most ski-specific type of training you will perform during the course of the program. You can perform the speed workouts after your weight training or on nonweight-training days. Always gauge your workouts by how you feel. If you have taxed your body physically moving furniture on Monday, you might want to wait an extra day before your next hard workout.

That is the Advanced FitSkiing program. Now get started so you can be ready to make some tracks when the snow starts falling. Your weekly schedule for stage 3 follows.

Day	Weight Training/Plyometrics	Speed Training
Monday	Workout One	None
Tuesday	None	Speed Intervals
Wednesday	Workout Two	None
Thursday	None	Speed Intervals
Friday	Workout Three	None
Saturday	None	Speed Intervals
Sunday	None	None

Next you will find quick reference guides to the workouts in this chapter. These visual guides will assist you in keeping track of which exercises to perform and in what sequence to complete them. Each stage of the FitSkiing program is illustrated with photos and the corresponding number of the correct sequence. For example, if a number 1 is set below an exercise, it means it should be the first exercise performed. If a number two appears below a photo, then it is to be performed second in the sequence. Complete the recommended number of sets for each exercise before you move to the next exercise.

These guides also can be copied for a handy reference to take with you to the gym. You can post them on your refrigerator to help keep you motivated and on schedule to get in the best skiing shape of your life.

Basic Program Quick Reference Guide

Improve Strength and Overall Conditioning
Workout 1

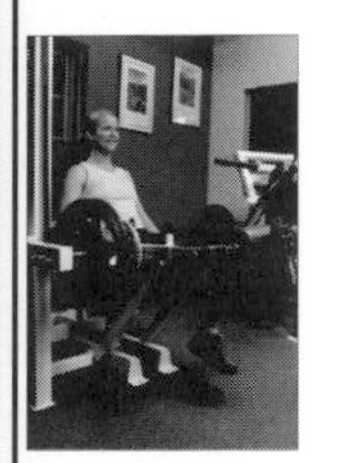
1

2

3

4

5

6

7

8

9

10

Improve Strength and Overall Conditioning
Workout 2

1

2

3

4

5

6

7

8

9

10

Basic Program Quick Reference Guide

Improve Strength and Overall Conditioning
Workout 3

1

2

3

4

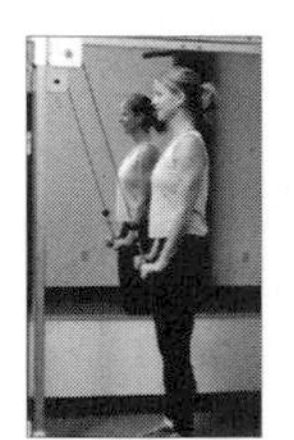
5

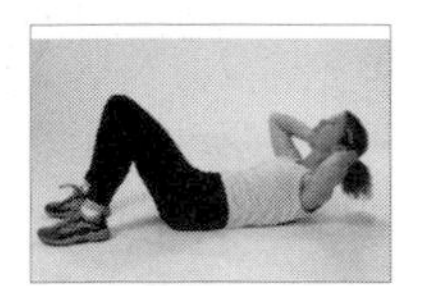
6

7

8

9

10

Improve Muscular and Aerobic Endurance
Workout 1

1

2

3

4

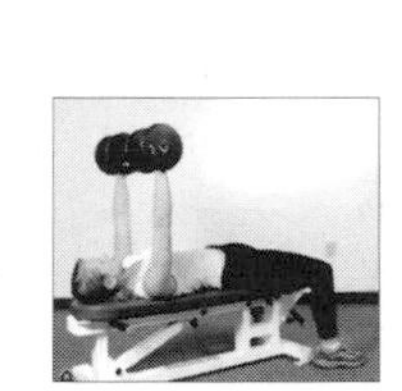
5

6

7

8

9

10

11

12

13

14

Basic Program Quick Reference Guide

Improve Muscular and Aerobic Endurance
Workout 2

1

2

3

4

5

6

7

8

9

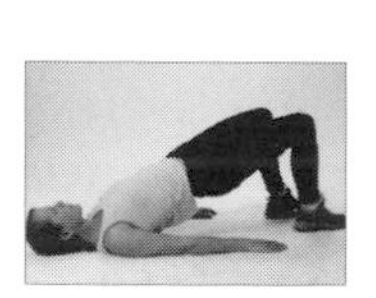
10

11

12

13

14

Improve Muscular and Aerobic Endurance
Workout 3

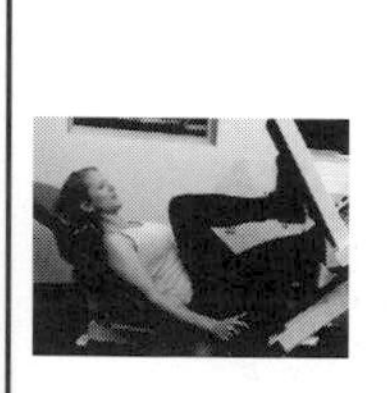
1

2

3

4

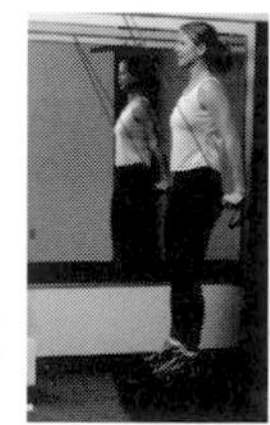
5

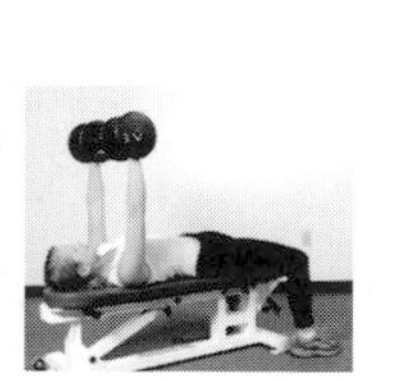
6

7

8

9

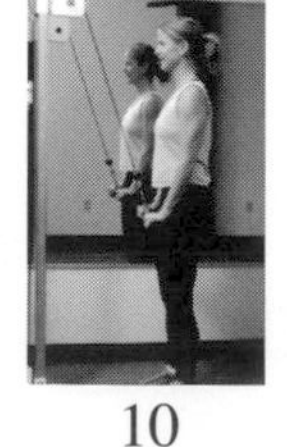
10

11

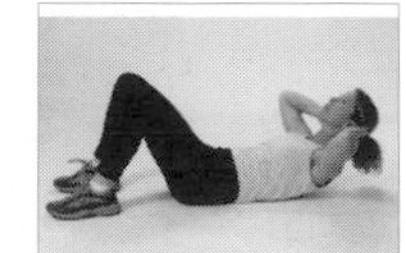
12

13

14

Basic Program Quick Reference Guide

Improve Power Endurance, Speed and Balance
Workout 1

1

2

3

4

5

6

7

8

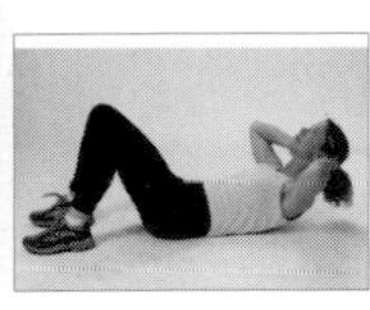
9

10

11

12

13

14

Improve Power Endurance, Speed and Balance
Workout 2

1

2

3

4

5

6

7

8

9

10

11

12

13

14

Basic Program Quick Reference Guide

Improve Power Endurance, Speed and Balance
Workout 3

1

2

3

4

5

6

7

8

9

10

11

12

13

14

Advanced Program Quick Reference Guide

Improve Overall Strength and Conditioning
Workout 1

1

2

3

4

5

6

7

8

9

10

11

12

13

Improve Overall Strength and Conditioning
Workout 2

1

2

3

4

5

6

7

8

9

10

11

12

Advanced Program Quick Reference Guide

Improve Overall Strength and Conditioning
Workout 3

1

2

3

4

5

6

7

8

9

10

11

12

Improve Muscular and Aerobic Endurance
Workout 1

1

2

3

4

5

6

7

8

9

10

11

12

13

14

Advanced Program Quick Reference Guide

Improve Muscular and Aerobic Endurance
Workout 2

1

2

3

4

5

6

7

8

9

10

11

12

13

14

Improve Muscular and Aerobic Endurance
Workout 3

1

2

3

4

5

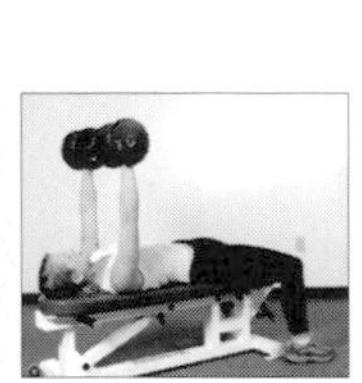
6

7

8

9

10

11

12

13

14

15

Advanced Program Quick Reference Guide

Improve Power Endurance, Speed and Balance
Workout 1

Improve Power Endurance, Speed and Balance
Workout 2

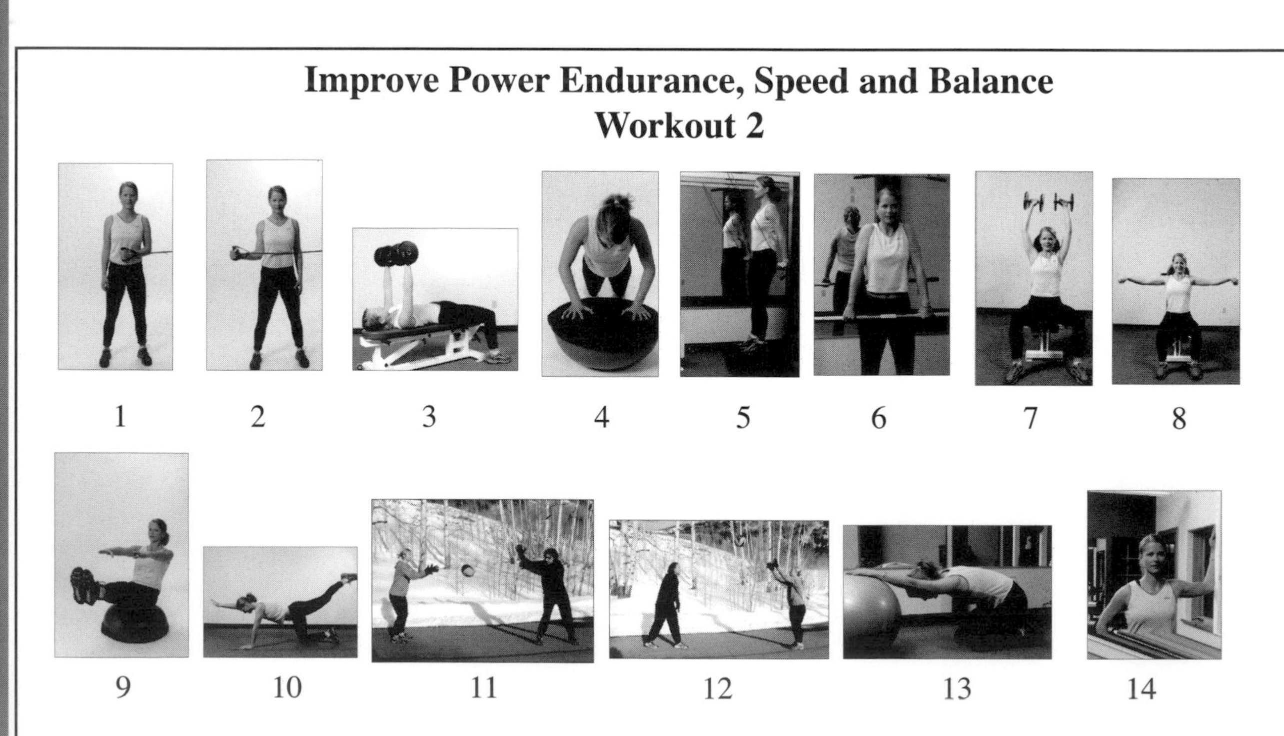

Advanced Program Quick Reference Guide

Improve Power Endurance, Speed and Balance
Workout 3

1  2  3  4  5  6  7

8  9  10  11  12  13  14

Pre-Ski Warm Up

You've heard it time and time again; warm up before you workout or ski. The FitSkiing program is no different. In fact if you warm up with these simple exercises you will perform better on the slopes and be at less risk for injury. Below is a chart that describes the general pre ski warm up.

Pre-Ski Warm Up
Before Hitting the Slopes
• 1 warm up set (50% of work set) • 1 work set • 30 seconds to 1 minute • Exercise RPE: 5 • Rest 1 minute between sets *Note: Remember you are warming up before you go skiing, this is not a workout, it is simply to get your body prepared for the slopes.*

On the following chart you will find the warm up exercises to perform before you head out to the lifts. You can also find the exercises in chapter eight. Those that are denoted with a coffee cup are the exercises you will be performing.

Pre-Ski Warm Up
Exercises Before Skiing
Transverse Abdominal Hold Leg Circles Back Extension Bridge Opposing Arm/Leg Extension Downward Dog

An illustrated guide to the exercises is on the following page. If you have further questions on how to perform the exercises turn to chapter eight for a more in depth description. You can copy it and bring it to the gym or post it on your refrigerator as an easy reminder of which exercises to complete.

Pre-Ski Warm Up

1

2

3

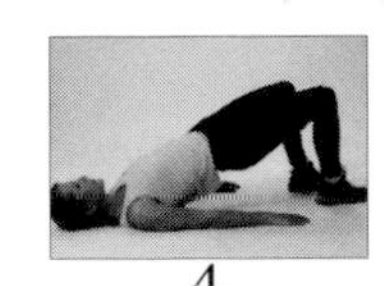
4

5

6

KEY SYMBOLS

WARNING

OUTDOOR ALTERNATIVE

EXERCISE EXPENSE

TARGET TRAINING TIP

IMPROVES BALANCE

PRE SKI WARM UP

EXERCISE ALTERNATIVE

CHAPTER EIGHT

FITSKIING EXERCISES

LEGS

1. Lunge
2. Lateral Lunge
3. Single Leg Curl
4. Single Leg Extension
5. Single Leg Press
6. Reverse Calf Raise
7. Single Leg Squat
8. Ski Tuck
9. Dumbbell Squat
10. Step Up
11. Wall Sit
12. Hip Abduction
13. Medicine Ball Reach/Squat
14. Bosu Ball Squat
15. Fit Ball Leg Curl
16. Single Leg Stability
17. Leg Circles

LUNGE

STRENGTHENS QUADRICEPS, HAMSTRINGS, AND GLUTES

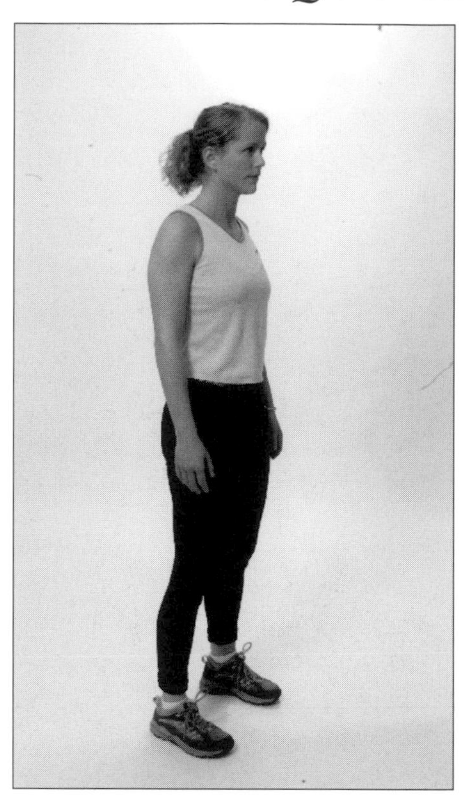

Exercise Description

1. With hands at your sides stand upright with your feet together.
2. Keeping your head forward, back upright, and chest out, bend your knees and bring your trailing knee almost to the floor.
3. Push back with your front foot to the starting position with one powerful movement, bringing feet together.
4. Step forward with your other foot and repeat.

Note: To make the exercise more difficult hold dumbbells at your sides.
Note: This exercise also can be done while walking (see outdoor alternative).

OUTDOOR ALTERNATIVE

WARNING!

Do not let the knee extend over the foot. This can apply unneeded pressure to the knee, specifically the patellar tendon.

LUNGE

STRENGTHENS QUADRICEPS, HAMSTRINGS, AND GLUTES

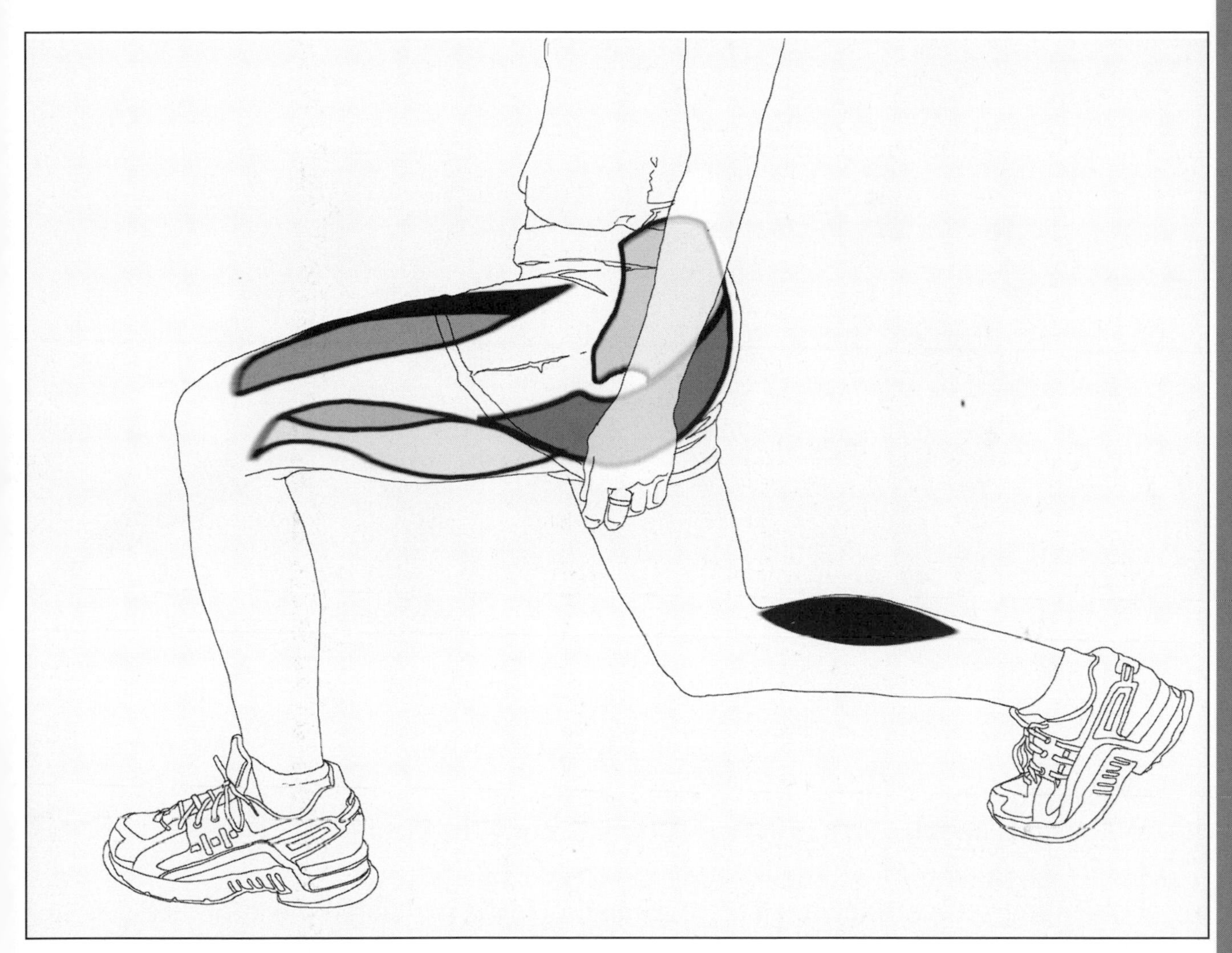

FITSKIING MUSCLES AT WORK

The lunge is a great all-around exercise for the entire leg. It works the quadriceps muscles, the hamstrings, and the calves. By performing the lunge, you are working the same muscles in a similar way to when you are skiing. This is a ski-specific movementt, especially for telemark skiers.

By improving muscular endurance in these areas, you will be more likely to have stability on your skis and to fatigue less. Because the lunge works so many of the leg muscles, your body will be at less risk of injury. When one or more of the muscle groups fatigues, you will have plenty of fibers recruited in other muscles to compensate.

By keeping the abdominal muscles contracted throughout the movement, you also will teach your core to work with your leg muscles. This will provide extra stability and support.

LATERAL LUNGE

STRENGTHENS QUADRICEPS, OUTER HIPS, AND CALVES

Exercise Description

1. With hands on hips, step off to one side abducting the hip.
2. Go into a squat position on the lunging side.
3. Lower yourself until the thigh of your lunging leg is parallel to the floor. Keep your head facing forward with your spine slightly arched.
4. After you reach the bottom position, push yourself upward and to the side, back to the initial position. Repeat with the other side.

Note: To make the exercise more difficult, hold dumbbells at your sides.

TARGET TRAINING TIP

To recruit more fast twitch fibers emphasize a fast push off at the midpoint of the movement. Always remember to use your abdominal muscles for stabilization of the body.

LATERAL LUNGE

STRENGTHENS QUADRICEPS, OUTER HIPS, AND CALVES

FITSKIING MUSCLES AT WORK

The lateral lunge is an effective exercise to get your body prepared for the ski season. When you are transferring weight from one ski to the other, your legs make a slight lateral adjustment. By adding the lateral lunge to your training program, you will improve your stability and strength during turns.

By completing this exercise, you also will strengthen those ski-specific muscles (quadriceps), which in turn will help you ski longer and prevent injuries. By increasing the strength in your outer hips, you will have more muscles to rely on, thereby decreasing the amount of direct fatigue applied to the quadriceps muscles.

SINGLE LEG CURL

STRENGTHENS HAMSTRINGS

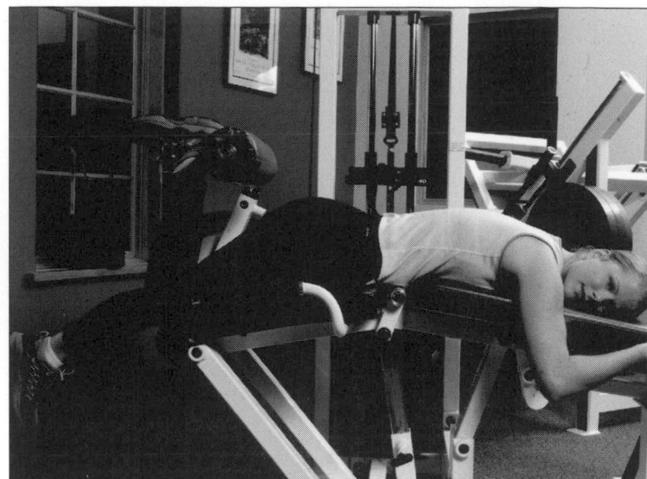

Exercise Description

1. Lie facedown on the leg curl machine and hook your heels under the padded lever.
2. Keeping your pelvis pressed into bench, curl your leg as far as it will go. Release and lower the weight slowly.
3. Repeat with the other leg.

Note: Remember to push your hips and pelvis into the bench because this provides greater focus on the hamstrings and away from the lower back.

TARGET TRAINING TIP

Consciously focus on the hamstring muscle while curling the weight. This will provide more focus on the muscle and help maintain proper form.

WARNING!

Do not lift your hips or pelvis off the bench. This exercise should be done strictly to eliminate potential back injuries.

ALTERNATIVE (STANDING LEG CURL)

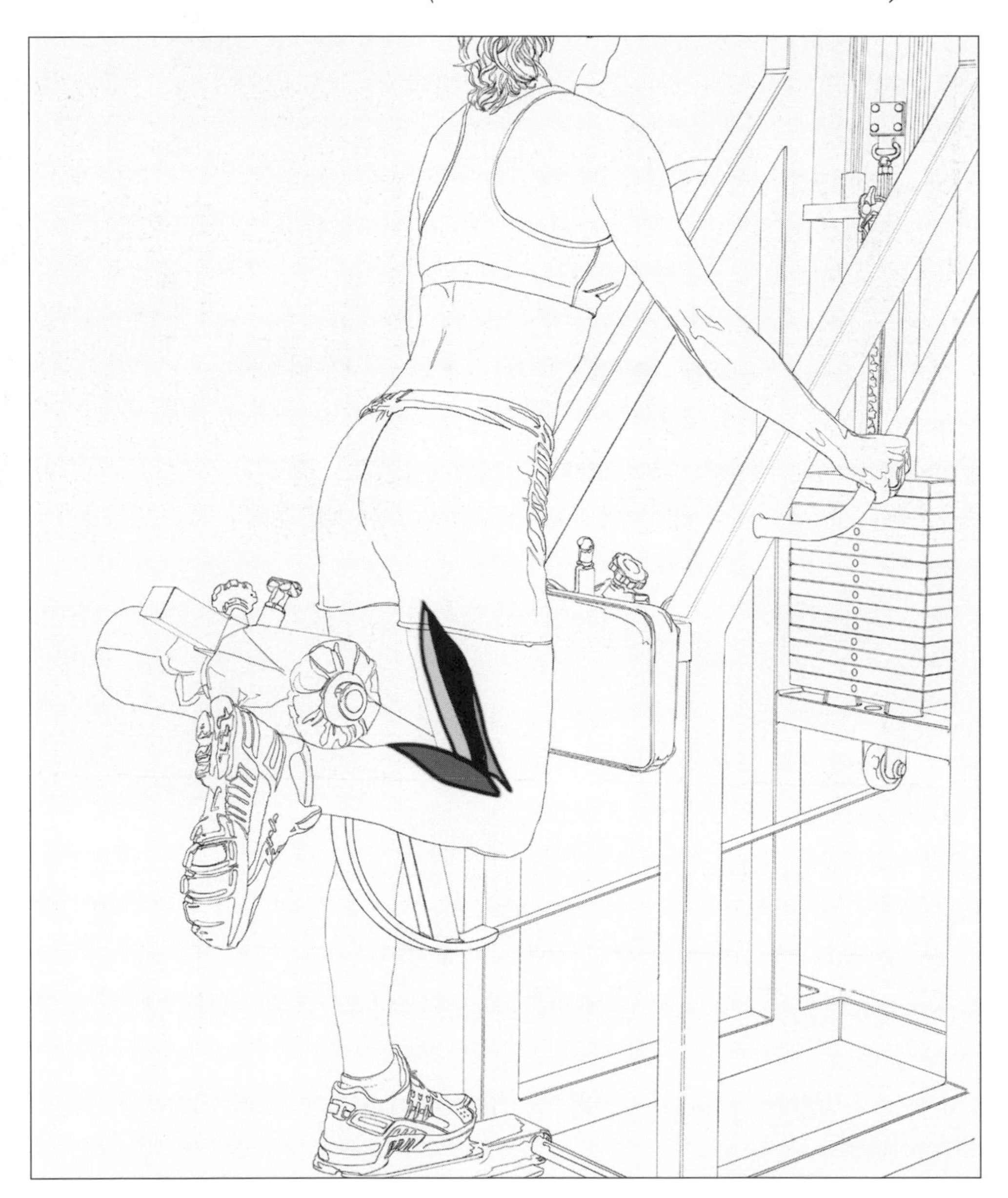

FITSKIING MUSCLES AT WORK

It is well-known in the sports medicine community that most people have imbalanced strength when comparing quadriceps (front part of leg) strength to hamstring (back part of leg) strength. This can lead to injury due to a large amount of force being applied from the quadriceps and not enough balance with regards to the hamstring muscles.

Skiing involves the hamstring muscles in stabilizing the body and flexing the knee. By strengthening the hamstring muscles, a skier will be more stable while skiing and will be able to absorb bumps (moguls) more easily.

The longer you ski, the more fatigued your abdominal and quadriceps muscles become. If your body, including the hamstring muscles is strong and has muscular endurance, you will be more likely to stay on your skis longer and prevent unwanted injuries.

SINGLE LEG EXTENSION

STRENGTHENS QUADRICEPS

Exercise Description

1. Using a leg extension machine, sit in the seat and hook your feet under the padded lever.
2. Extend your legs out to the maximum, making sure you remain sitting flat on the machine.
3. Lower the weight slowly until your feet are no farther back than the knees and the thighs are stretched.
4. Repeat with the other leg.

Note: Don't lift your hips off the seat and cheat the weight up

WARNING!

Do not lock out the knees at the top of the movement. Although this does provide greater stress on the muscles, it can injure the knee.

TARGET TRAINING TIP

As you extend your knee, contract the abdominal muscles. Teaching your body's core to work with other muscles will provide more stability and help prevent injuries.

LEG EXTENSION

STRENGTHENS QUADRICEPS

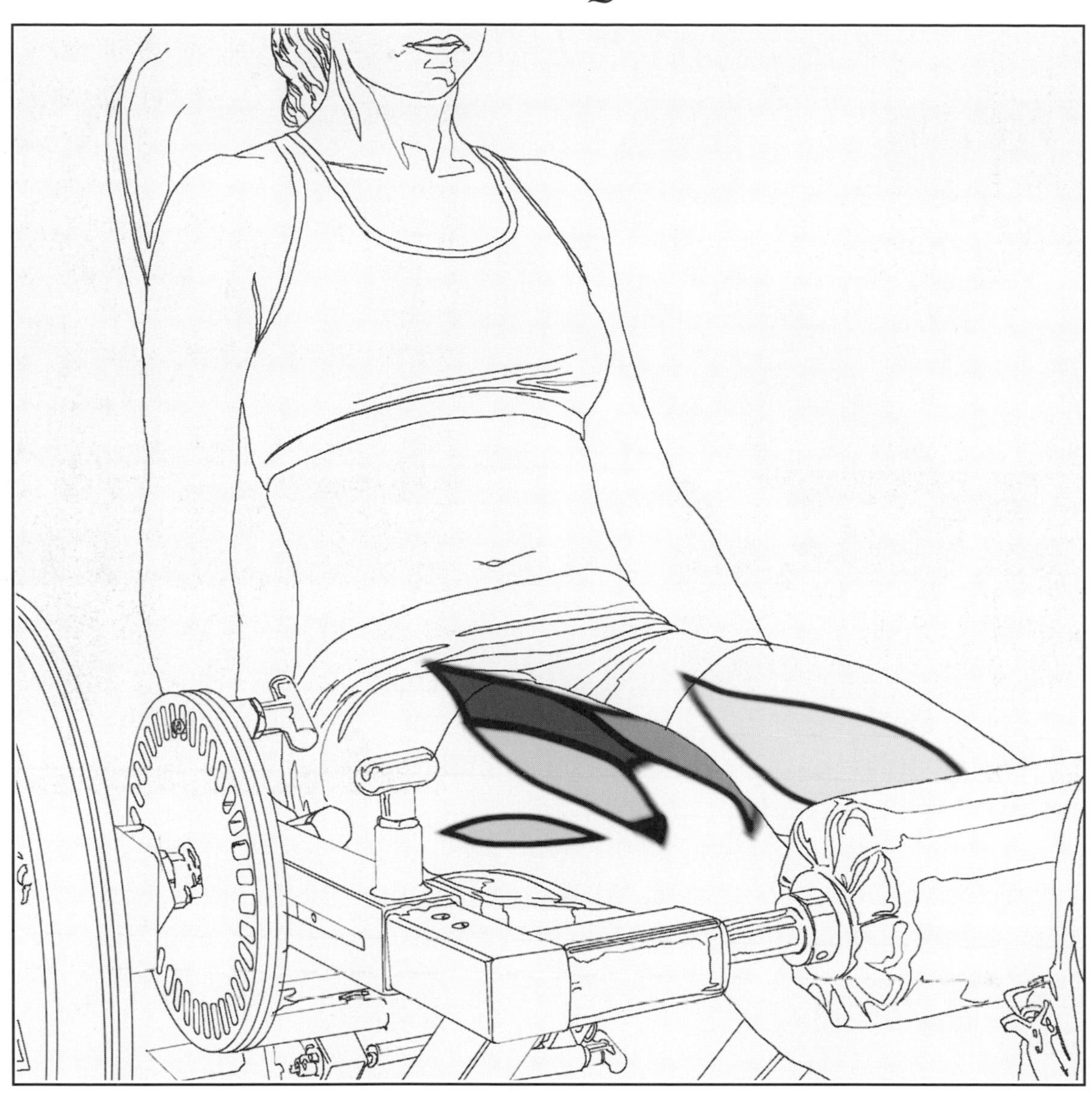

FITSKIING MUSCLES AT WORK

Many physicians and physical therapists would throw every leg extension machine out of the gym if they could. They believe that it applies too much stress to the knees. Remember that the actual movement of the quadriceps muscles is to extend the knee, and the leg extension is one of the few exercises that isolates only these muscles. The leg extension works the entire front part of your thigh and is a good warm-up exercise to get your leg muscles fired before performing other leg exercises like the squat or lunge. By warming up your quadriceps first, you will be stronger for other movements that use the same muscles. You also put yourself at less risk of injury.

SINGLE LEG PRESS

STRENGTHENS QUADRICEPS, HAMSTRINGS, HIP FLEXORS, AND GLUTES

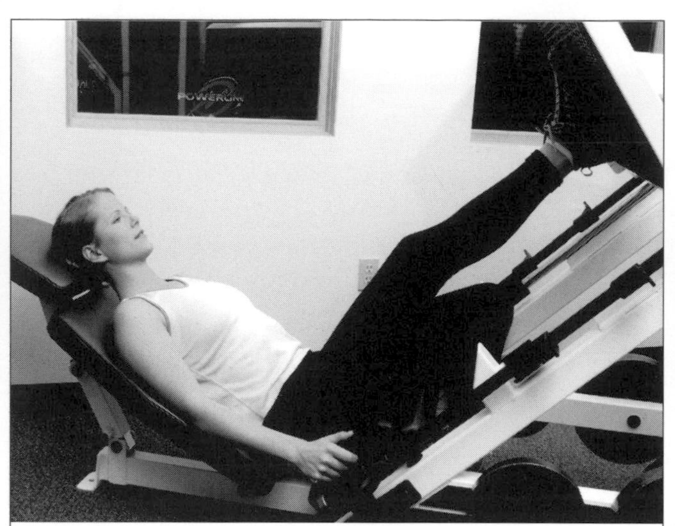

Exercise Description

1. Adjust the leg press machine so there is a slight (10 degree) bend at the knee when your feet are placed against the pad.
2. Make sure your back is flat against the seat. Press and release safety restraints.
3. Lower weight till the knees are at 90 degrees. Pause briefly at the bottom of the movement and press weight back up. Remember not to lock the knees at the top of the movement.
4. Repeat with the other leg.

WARNING!

Do not lock knees at the top of the movement. This can place unneeded stress on the knee joint.

Keep you abdominal muscles contracted to ease any stress placed on the lower back.

OUTDOOR ALTERNATIVE

SINGLE LEG PRESS

STRENGTHENS QUADRICEPS, HAMSTRINGS, HIP FLEXORS, AND GLUTES

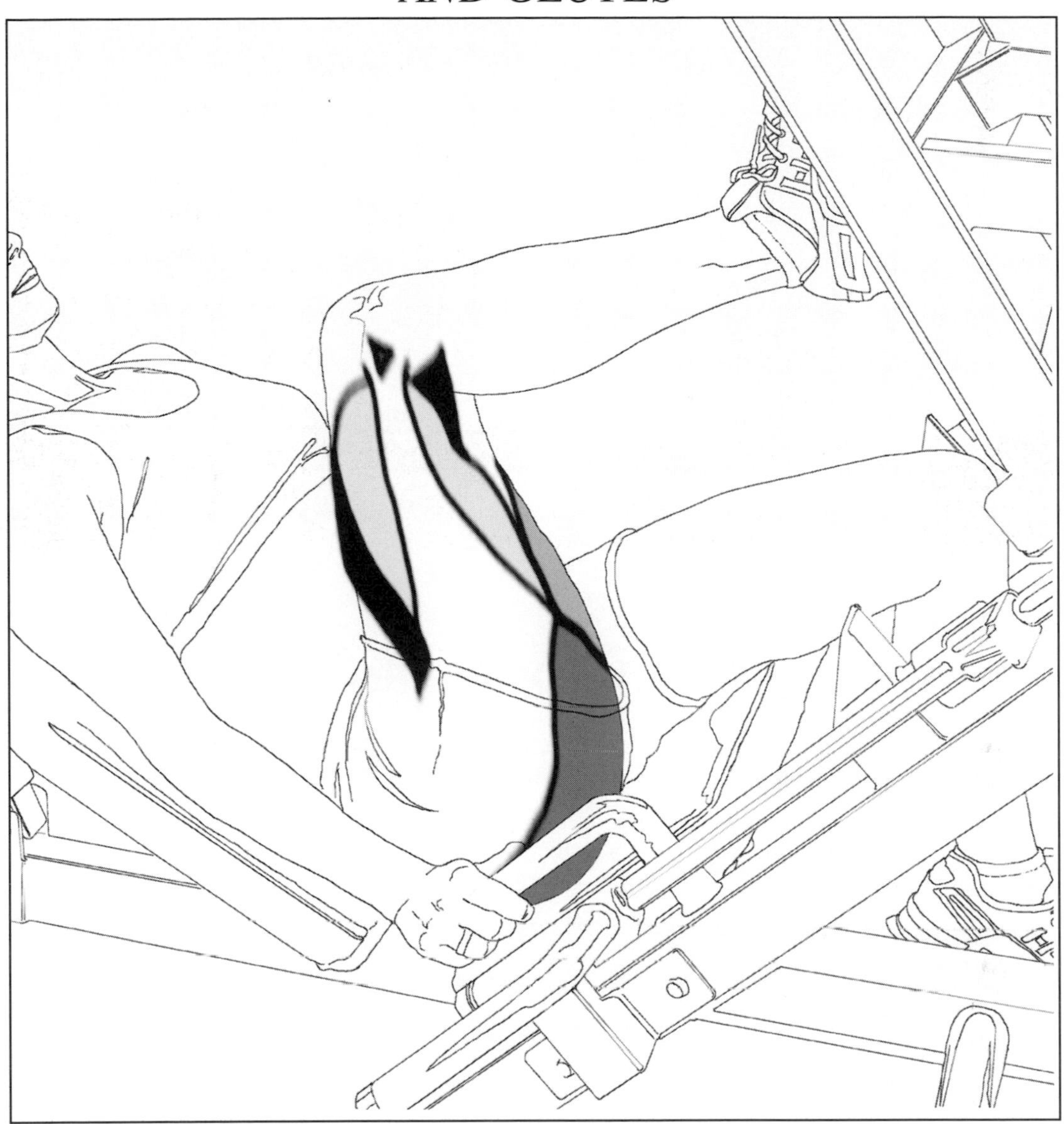

FITSKIING MUSCLES AT WORK

The leg press is a great overall exercise for the legs. It strengthens the quadriceps, hip flexors, gluteus maximus, and to some extent the hamstrings. This is a great overall exercise for the leg muscles. All these muscles are used while skiing. Although many consider this an alternative to the squat, it is more leg specific because of the position your body is in. When performing the squat, you are working not only your legs but your entire body because you are standing as opposed to lying in a fixed position. The squat also applies more stress to the glute muscles as opposed to the quadriceps (although it does apply significant stress to the quadriceps). The leg press is a good alternative to the squat if you have lower back problems or weaker leg muscles.

REVERSE CALF RAISE

STRENGTHENS SHINS (ANTERIOR TIBIALIS)

Exercise Description

1. Sit on the edge of a bench or chair with your legs extended. Place a dumbbell between your feet and extend them as far as they will go.
2. Slowly raise your feet toward your body, contracting the shin (anterior tibialis) muscles).
3. Repeat for a set number of repetitions.

TARGET TRAINING TIP

Always remember to keep the abdominal muscles tight or contracted to support the lower back. Doing so also teaches the body to utilize its core when using other muscles.

IMPROVES BALANCE

Strengthening your shins or anterior tibialis muscles can create more balance and stability. It also may reduce shin splints when you first begin your training.

REVERSE CALF RAISE

STRENGTHENS SHINS (ANTERIOR TIBIALIS)

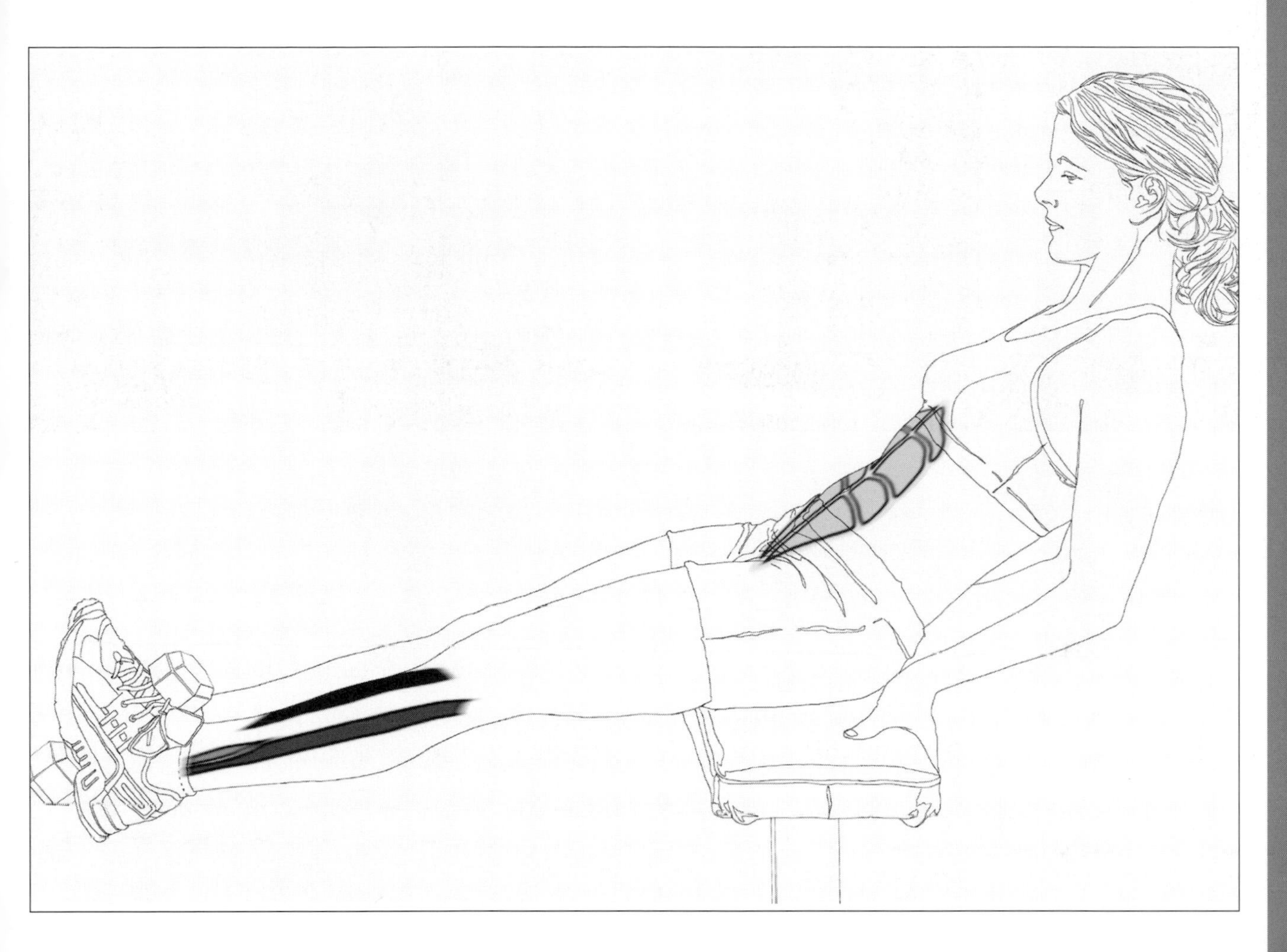

FITSKIING MUSCLES AT WORK

The reverse calf raise is essential to a good ski-conditioning program. The anterior tibialis muscles, or shins as they are commonly called, are important to strengthen because they help in the stability while you are on your skis. When your lower leg is locked into a ski boot, it is automatically dorsiflexed (foot is pulled toward the body). Because of that, the shins can fatigue quickly if they have not been strengthened. This is commonly called shin splints. By adding this exercise to your workout you will be more stable on your skis and be less likely to have pain in your shins.

SINGLE LEG SQUAT

STRENGTHENS HAMSTRINGS, QUADRICEPS, AND GLUTES

Exercise Description

1. Begin by standing on one foot. Stabilize on the leg until you feel comfortably balanced.
2. Contract the abdominal muscles and take a deep breath. Slowly lower the body till the leg is at 90 degrees or until you begin to feel unstable.
3. At the bottom of the movement, pause for a moment and then breathe out while extending the leg until you are at the starting position.
4. Repeat with the other leg.

Note: Always make sure you feel balanced before going into the squat. Place dumbbells in hands and hold at your sides to make the exercise more difficult.

IMPROVES BALANCE

Single leg training improves independent leg stability and balance. By incorporating single limb work in your training, you may also help prevent injury.

TARGET TRAINING TIP

Put most of the pressure on the heel of the foot as opposed to the toe. This will place more stress on the appropriate leg muscles as opposed to the knee joint.

SINGLE LEG SQUAT

STRENGTHENS HAMSTRINGS, QUADRICEPS, AND GLUTES

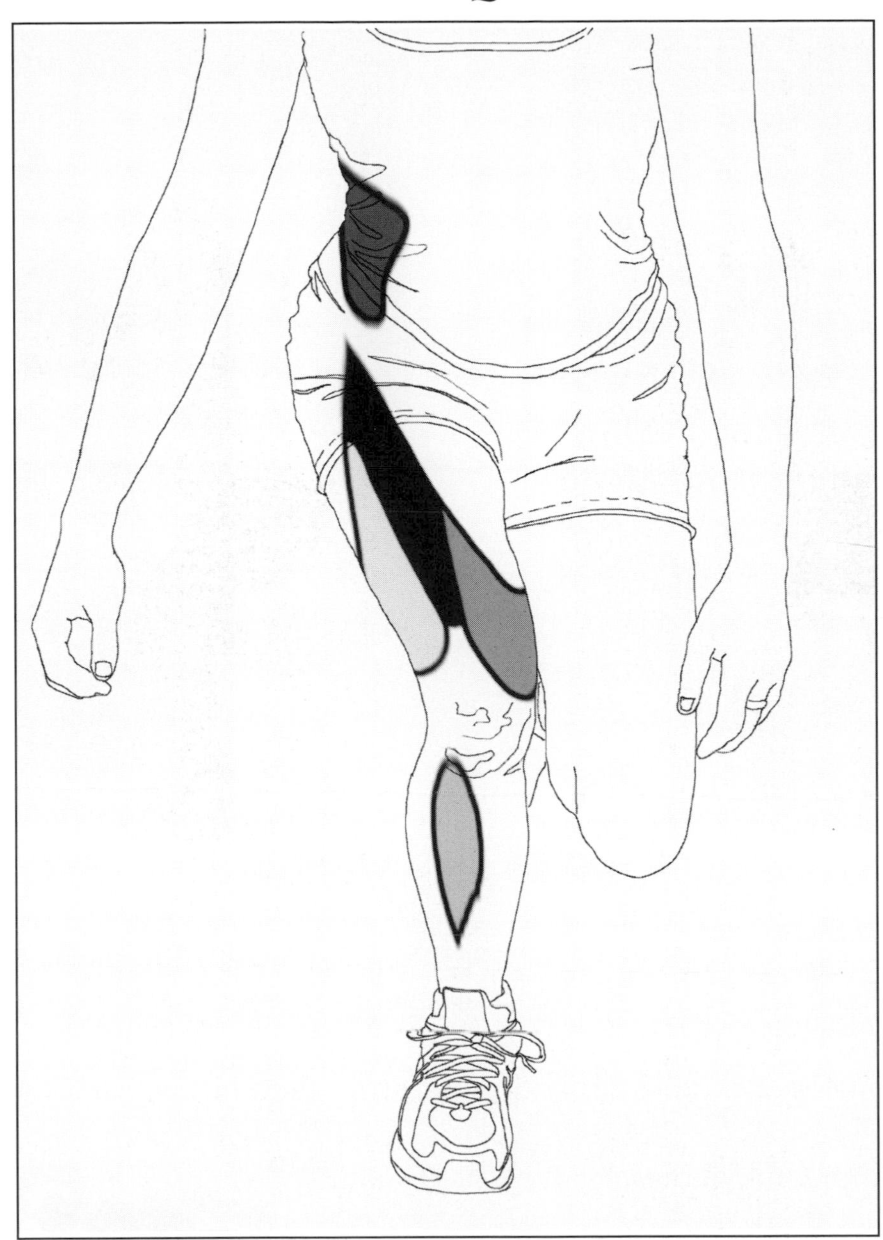

FITSKIING MUSCLES AT WORK

The single leg squat is a unilateral (one leg at a time) movement that is a great overall performance enhancer for skiing. Because we have independent leg action in skiing (as opposed to snowboarding where both legs work in a larger part together), the single leg squat is a great specific exercise because you are using independent leg action, as well. This exercise also requires the oblique muscles (side part of the torso) to engage. This teaches the legs and core to work together to perform one motion. By getting more muscles to work together, you will have more stability on your skis and be at less risk of injury.

SKI TUCK

STRENGTHENS BALANCE, HAMSTRINGS, AND QUADRICEPS

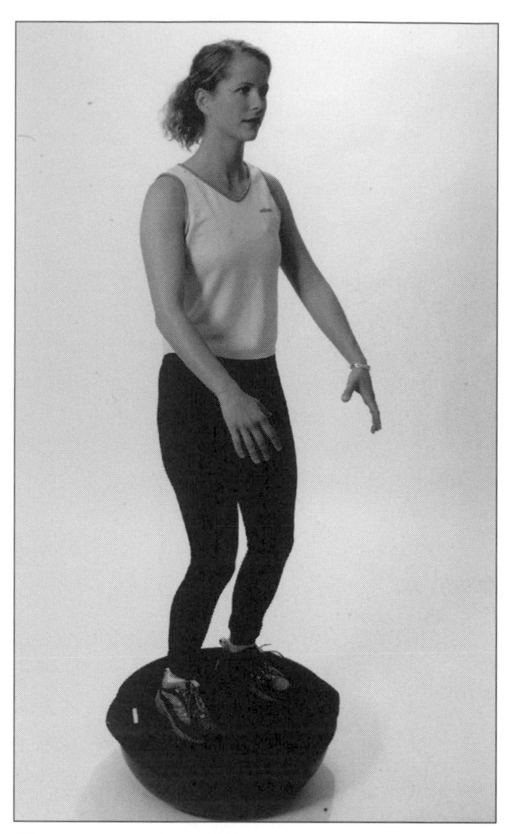

Exercise Description

1. Flip the Bosu Ball over so the base is on top. Place one foot on the base, and then bring the other onto it. Make sure you are stable and comfortable with your balance before you begin.
2. Squat down into a tuck position with your arms slightly bent and tucked in to the sides.
3. Contract your abdominal muscles for added stability. Maintain pressure through the heels of your feet.
4. Hold this position for the recommended time.

Note: Return to the upright position and step off the Bosu Ball.

OUTDOOR ALTERNATIVE

IMPROVES BALANCE

The bosu Ball provides a safe, unstable surface. It assists in improving overall balance on skis and in daily life. The ski tuck improves muscular endurance and balance.

SKI TUCK

STRENGTHENS BALANCE, HAMSTRINGS, AND QUADRICEPS

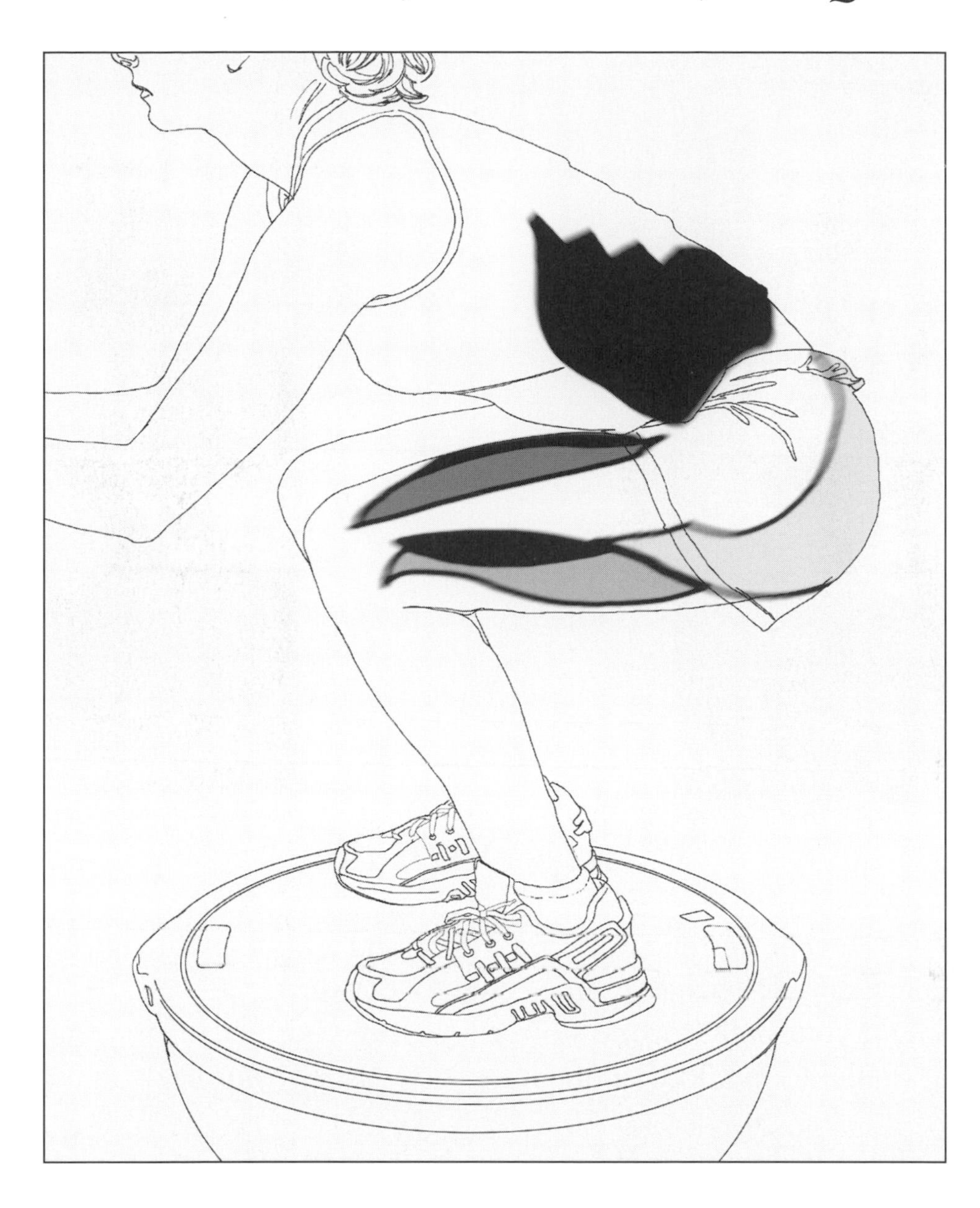

FITSKIING MUSCLES AT WORK

The ski tuck is very ski specific. When skiing, you are flexed at the knee or squatting a majority of the time. By including this exercise in your training program, you will apply stress to the same muscles that you use more than 50 percent of the time when skiing. By using the Bosu Ball, you create an unstable surface, similar to that of the terrain you ski on. If you don't have a Bosu Ball you can stand on a couch cushion. If you haven't achieved a comfortable sense of balance yet, you may want to consider holding the ski tuck on a flat surface like the photograph at the right shows.

DUMBBELL SQUAT

STRENGTHENS QUADRICEPS, HAMSTRINGS, AND GLUTES

Exercise Description

1. Stand with your feet placed shoulder width apart and dumbbells at your sides. Your feet should be pointed straight ahead or turned slightly outward.
2. Inhale and hold your breath while slowly lowering your body. You should have a 90 degree bend (parallel to the floor) at the knee joint. Keep your heels in contact with the floor.
3. With your abdominals still contracted, begin the upward portion of the movement, slowly extending the legs while exhaling.

EXERCISE ALTERNATIVE

WARNING!

If you have lower back or recent knee-related injuries, do not perform the barbell squat. Depending on the severity of knee or back injuries, you might want to avoid the squat completely.

DUMBBELL SQUAT

STRENGTHENS QUADRICEPS, HAMSTRINGS, AND GLUTES

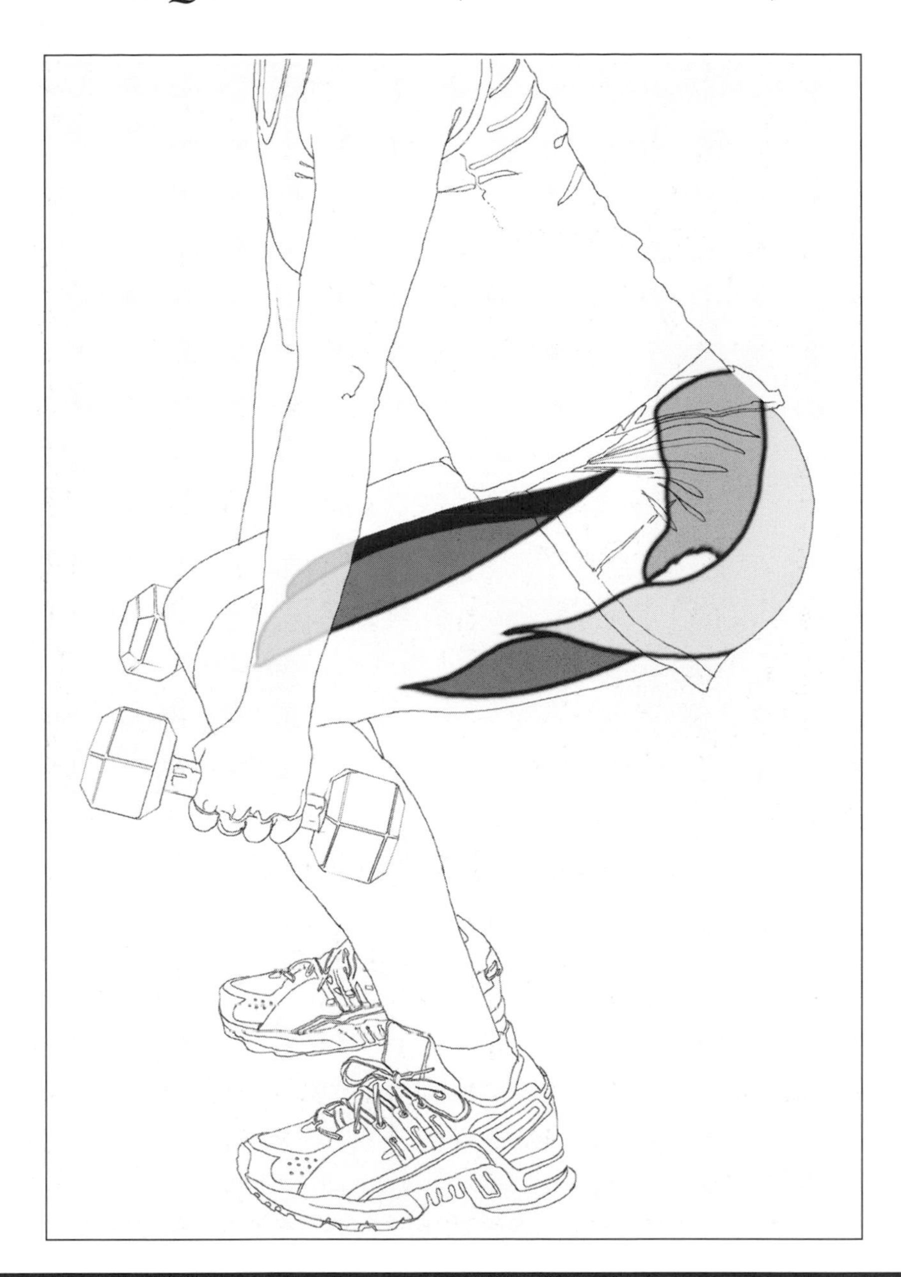

FITSKIING MUSCLES AT WORK

A favorite of professional ski racers, the squat improves strength and power in the quadriceps, hamstrings, and glute muscles. The squat is a somewhat unstable exercise at first. It requires a lot of balance and core strength. By performing the squat, you engage your core muscles while at the same time using your legs. This teaches the leg muscles and the core muscles to work together, which provides more stability and can put you at less risk of injury. If you want to apply more stress to the entire body, try the exercise pictured at left. The squat also helps the body learn to transition quickly from side to side, which can help on fresh groomed snow, as well as in deep powder..

STEP UP

STRENGTHENS QUADRICEPS, GLUTES, AND CALVES

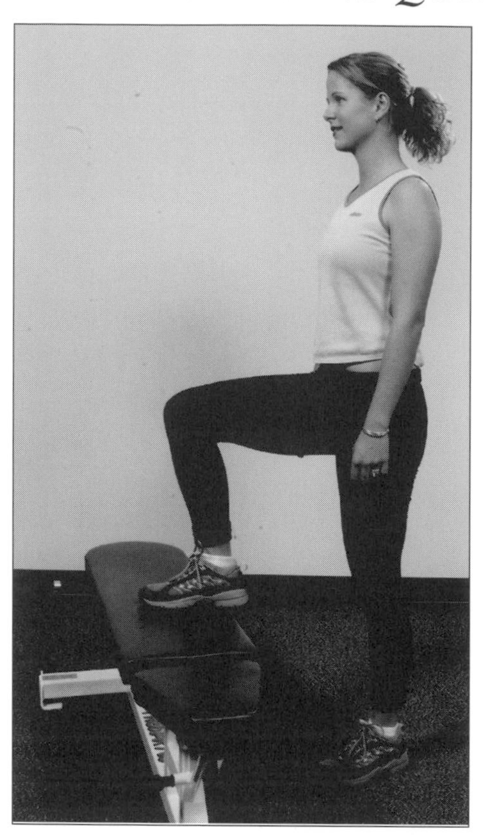

Exercise Description

1. Find a box or bench that lines up just below the knees.
2. Step onto the bench with one foot and powerfully bring the other foot off the floor. Keep your abdominal muscles contracted throughout the entire movement.
3. As you reach the top of the movement, extend the trailing leg's hip backward to contract the glute muscles.
4. Step down and repeat with the other leg.

Note: Always drive through the heel. This applies more stress to the leg muscles as opposed to the knee joint.

OUTDOOR ALTERNATIVE

TARGET TRAINING TIP

The more hip flexibility you have, the more your muscles can be recruited. This can lead to quicker strength gains. Remember to stretch after training with weights.

STEP UP

STRENGTHENS QUADRICEPS, GLUTES, AND CALVES

FITSKIING MUSCLES AT WORK

The step up improves the power of your legs, which in turn assists in your skiing power. While completing this exercise, you engage your quadriceps, glutes, and calf muscles. These are the same muscles you use when skiing. By improving power within these muscles, you will be able to make quicker turns and improve your balance and stability on the slopes. If you don't have a bench to use, you can use a set of stairs.

WALL SIT

STRENGTHENS QUADRICEPS AND HAMSTRINGS

Exercise Description

1. Begin by finding a solid, straight wall to sit against. Position your back firmly against the wall and squat to a 90 degree angle at the knee joint.
2. Make sure that your lower back is flush with the wall and that no space is between you and the supporting structure.
3. Hold for the specified time.
4. When you are finished, push through the heels of your feet and drive yourself to the upright position.

WARNING!
The picture at left was shot to demonstrate hazardous conditions that should not be used for exercises. Make sure you find a solid non-slippery surface to perform exercises.

TARGET TRAINING TIP
Remember that keeping the pressure on your heels keeps the focus on your legs and away from your knees. Always contract your abdominals for extra back support.

WALL SIT

STRENGTHENS QUADRICEPS AND HAMSTRINGS

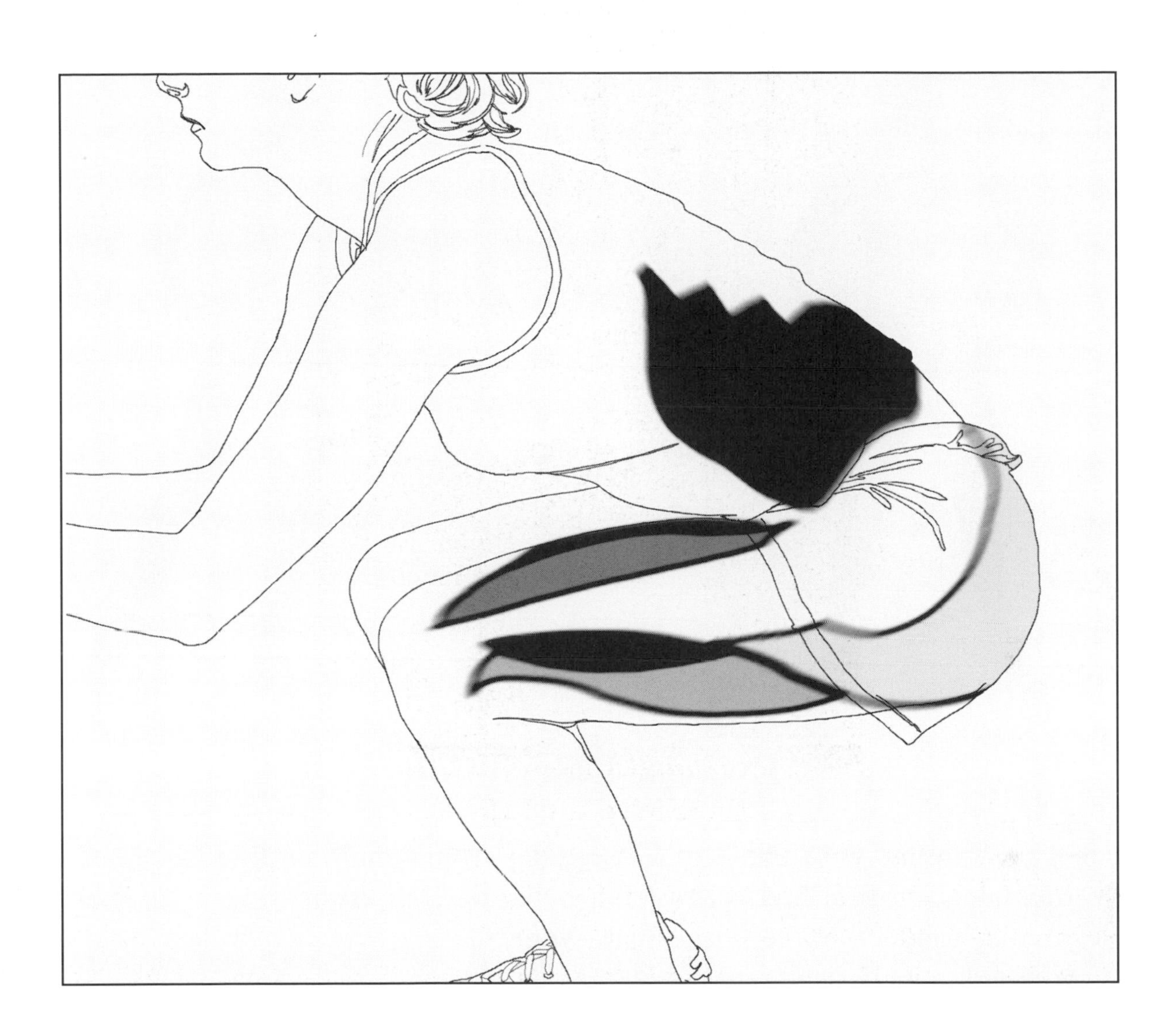

FITSKIING MUSCLES AT WORK

This is a favorite of skiers everywhere, because it improves the amount of muscular endurance in the muscles. When skiing, you may find that your leg muscles start to burn. This is due to fatigue and a lack of oxygenated blood available to help the muscles recover. Therefore, your muscles produce lactic acid as a protective mechanism so you stop what you are doing and will recover. This exercise improves your ability to buffer the lactic acid and therefore allows you to ski longer. The wall sit applies stress to all the major muscles you use while skiing.

HIP ABDUCTION

STRENGTHENS OUTER HIP

Exercise Description

1. Attach a band around your ankles or a low pulley from a multipurpose machine.
2. Place your hands on your hips or grasp a firm bar for stability.
3. Raise your leg (abduct) to the side as far as you can.
4. Bring your feet together and repeat with the other side.

Note: To make the exercise more difficult, increase the band tension. Resistance bands come in many different tension levels.

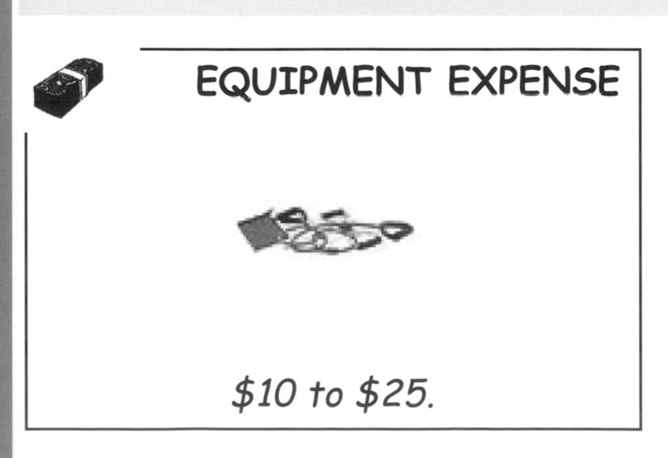

EQUIPMENT EXPENSE

$10 to $25.

TARGET TRAINING TIP

Remember to focus on the hip muscle. The more you think about the muscle you are working the more effective the exercise will be.

MEDICINE BALL REACH/SQUAT

STRENGTHENS COORDINATION, QUADRICEPS, AND GLUTES

EXERCISE DESCRIPTION

1. Stand on one leg in a squatting position with thc ball to the outside of the opposite leg.
2. Bring the ball in a diagonal angle toward the opposing shoulder.
3. Look straight ahead when first attempting this movement, but you should later progress so the eyes follow the movement of the ball.
4. Repeat with the opposite side.

TARGET TRAINING TIP

Keep your abdominals contracted throughout the movement to maintain stability. Push through your heel to keep the tension on the leg and not the knee.

IMPROVES BALANCE

The reach and squat improves coordination and balance by training the body to work in diagonal patterns. When reaching across your body to pick up your pole or ski, you will better maintain your balance.

BOSU BALL SQUAT

STRENGTHENS BALANCE, QUADRICEPS, AND HAMSTRINGS

Exercise Description

1. Prepare by placing the Bosu Ball so the platform is on a flat, solid surface with the ball portion right side up.
2. Step onto the ball and get comfortable with your balance. With feet about shoulde-width apart, contract your abdominals while breathing in.
3. Squat to a 90 degree angle at the knee joint while keeping your abdominal muscles contracted.
4. Hold for a moment and begin the upward portion of the movement. Repeat for the specified number of repetitions.

EQUIPMENT EXPENSE

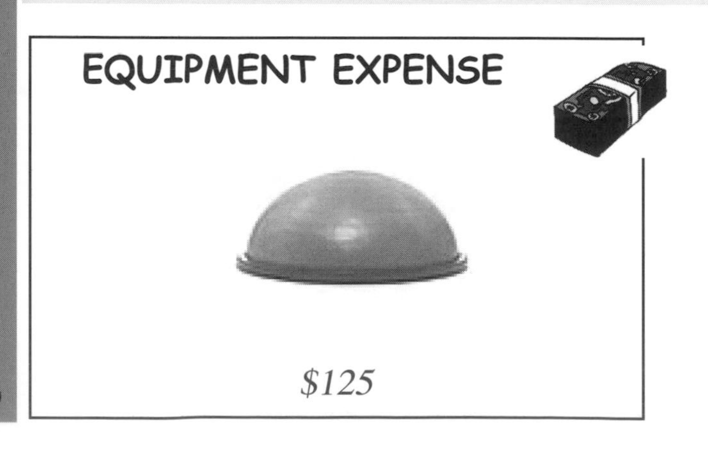

$125

WARNING!

Remember to get comfortable standing on the Bosu Ball before you begin the squat. Push through your heels to avoid injuring the knees.

BOSU BALL SQUAT

STRENGTHENS BALANCE, QUADRICEPS, AND HAMSTRINGS

FITSKIING MUSCLES AT WORK

This exercise is similar to a regular squat, with one minor change. To make the squat even tougher, try using the Bosu Ball to create a less stable surface. By doing so you create a similar environment to what you will find when you are skiing. This exercise utilizes the same muscles as the squat, which was described earlier in this chapter.

FIT BALL LEG CURL

STRENGTHENS HAMSTRINGS AND GLUTES

EXERCISE DESCRIPTION

1. Lie on your back with your arms outstretched and your palms facing downward. Place your heels on the ball.
2. Curl your heels toward your glutes by bending your knees.
3. Return to the start position while maintaining the level of your hips throughout the entire exercise.
4. Do not allow the feet to rotate outward while flexing the legs (keep your toes pointing straight up).

WARNING!

Remember to get comfortable with the fit ball before you begin the exercise. Don't hyperextend your back when performing the fit ball leg curl.

EQUIPMENT EXPENSE

$25 to $40

FIT BALL LEG CURL

STRENGTHENS HAMSTRINGS, AND GLUTES

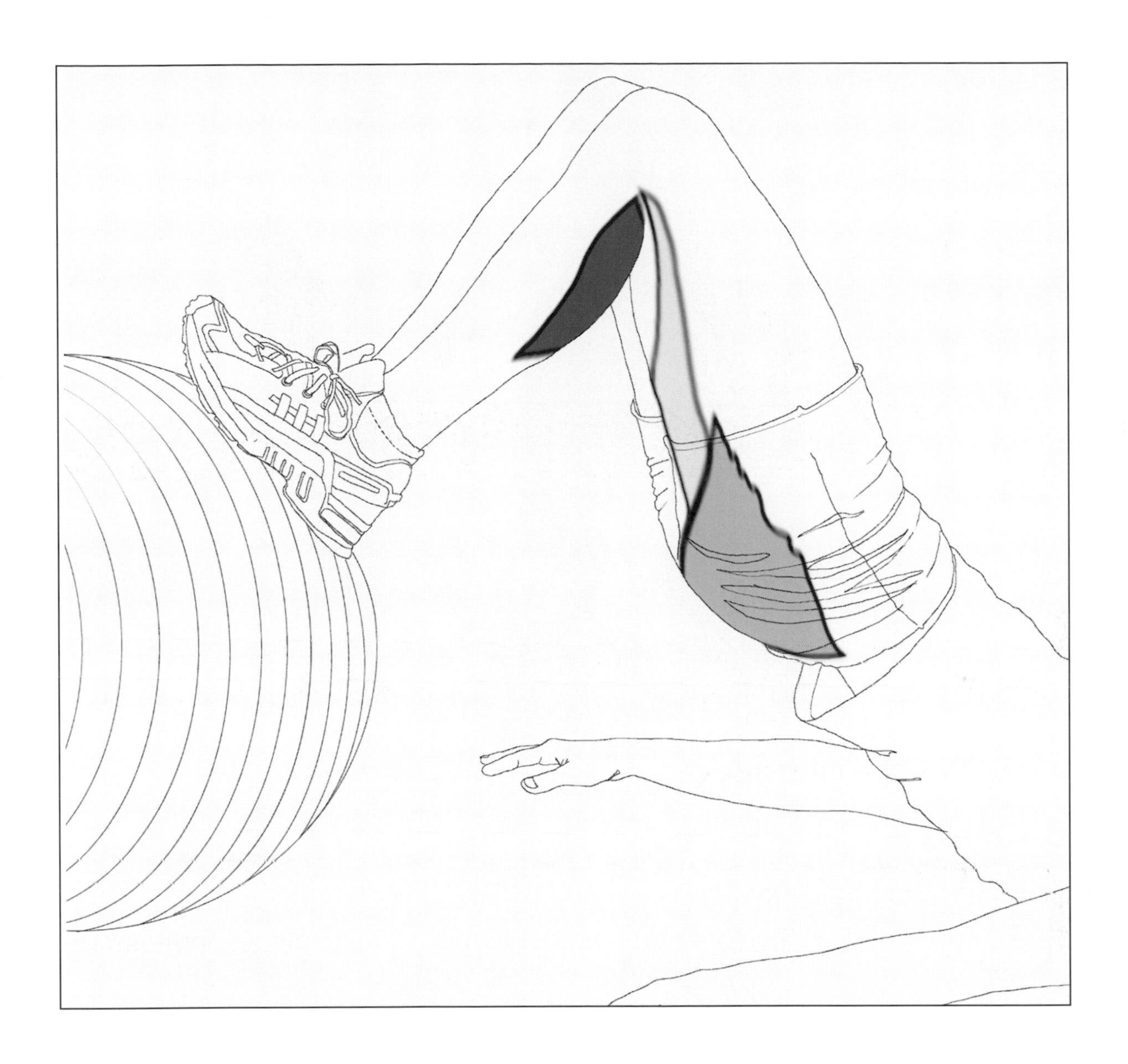

FITSKIING MUSCLES AT WORK

This is a great exercise to develop the hamstring and lower back muscles. The hamstring muscles are used on the downward, or compression, portion of skiing. This is why strengthening this area is so important. By using a fit ball, you provide a more independent and unstable environment, similar to that on the slopes. This exercise also improves strength in your lower back, which helps provide support while skiing.

SINGLE LEG STABILITY

STRENGTHENS BALANCE AND ANKLES

EXERCISE DESCRIPTION

1. Stand on the Bosu Ball with a single leg and your foot pointing straight ahead keeping the knee slightly flexed maintaining a stable position on the ball.
2. Keep the opposing leg directly beside the stable one, to maintain an optimum center of gravity.
3. Keep your hips and shoulders level throughout the exercise, while at the same time contracting your abdominals.
4. Repeat with the other leg.

TARGET TRAINING TIP
Make sure you feel comfortable standing on the Bosu Ball before attempting the single leg stability exercise. Step on the center of the ball before beginning the exercise.

IMPROVES BALANCE
The single leg stability exercise requires the body to get used to an unstable plane. By balancing on one foot and strengthening the ankle, you will have more stability on your skis.

LEG CIRCLES

STRENGTHENS HIPS AND IMPROVES OVERALL FLEXIBILITY

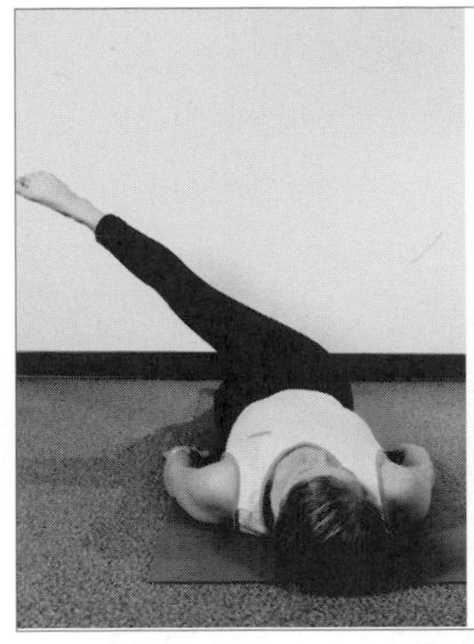
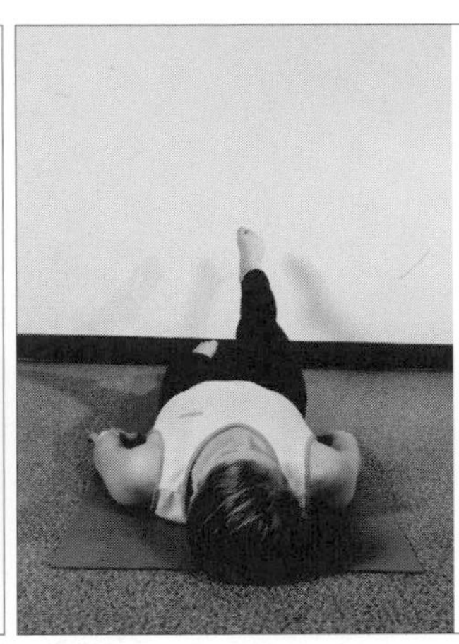
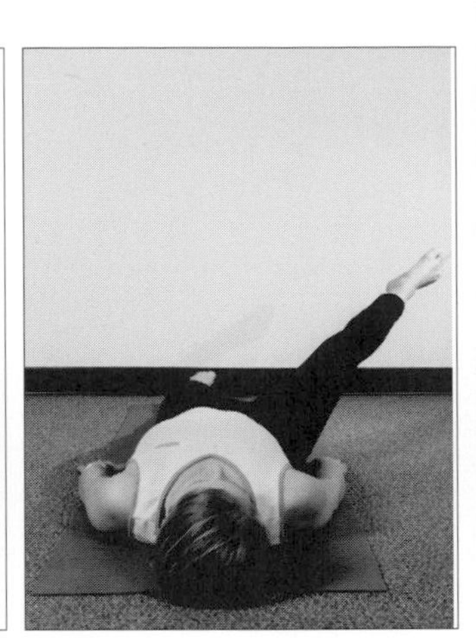

EXERCISE DESCRIPTION

1. While lying on your back, bring one leg to 90 degrees or as close as you can get it to a right angle.
2. It helps to press the back of your neck into the mat to assist in lengthening it.
3. Point your toe toward the ceiling and stretch your leg across your body, then straight in front of you and back to the top. Make sure you maintain stabilization at the hips.
4. Repeat with the other leg.

TARGET TRAINING TIP

The more flexibility you have, the better range of motion you will be able to obtain. Make sure to keep your lower back pressed into the floor.

PRE-SKI WARM-UP

Leg circles are a great way to warm up the hips and thighs before skiing. Try this exercise 20 to 30 minutes before hitting the slopes.

1. Lat Pull-down
2. Shrug
3. Straight Arm Pull-down
4. Scapular Retraction

LAT PULL-DOWN

STRENGTHENS LATISIMUS AND BICEPS

EXERCISE DESCRIPTION

1. Seated on a lat pull-down machine, lean back from the hips.
2. Grip the bar with your hands positioned about 6 inches. Outside the shoulders.
3. Contract the abdominals while beginning to pull the bar down. Keeping your arms straight, begin to pull the arms toward your body.
4. Continue as far as you can control. Contract the lats at the bottom of the movement.
5. Return to the beginning of the movement by slowly letting the bar rise to its initial position. Motion is stopped just before the muscles relax.

WARNING!

It is important not to let your back arch at any time during the movement. Doing so can create unneeded stress on the lumbar and thoracic spine.

TARGET TRAINING TIP

Remember to focus on the outer back (lat) muscles when pulling the weight towards the chest. This will assist in making sure the correct muscles are being worked.

LAT PULL-DOWN

STRENGTHENS LATISIMUS AND BICEPS

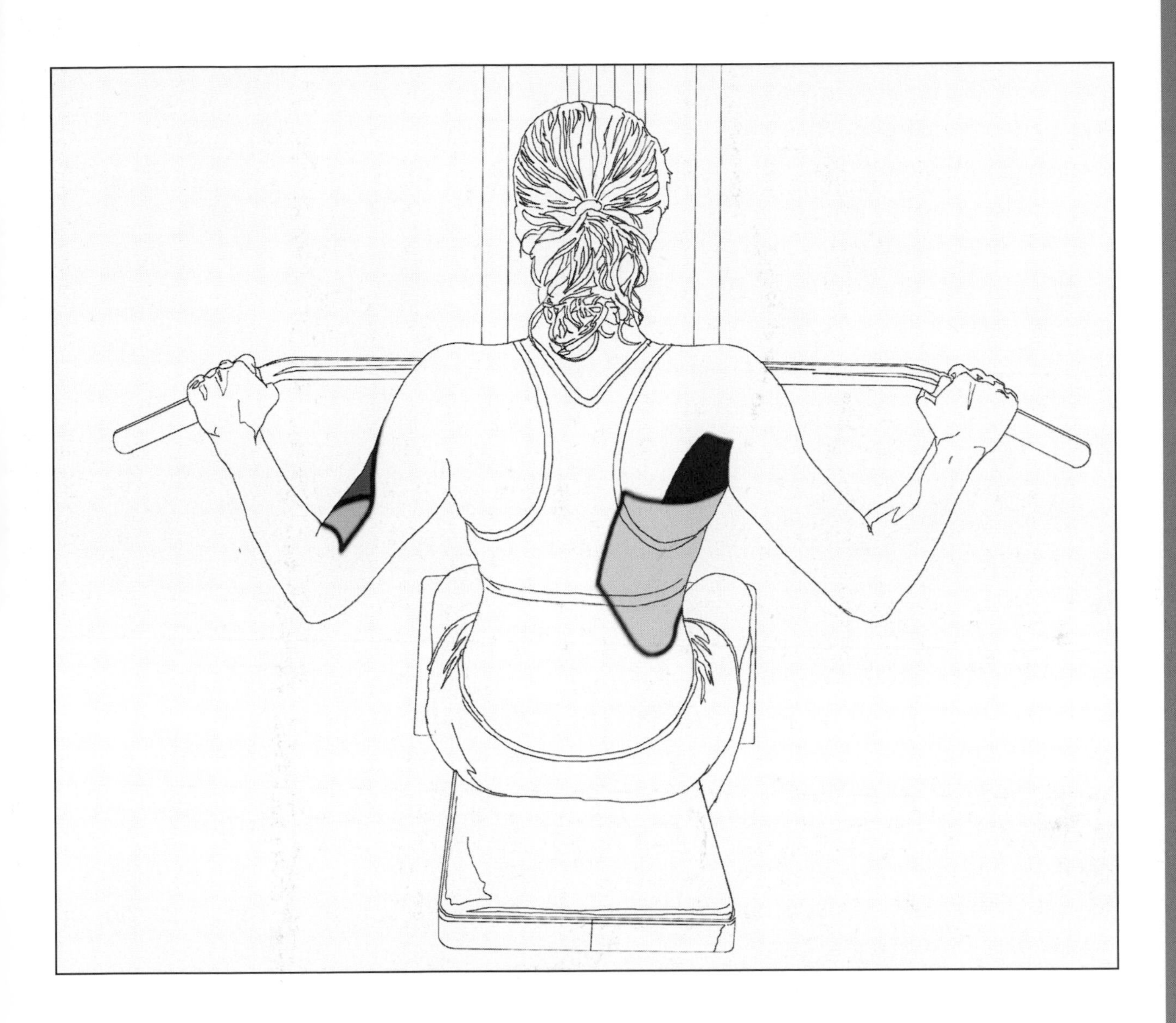

FITSKIING MUSCLES AT WORK

It is important to have balance among all muscles in your body. By having balanced strength, you will be at less risk of injury. The lat pull-down incorporates your latisimus dorsi muscles as well as your biceps and to some extent smaller back muscles. If you are hiking back up to get your skis after a fall, your lat muscles engage to help pull you up the mountain or slope. Your back muscles also help when pushing yourself on the cat tracks from one ski run to the next.

SHRUG

STRENGTHENS TRAPEZIUS

EXERCISE DESCRIPTION

1. Standing with your feet firmly planted on the floor, grasp a bar and/or weight that you feel comfortable with.
2. Begin by inhaling and contracting the abdominal muscles. Roll the shoulders back slightly.
3. Elevate the bar as far as you can until you get a good contraction of the upper trapezius muscles.
4. Return to the beginning of the movement by slowly lowering the bar to its initial position.

TARGET TRAINING TIP

Squeeze your trapezius muscles at the top of the movement to place extra emphasis on that area. For lifting heavier weight, you might want to consider lifting straps.

WARNING!

Do not roll your shoulders back when performing a shrug. On the first repetition, retract your scapula and then elevate your shoulders as high as you can.

STRENGTHENS TRAPEZIUS

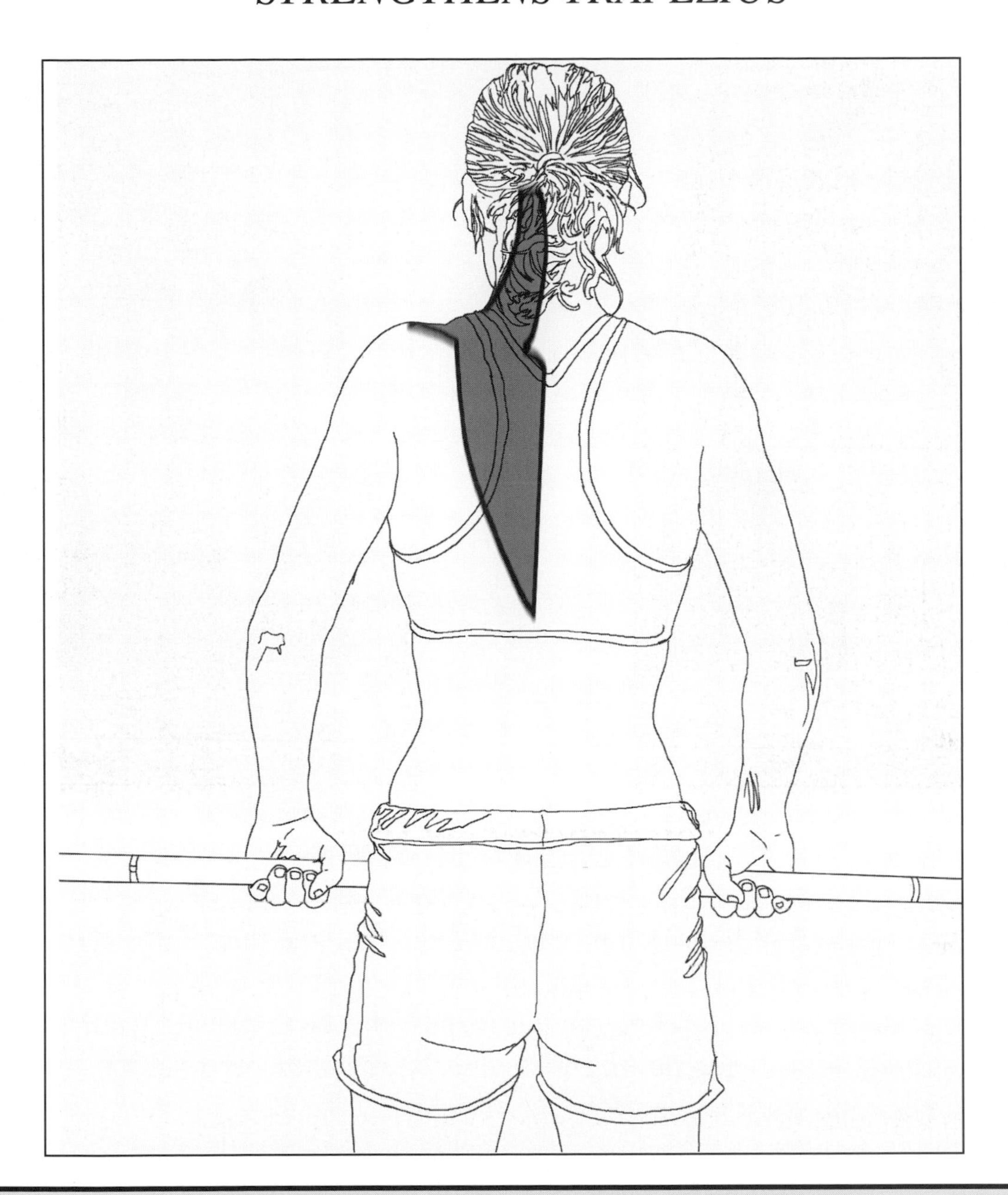

FITSKIING MUSCLES AT WORK

Many people have week trapezius muscles and, therefore, put their neck and shoulders at greater risk of injury. By improving the strength in the upper portion of your traps you will provide more stability to your neck and shoulders. Did you ever wonder why football players have such big trap muscles? They develop them so they have more support when they get hit by another player or land on their neck or shoulders. In the same respect, if you collide with another skier or take a fall, you will be less susceptible to injury in these areas.

STRAIGHT ARM PULL-DOWN

STRENGTHENS BALANCE AND LATISIMUS

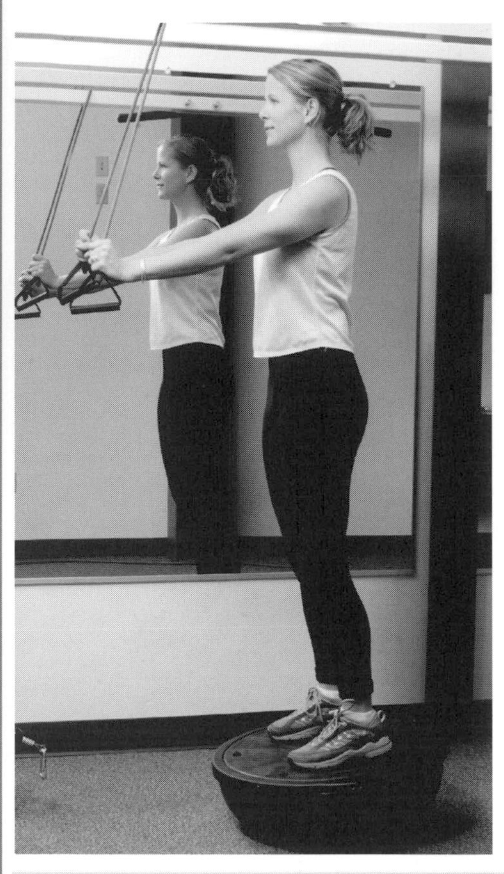

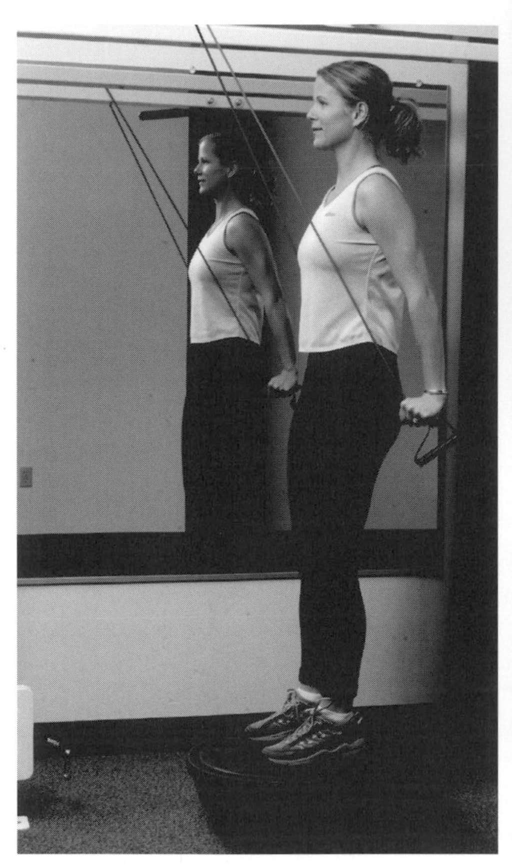

EXERCISE DESCRIPTION

1. Begin with the Bosu Ball flat side up. Stand on the ball and get comfortable with your balance.
2. Contract the abdominals while beginning to pull the band toward your midsection. Maintaining straight arms, keep pulling with your lat muscles. Extend the arms beyond your glutes to get a full contraction of the lat muscles.
3. Return to the beginning of the movement by slowly releasing the bands to their initial position. Motion is stopped just before your muscles relax.

WARNING!

Make sure you feel comfortable with your balance on the Bosu Ball before beginning this exercise. Keep your feet on the center of the ball to maintain safety and balance.

IMPROVES BALANCE

The Bosu Ball provides an unstable surface which can improve balanc,e. The straight arm pull-down also teaches the body to use ski-specific muscles while requiring it to maintain stability.

STRAIGHT ARM PULL-DOWN

STRENGTHENS BALANCE AND LATISIMUS

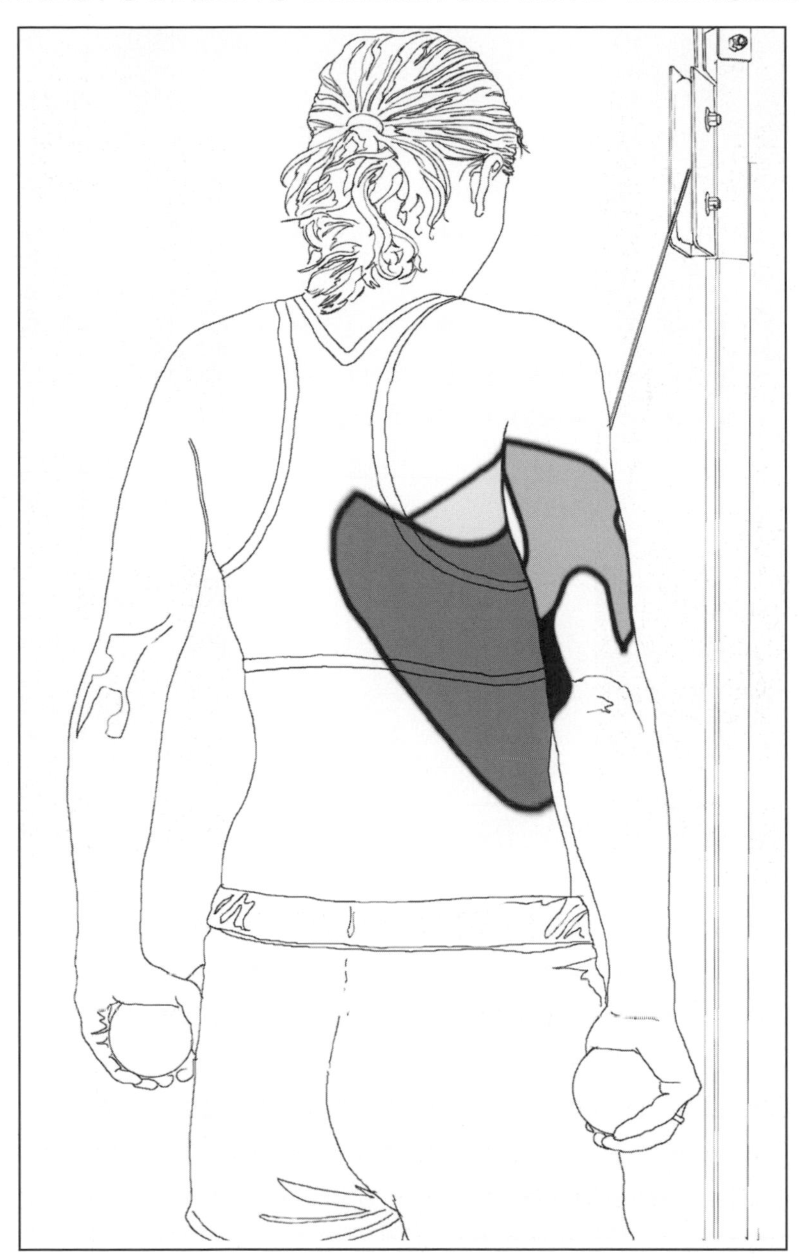

FITSKIING MUSCLES AT WORK

This is by far one of my favorite exercises to develop strong muscles for those long cat tracks we push along to get to the really good snow. By using the Bosu Ball, you provide an unstable surface that is more similar to that of snow. It also helps engage the core more so you divert energy from your back muscles to your abdominals.

This exercise is also great for cross-country skiers because it simulates a similar action to skate skiing. Remember to always use your core muscles to help stabilize your body. If you engage your core, you will use less energy and have a more enjoyable time on skis.

SCAPULAR RETRACTION

STRENGTHENS SUBSCAPULAR MUSCLES, REAR DELTOIDS

EXERCISE DESCRIPTION

1. Seated on a fit ball, grasp a two-handled rope. Place hands so the palms are facing down and the elbows are turned to the outside of the body.
2. Contract the abdominals while beginning to pull the rope toward your body. Keeping your arms straight, begin to pull your arms toward your body.
3. Continue as far as you can control. Squeeze your shoulder blades together at the end of the movement.
4. Return to the beginning of the movement by slowly releasing the bar to its initial position. Motion is stopped just before your muscles relax.

EQUIPMENT EXPENSE

$25 to $40

TARGET TRAINING TIP

Remember to keep your abdominals contracted during the movement. This will not only teach your core to work with your scapular muscles and rear deltoids, but it also will provide extra stability when performing the exercise.

1. Dumbbell Bench Press
2. Bosu Ball Push Up

DUMBBELL BENCH PRESS

STRENGTHENS CHEST, ANTERIOR DELTOIDS, AND TRICEPS

EXERCISE DESCRIPTION

1. Begin by laying flat on a bench with your elbows at a 90 degree angle.
2. Contract the abdominal muscles and press the dumbbells toward the ceiling. At the top of the movement, bring the dumbbells together to get a full contraction of the chest muscles.
3. After fully extending the arms, lower the weight slowly until the elbows return to a 90 degree angle.
4. Step down and repeat with your other leg.

WARNING!

Do not let your elbows drop below your shoulders. This can cause unneeded stress and possible injury to the shoulder joint. The elbows should be in line with the shoulders at the bottom of the movement.

TARGET TRAINING TIP

If you have lower back pain, try putting your feet up on the bench. This will take some of the pressure off your lumbar spine.

DUMBBELL BENCH PRESS

STRENGTHENS CHEST, ANTERIOR DELTOIDS, AND TRICEPS

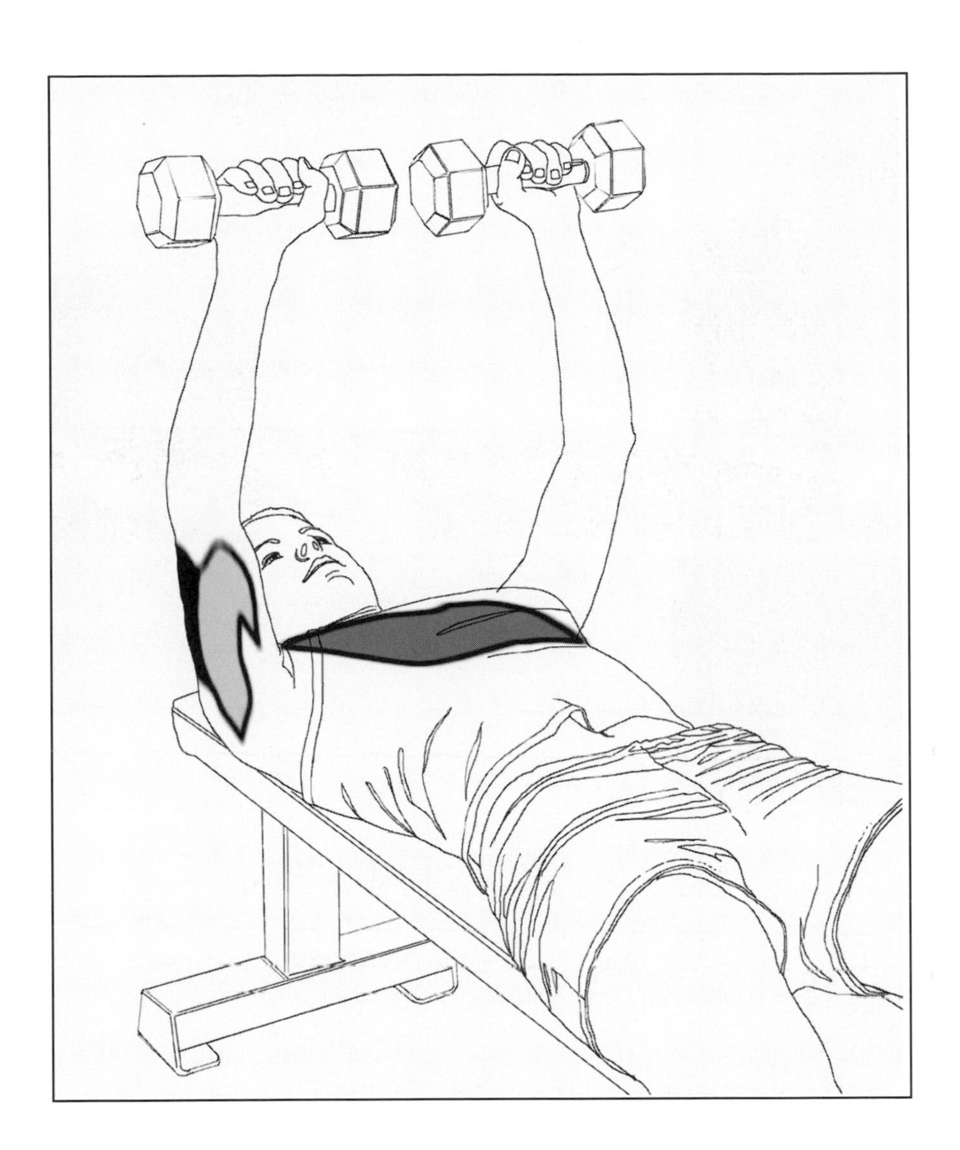

FITSKIING MUSCLES AT WORK

The dumbbell bench press is a great exercise for skiers because it improves overall upper body strength and independent arm strength. Many people use the barbell bench press; however, this exercise is more for those who need to provide a couple of powerful motions using the entire upper body at once. By using each arm independently, you will make sure that each arm has balanced strength. By developing strength in the chest and the triceps, you will have an easier time pushing yourself up off the snow if you fall or if you are simply taking a break.

BOSU BALL PUSH UP

STRENGTHENS BALANCE, CHEST, SHOULDERS AND TRICEPS

EXERCISE DESCRIPTION

1. Begin with the Bosu Ball flat side up. Kneel down (beginning) or extend your legs so the balls of your feet are firmly positioned on the floor.
2. Place both hands shoulder width apart on the Bosu Ball and slowly lower your body toward the floor until your chest almost touches the ball.
3. Keeping your abdominal muscles flexed, push yourself back to the starting position. Make sure to keep a slight bend to the elbow.

EXERCISE ALTERNATIVE

WARNING!

Make sure you feel comfortable with the Bosu Ball before you begin this exercise. Make sure your elbows do not go beyond the shoulders.

BOSU BALL PUSH UP

STRENGTHENS BALANCE, CHEST, SHOULDERS, AND TRICEPS

FITSKIING MUSCLES AT WORK

Although this exercise uses similar muscles to those the bench press incorporates, it has one major difference: the instability of the Bosu Ball. By using the Bosu Ball, you provide an unstable surface that requires your core to engage. By engaging your core, your body learns to use energy from this area and less energy from your chest, shoulders, and triceps.

If it is a little tough at first, try putting your knees on the floor to take away some of the weight of your body. As with the bench press, the Bosu Ball push up, assists in pushing up off the snow when you have fallen or are simply taking a break.

SHOULDERS

1. Dumbbell Shoulder Press
2. External Rotation
3. Internal Rotation
4. Front Raise
5. Lateral Raise

DUMBBELL SHOULDER PRESS

STRENGTHENS SHOULDERS

EXERCISE DESCRIPTION

1. Begin by sitting on an upright bench. Hold dumbbells just outside of your shoulders.
2. Press the dumbbells toward the ceiling. Bring them together at the top for a better contraction of the deltoid muscles.
3. Slowly lower the dumbbells back to their initial starting position.

Note: Always remember to keep your abdominal muscles contracted through the entire movement.

WARNING!

Remember not to lock the elbows at the top of the movement. This can place unneeded stress on the elbow joint.

TARGET TRAINING TIP

Focus on the shoulders to make sure the proper muscles are being worked. Keep the abdominals contracted to maintain stability and relieve pressure from the lower back.

DUMBBELL SHOULDER PRESS

STRENGTHENS SHOULDERS

FITSKIING MUSCLES AT WORK

The dumbbell shoulder press helps develop strength in the anterior and medial deltoids. It is a good exercise for skiers to perform because it helps in the overall stability of the body and assists when pushing off while skiing on cat tracks from run to run.

EXTERNAL ROTATION

STRENGTHENS ROTATOR CUFF MUSCLES

EXERCISE DESCRIPTION

1. Begin by finding the right tension of band for your rotator cuff strength. As an alternative you can use a multipurpose machine with a cable.
2. Attach the band to a secure surface such as a pole or doorknob when the door is completely open. With abdominal muscles flexed, pull the band away from the body using your deep shoulder muscles (rotator cuff). Keep your elbow locked against your body so your muscles get the most work.
3. After completing the movement, slowly bring your arm back toward the body.
4. Repeat with your other arm.

EQUIPMENT EXPENSE

$10 to $25

TARGET TRAINING TIP

Make sure you keep your elbow against the side of your body. You might want to roll up a towel and slide it under your arm to assist in maintaining proper stability.

EXTERNAL ROTATION

STRENGTHENS ROTATOR CUFF MUSCLES

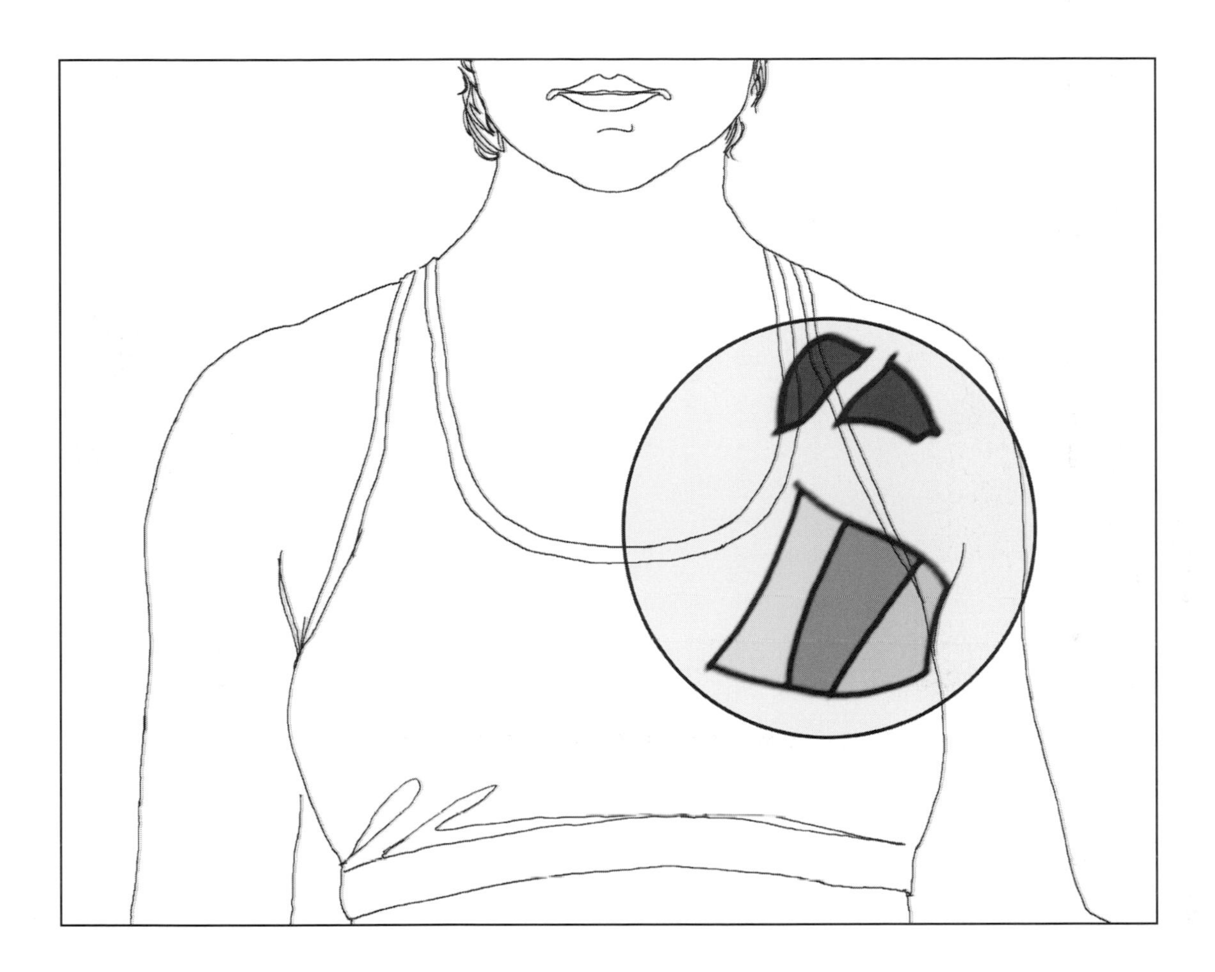

FITSKIING MUSCLES AT WORK

You might be wondering why there is a circle around this group of muscles. It simply means that you are looking at the posterior and deep portion of the shoulder and scapular area. The rotator cuff muscles are commonly injured because they are so small, yet they are required to stabilize the shoulder area. By improving rotator cuff strength you will be at less risk of injury when performing other exercises like the bench press or shoulder press.

INTERNAL ROTATION

STRENGTHENS ROTATOR CUFF MUSCLES

EXERCISE DESCRIPTION

1. Begin by finding the right tension of band for your rotator cuff strength. As an alternative you can use a multipurpose machine with a cable.
2. Attach the band to a secure surface such as a pole or doorknob when the door is completely open. With abdominal muscles flexed, pull the band toward the body using your deep shoulder muscles (rotator cuff). Keep your elbow close to your body so your muscles get the most work.
3. After completing the movement, slowly bring your arm to its initial starting position.
4. Repeat with your other arm.

EQUIPMENT EXPENSE

$10.00-$25.00

TARGET TRAINING TIP

Make sure you keep your elbow close to your body. You might want to roll up a towel and slide it under your arm to assist in maintaining proper stability.

INTERNAL ROTATION

STRENGTHENS ROTATOR CUFF MUSCLES

FITSKIING MUSCLES AT WORK

You might be wondering why there is a circle around this group of muscles. It simply means that you are looking at the posterior and deep portion of the shoulder and scapular area. The rotator cuff muscles are commonly injured because they are so small, yet they are required to stabilize the shoulder area. By improving rotator cuff strength, you will be at less risk of injury when performing other exercises like the bench press or shoulder press.

FRONT RAISE

STRENGTHENS ANTERIOR DELTOIDS

Exercise Description

1. Begin by finding the right tension of band for your anterior deltoid strength. As an alternative you can use a multipurpose machine with a cable or dumbbells.
2. Attach the band under your feet. With your abdominal muscles flexed and palms facing down, raise your arms to shoulder level. Your hands should be in line with your shoulders.
3. After completing the movement slowly bring the arm down to the sides of your body.

Note: If you can't bring your arms to shoulder level, you should choose a band with less tension.

EQUIPMENT EXPENSE

$10.00-$25.00

TARGET TRAINING TIP

Make sure you keep your abdominals contracted throughout the entire movement. By engaging the abdominal muscles, you work your midsection and you also teach the shoulder muscles to work with them. This provides more balance and stability.

FRONT RAISE

STRENGTHENS ANTERIOR DELTOIDS

FITSKIING MUSCLES AT WORK

The front raise is a good exercise to isolate the anterior portion of the shoulder muscles. By strengthening the anterior deltoid muscles, you will have an easier time picking up your skis and putting them in your storage box on top of your vehicle.

LATERAL RAISE

STRENGTHENS LATERAL DELTOIDS

Exercise Description

1. Sit on an upright bench with your arms at your sides. Push the small of your back into the bench.
2. Contract your abdominal muscles and slowly raise the dumbbells to shoulder level.
3. After completing the movement, slowly bring the arms to your sides.
4. Repeat for the suggested number of repetitions.

WARNING!

Remember to press the lower back and spine into the back of the bench. This will help maintain proper form, as well as minimize potential injury to the lower back.

TARGET TRAINING TIP

Keep your elbows slightly bent throughout the entire movement. This will take the pressure off the elbow joint and help maintain tension on the shoulders.

LATERAL RAISE

STRENGTHENS LATERAL DELTOIDS

FITSKIING MUSCLES AT WORK

The lateral raise develops the lateral deltoids, anterior deltoids, and to some extent the upper trapezius muscles. This is a good exercise because it helps you gain overall upper body stability. When skiing, you should try to keep your poles in front of you. This exercise improves muscular endurance in these muscles so you have an easier time keeping them in front of thc body and not behind you. Many times, skiers' shoulders begin to fatigue and then their poles drop. The next thing they know, they catch the pole in the snow and end up falling. The higher you raise the dumbbells the more you engage your traps.

ARMS

1. Barbell Curl
2. Triceps Extension
3. Triceps Press-down

BARBELL CURL

STRENGTHENS BICEPS

Exercise Description

1. Begin with your feet firmly planted on the floor. Grasp a bar with your palms facing outward.
2. Flex your abdominal muscles and curl the bar toward your chest. Remember to keep most of the pressure on your heels and not on your toes. This keeps the tension away from your lower back.
3. After completing the movement, slowly lower the bar to its starting position.
4. Repeat for the suggested number of repetitions.

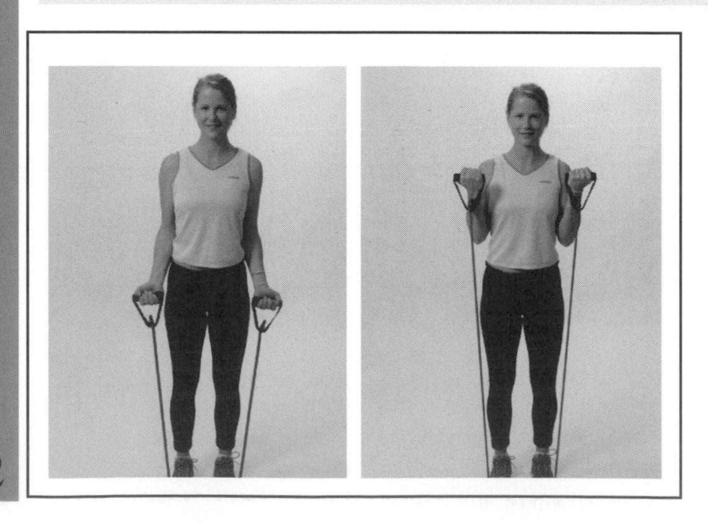

WARNING!

Keep your feet firmly placed on the floor for stability. Remember to keep the abdominals tight to prevent low back injury. Keep strict form and don't swing (hyper extend) the weight up.

BARBELL CURL

STRENGTHENS BICEPS

FITSKIING MUSCLES AT WORK

The biceps curl is an important exercise for providing balance and stability to the upper body muscles. Skiers use their biceps to help push themselves on cat tracks, as well as maintain their poles in front of their body. It is also a great exercise to help you lift your ski equipment into your vehicle.

TRICEPS EXTENSION

STRENGTHENS TRICEPS

Exercise Description

1. Lay on a fit ball, making sure the small of your back is supported.
2. Contract your abdominal muscles. Hold the bar just above your nose or forehead (depending on your arm length).
3. Slowly extend the elbows toward the ceiling, contracting the triceps muscles.
4. When your arms are fully extended, slowly lower the bar back to your nose or forehead.

WARNING!

Keep the lower back pressed into the fit ball. This will help maintain stability and prevent back injuries. Remember to get your balance on the ball before you begin the exercise.

EQUIPMENT EXPENSE

$25. to $40

TRICEPS EXTENSION

STRENGTHENS TRICEPS

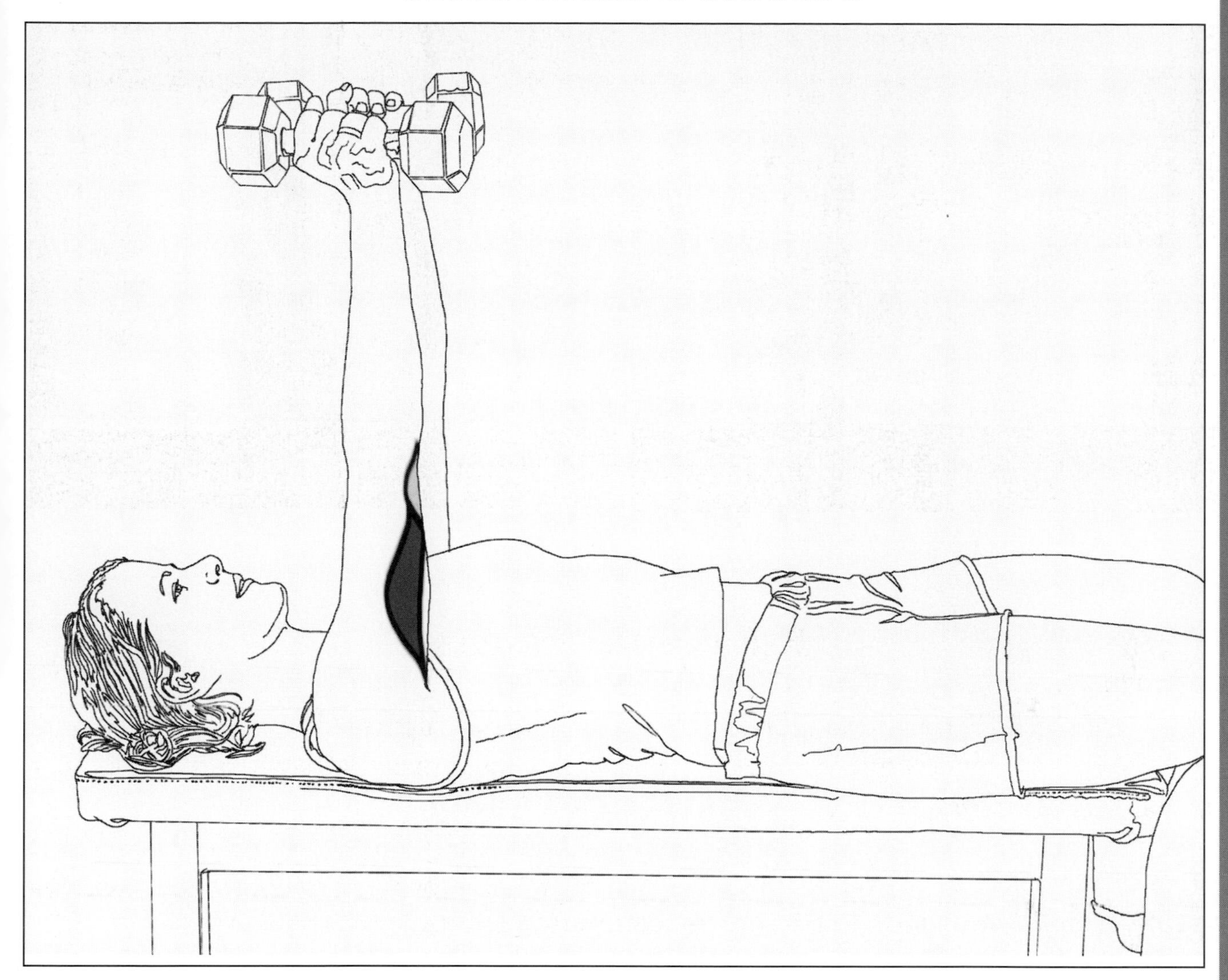

FITSKIING MUSCLES AT WORK

This exercise improves strength to the back of the arm, or the triceps muscles. These muscles are important in helping you push up off the snow when you have fallen. They are also important in helping you push your way along cat tracks or to the the lift line.

TRICEPS PRESS-DOWN

STRENGTHENS TRICEPS

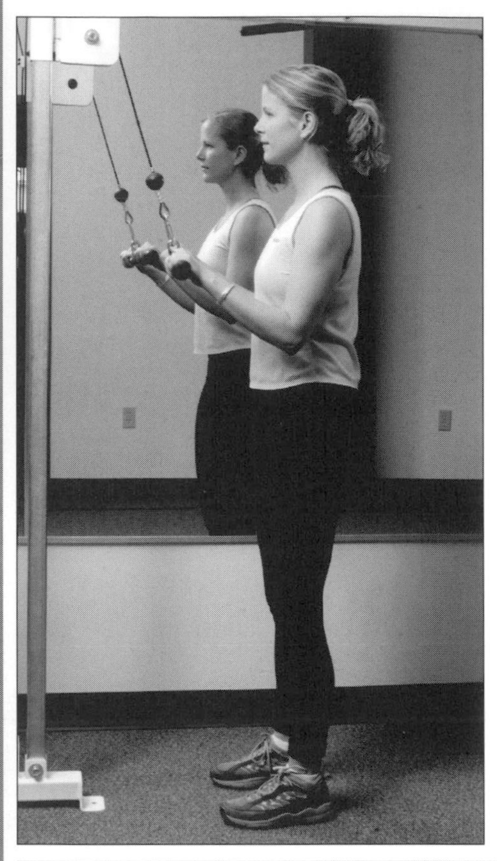

Exercise Description

1. Place your feet firmly on the floor. Grasp a straight or slightly cambered bar with your palms facing downward. Make sure the bar is at mid-chest level.
2. Contract your abdominal muscles and extend the arms downward, flexing the triceps muscles. Remember to keep your elbows locked at your sides.
3. When the elbows are fully extended, slowly raise them back to their starting position.
4. Repeat for the suggested number of repetitions.

WARNING!

Remember to keep the abdominals tight to help support the lower back. Keep a slight bend at the knee to relieve pressure from the back.

TARGET TRAINING TIP

Keep your elbows locked at your sides. This will help keep the emphasis on the triceps muscles. Remember to keep the abdominals tense so the triceps muscles and your core muscles learn to work together. This will eventually lead to more stability on your skis.

TRICEPS PRESS-DOWN

STRENGTHENS TRICEPS

FITSKIING MUSCLES AT WORK

Similar to the triceps extension, the triceps press-down works the muscles along the back of the arm. It is, however, more ski specific because you are standing as opposed to lying down. Try engaging your abdominal or core muscles when pressing the weight down. This will assist your body in learning to use both sets of muscles together so you use your energy more efficiently.

1. Back Extension
2. Bridge
3. Crunch
4. Oblique Crunch
5. Opposing Arm/Leg Extension
6. Fit Ball Reverse Crunch
7. Transverse Abdominal Hold
8. Bosu Ball Abdominal Stability
9. Side Plank
10. Decline Sit-Up
11. Fit Ball Rotation
12. Medicine Ball Crunch
13. Plank
14. Rope Crunch
15. Fit Ball Ski Crunch
16. Wood Chop
17. Medicine Ball Rotation

BACK EXTENSION

STRENGTHENS LOWER BACK

Exercise Description

1. Begin by lying flat on your stomach, relaxing the arms and legs.
2. Slowly extend the arms and legs upward toward the ceiling. You should feel your glute muscles and lower back muscles flexing.
3. After completing the movement, slowly let your body relax to a flat starting position.
4. Repeat for the suggested number of repetitions.

PRE-SKI WARM UP

The back extension is a great exercise to warm up some of your core muscles, specifically the low back and glutes. By firing these muscles before you begin your day on the slopes you will be less likely to be injured.

TARGET TRAINING TIP

Contract your gluteus maximus muscles when at the midpoint of the movement. This will provide more work for your core and those-all important ski muscles.

BACK EXTENSION

STRENGTHENS LOWER BACK

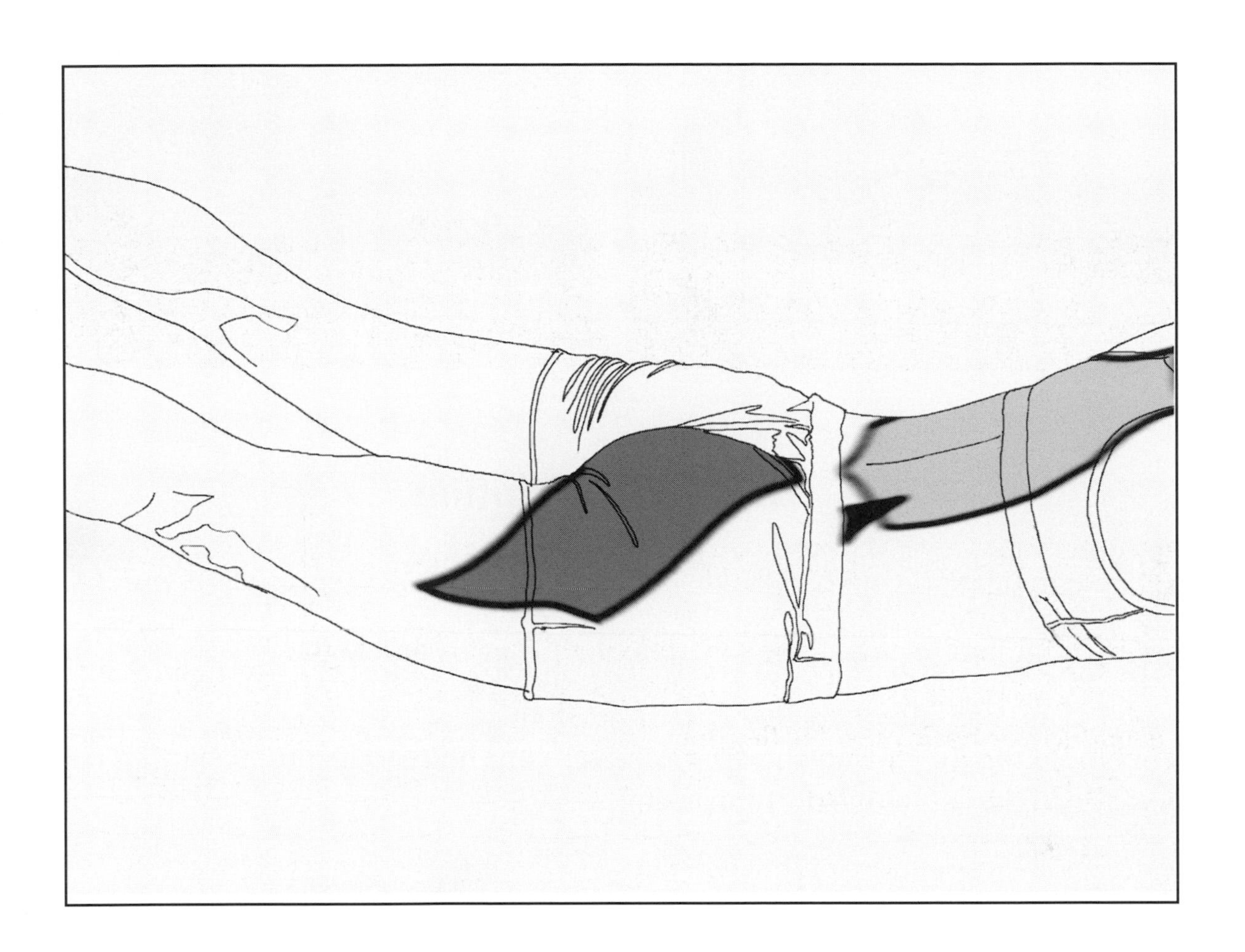

FITSKIING MUSCLES AT WORK

The back extension strengthens the lower back muscles as well as the gluteus maximus muscles. By improving strength in these areas, you will provide more stability while on your skis. If you ever get lower back pain, this is an important exercise. By strengthening the muscles shown above, you will provide more strength to the back, thereby lessening your risk of injury and pain.

Your core is your power source. By strengthening this area you also will increase the amount of power you have while skiing steep terrain or powder.

BRIDGE

STRENGTHENS LOWER BACK AND GLUTES

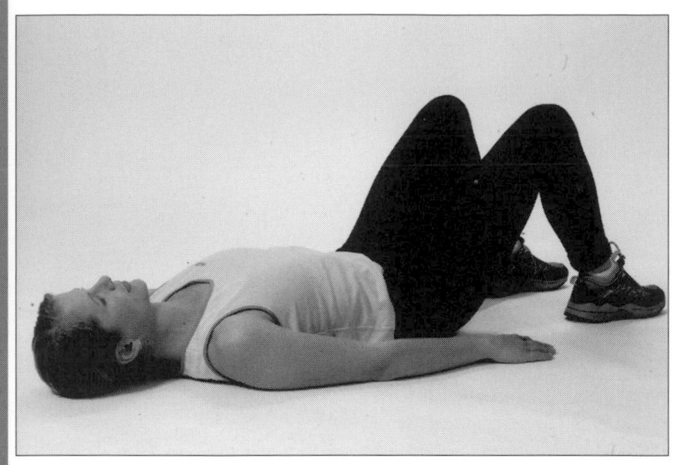

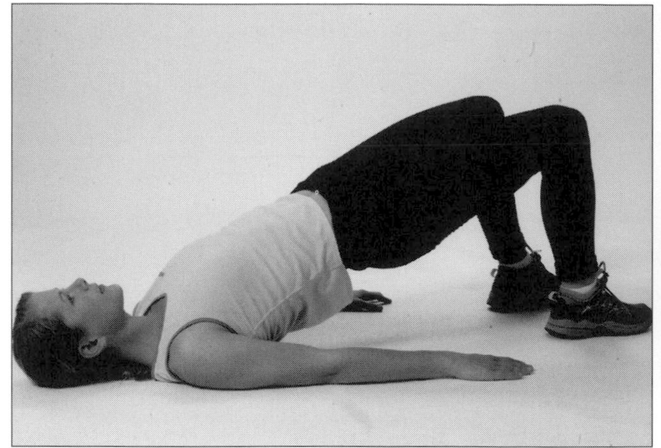

Exercise Description

1. Begin by lying flat on your back with your knees bent. Press the small of your back into the floor.
2. Driving through your heels, push your pelvis upward, contracting your glutes and lower back. Your arms should remain flat against the floor.
3. After completing the movement, slowly lower your body to its initial starting position.
4. Repeat for suggested number of repetitions.

PRE-SKI WARM UP

The bridge is a great exercise to get your lower back, hamstrings, and glutes firing properly. By warming up these muscles first, you will have more stability on your skis and less chance of injury on the slopes.

TARGET TRAINING TIP

Make sure you keep your feet pressed in the floor. This will help keep the emphasis on the hamstrings and glutes. Remember to focus on the hamstrings, glutes, and lower back. Focusing on the muscle will provide more emphasis on them and help you maintain form.

BRIDGE

STRENGTHENS LOWER BACK AND GLUTES

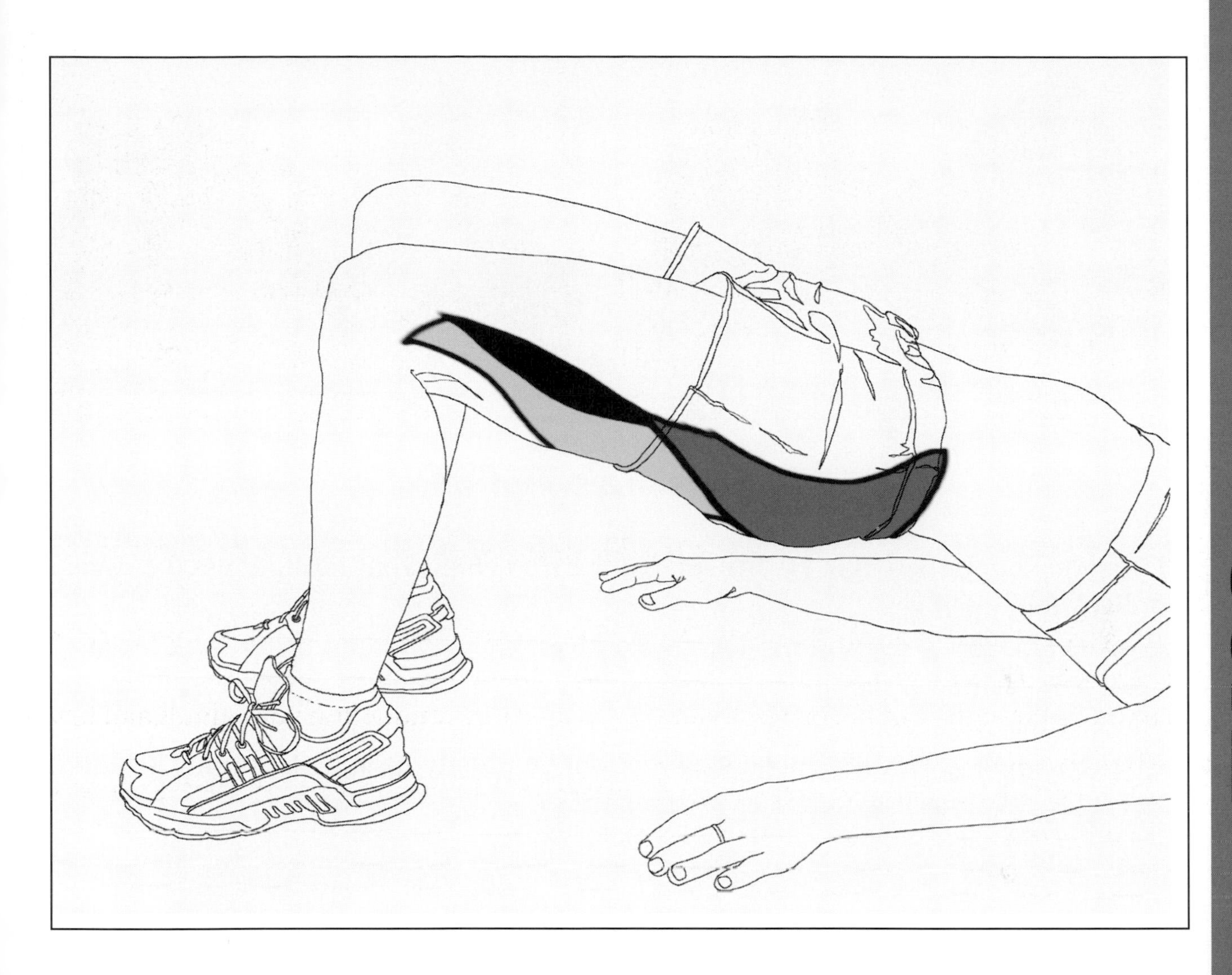

FITSKIING MUSCLES AT WORK

This is a great exercise for the hamstrings, glutes, and to some extent your lower back muscles. All these muscles are important in providing stability while skiing. Your hamstrings assist in flexing your leg, and your gluteus maximus muscles help in extending your hip. Both movements are used while skiing.

CRUNCH

STRENGTHENS RECTUS ABDOMINUS ("SIX-PACK")

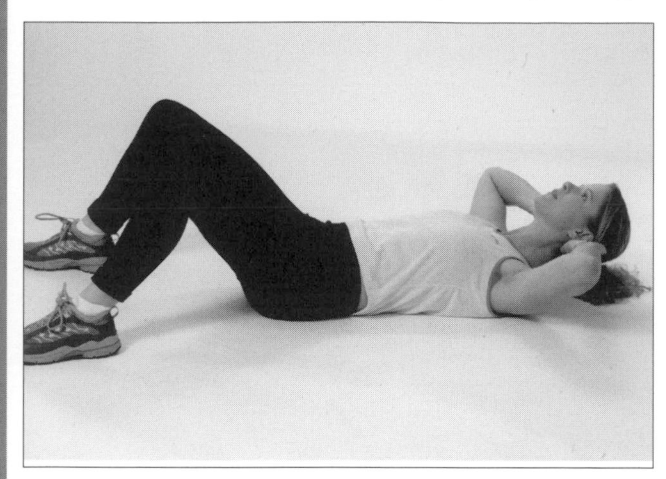

Exercise Description

1. Lying on your back, begin by bringing your arms behind your head. Press the small of your back into the floor.
2. Elevate your body slightly by flexing the trunk. Your mid and upper back should be about 4 to 6 inches off the floor. Remember to keep the small of your back pressed into the floor while crunching.
3. After completing the movement, slowly lower your body back to its starting position.
4. Repeat for the suggested number of repetitions.

WARNING!

Don't lift with your neck; focus your attention on the abdominal muscles. Remember to focus on a point on the ceiling to help mitigate neck strain. Keep the lower back pressed to the floor. This will help prevent straining the low back.

TARGET TRAINING TIP

Pick a point on the ceiling and maintain focus on it throughout the entire set. This will help keep the focus on the abdominal muscles and not the neck. If you feel that you are straining your neck, try placing your tongue against the roof of your mouth.

CRUNCH

STRENGTHENS RECTUS ABDOMINUS ("SIX-PACK")

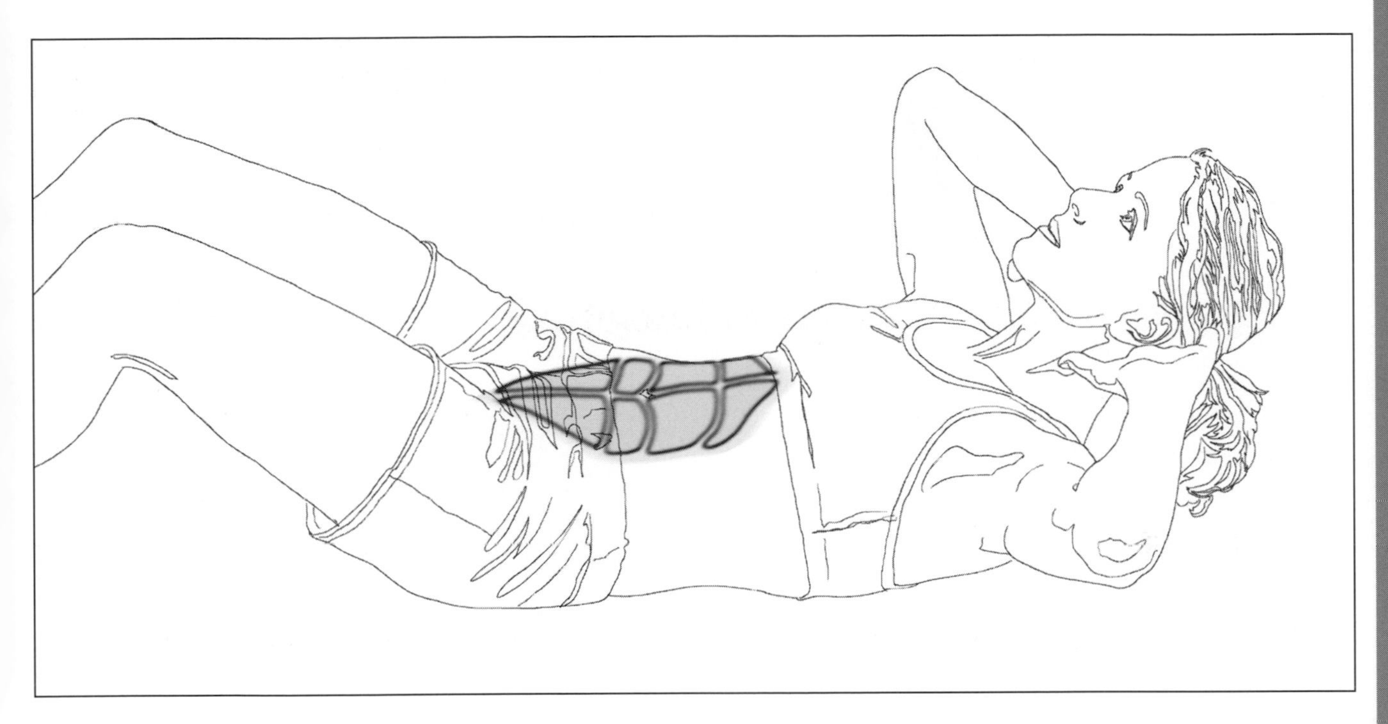

FITSKIING MUSCLES AT WORK

The crunch is a good exercise to start your abdominal workout. If you've never engaged your abdominals properly, this is a great exercise to learn with. At the top of the movement, remember to focus on your midsection and squeeze until you feel them work. On the way down, keep your focus on your abdominals. By strengthening your rectus abdominus muscles you will have more stability and power on your skis. You also will fatigue less because your core will pick up some of the slack when your legs begin to fatigue.

OBLIQUE CRUNCH

STRENGTHENS OBLIQUE MUSCLES

Exercise Description

1. Begin by positioning the side of your body on a fit ball. Your hips should be firmly placed against the ball. Cross your feet and drive them in the floor for support.
2. Flex your oblique muscles by bringing your elbows toward your hips. The total amount of movement depends on your flexibility; however, most people typically don't need to move that far.
3. After completing the movement, slowly lower your body to the starting position.
4. Repeat for the desired number of repetitions.

WARNING!

Remember to get your balance before beginning this exercise. This will help prevent possible injury and also enable you to use proper form.

TARGET TRAINING TIP

Keep your focus on the sides of your body (obliques). This will help provide proper form and work for the muscles. If you find it hard to stabilize yourself, put your feet against a wall.

OBLIQUE CRUNCH

STRENGTHENS OBLIQUE MUSCLES

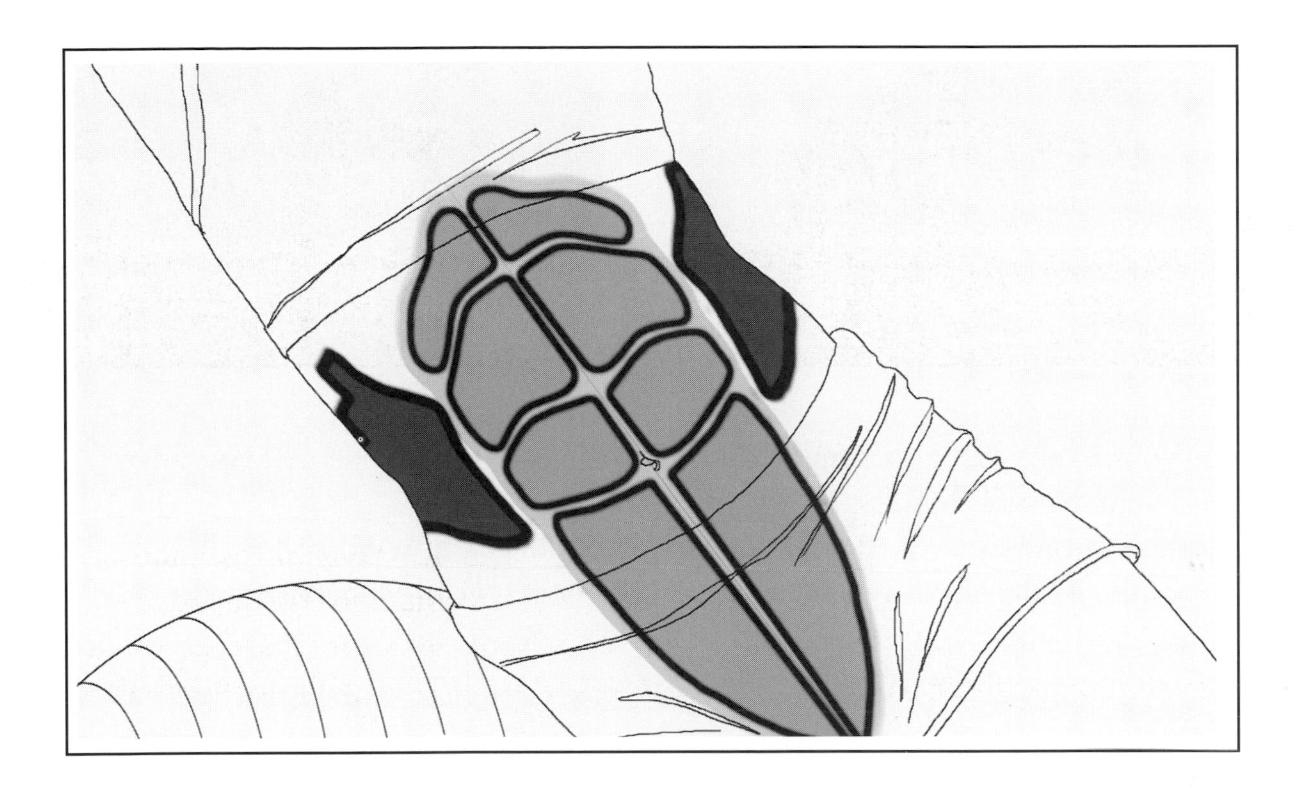

FITSKIING MUSCLES AT WORK

The oblique crunch strengthens the large muscles in your midsection. Your oblique muscles provide a large amount of power and stability to the rest of your body. By improving strength in this area, you will be at less risk of injury and have more stability while on your skis. Your oblique muscles are the primary stabilizers of your body.

OPPOSING ARM/LEG EXTENSION

STRENGTHENS HIPS, GLUTES, AND ABDOMINALS

Exercise Description

1. Place your hands and knees on the floor. Your hands should be just below your shoulders, and your knees should be below your hips.
2. Contract your abdominal muscles and extend your leg upward contracting your glutes and low back. At the same time, extend the opposing arm outward contracting your upper back muscles.
3. After completing the movement, slowly lower your arm and leg to their starting position.
4. Repeat with the opposite arm and leg.

PRE-SKI WARM UP

By extending the opposing arm and leg, you will help the neuromuscular system adapt better to unstable situations (in other words if one side of the body loses balance, the other will pick up the slack).

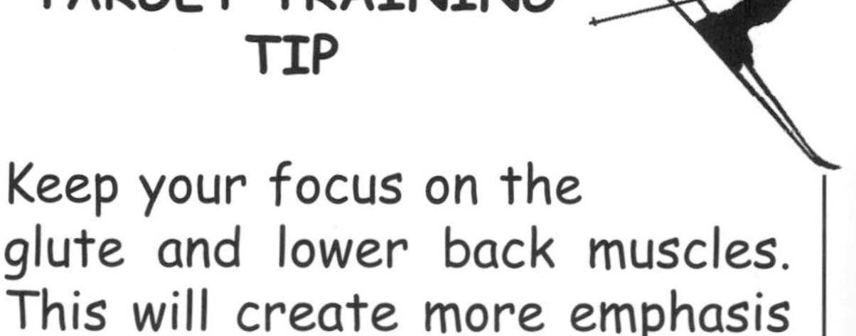

TARGET TRAINING TIP

Keep your focus on the glute and lower back muscles. This will create more emphasis on the muscles being worked. Remember not to extend further than your flexibility allows. This can potentially lead to extra injury.

OPPOSING ARM/LEG EXTENSION

STRENGTHENS HIPS, GLUTESS, AND ABDOMINALS

FITSKIING MUSCLES AT WORK

The opposing arm and leg extension helps your muscles connect from both sides, which will improve your strength and stability. By teaching opposite sides of the body to work together, you will improve your balance on the slopes. If you catch an edge, you will be less likely to fall; the other side of the body will react because it has learned to work with the opposite side. This exercise strengthens the glutes, lower and mid back muscles, traps and to some extent the hamstrings.

FIT BALL REVERSE CRUNCH

STRENGTHENS RECTUS ABDOMINUS (EMPHASIS ON LOWER)

Exercise Description

1. Lying on your back, grab a fit ball between your ankles. Press the small of your back to the floor.
2. Contract your abdominal muscles while bringing your legs toward your body. Remember to keep your hands pressed against the floor.
3. Slowly lower your legs to the floor after your legs reach a 90 degree angle.
4. Repeat for the desired number of repetitions.

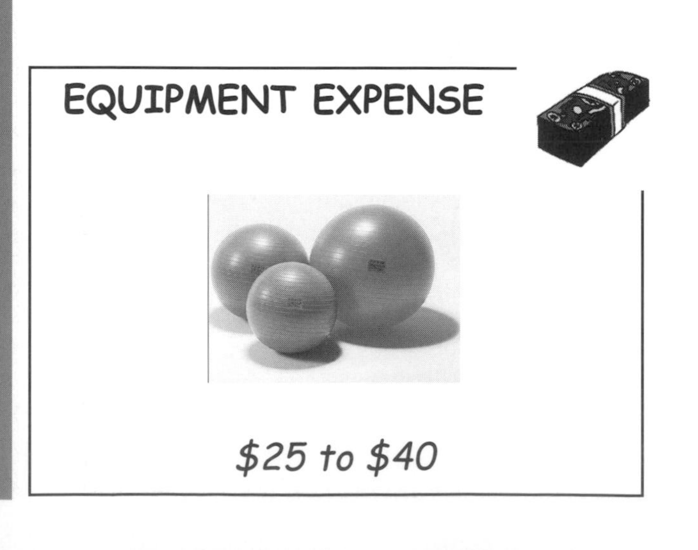

EQUIPMENT EXPENSE

$25 to $40

TARGET TRAINING TIP

Keep all the attention on the lower portion of your rectus abdominus (six-pack). This will provide more work and better form to that area.

FIT BALL REVERSE CRUNCH

STRENGTHENS RECTUS ABDOMINUS (EMPHASIS ON LOWER)

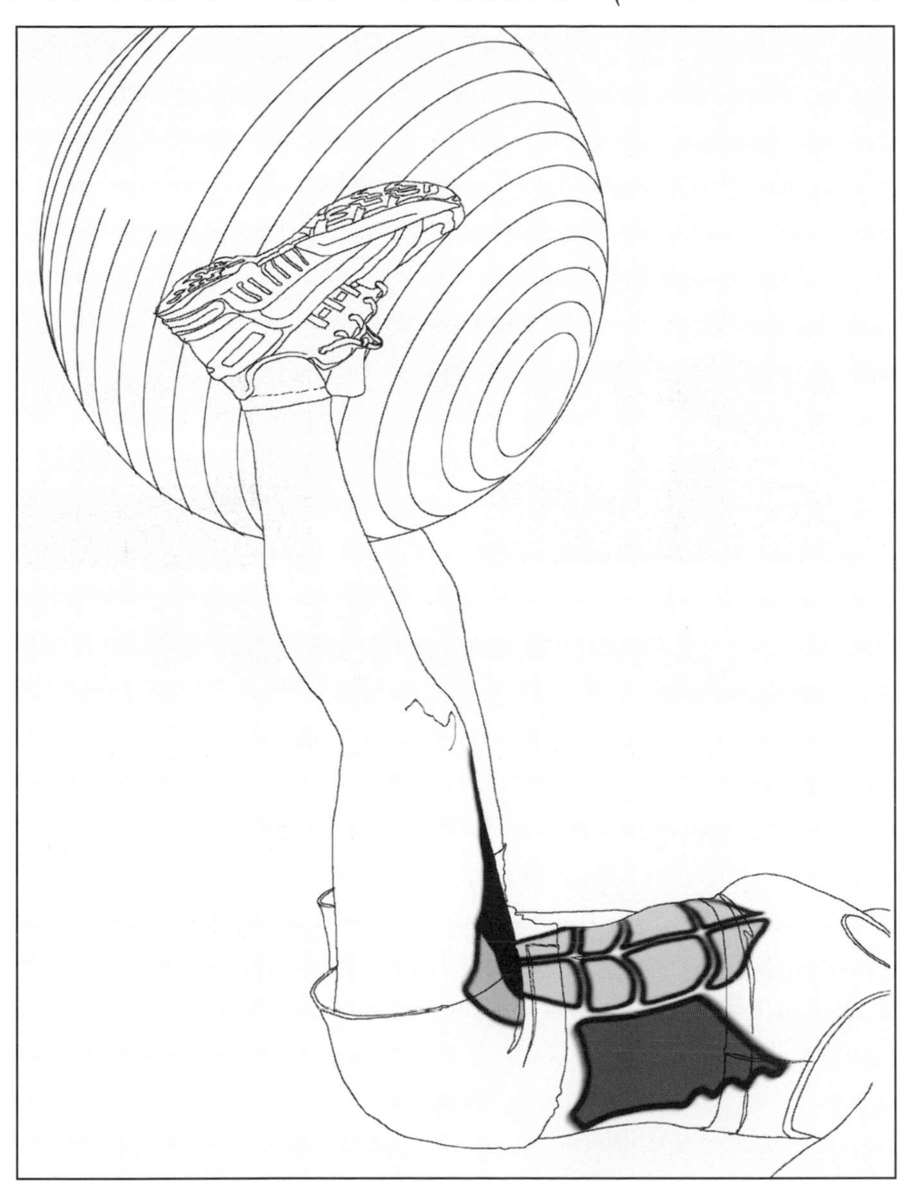

FITSKIING MUSCLES AT WORK

The reverse crunch is a great exercise to help develop your rectus abdominus muscles, as well as your hip flexors. Although you don't technically have lower abdominal muscles, you can target the lower portion of the rectus abdominus muscles. This is a great exercise to improve strength and stability on the slopes.

TRANSVERSE ABDOMINAL HOLD

STRENGTHENS TRANSVERSE ABDOMINUS

Exercise Description

1. Begin by placing your hands and feet on the floor. Your hands should be lined up below your shoulders. The legs should be placed in line below the hips.
2. Take a deep breath, letting your stomach expand.
3. Exhale all the air in your lungs while drawing your belly button toward your spine.
4. Hold for 10 seconds. Relax and breathe normally.
5. Repeat for the suggested number of sets and repetitions.

TARGET TRAINING TIP

Pull your stomach toward the spine as much as possible. This will guarantee that the transverse abdominus muscles are worked.

PRE-SKI WARM-UP

The transverse abdominus muscles are extremely important to the overall strength and stability of the core. By warming up these muscles before you hit the slopes you will reduce your risk of injury,.

TRANSVERSE ABDOMINAL HOLD

STRENGTHENS TRANSVERSE ABDOMINUS

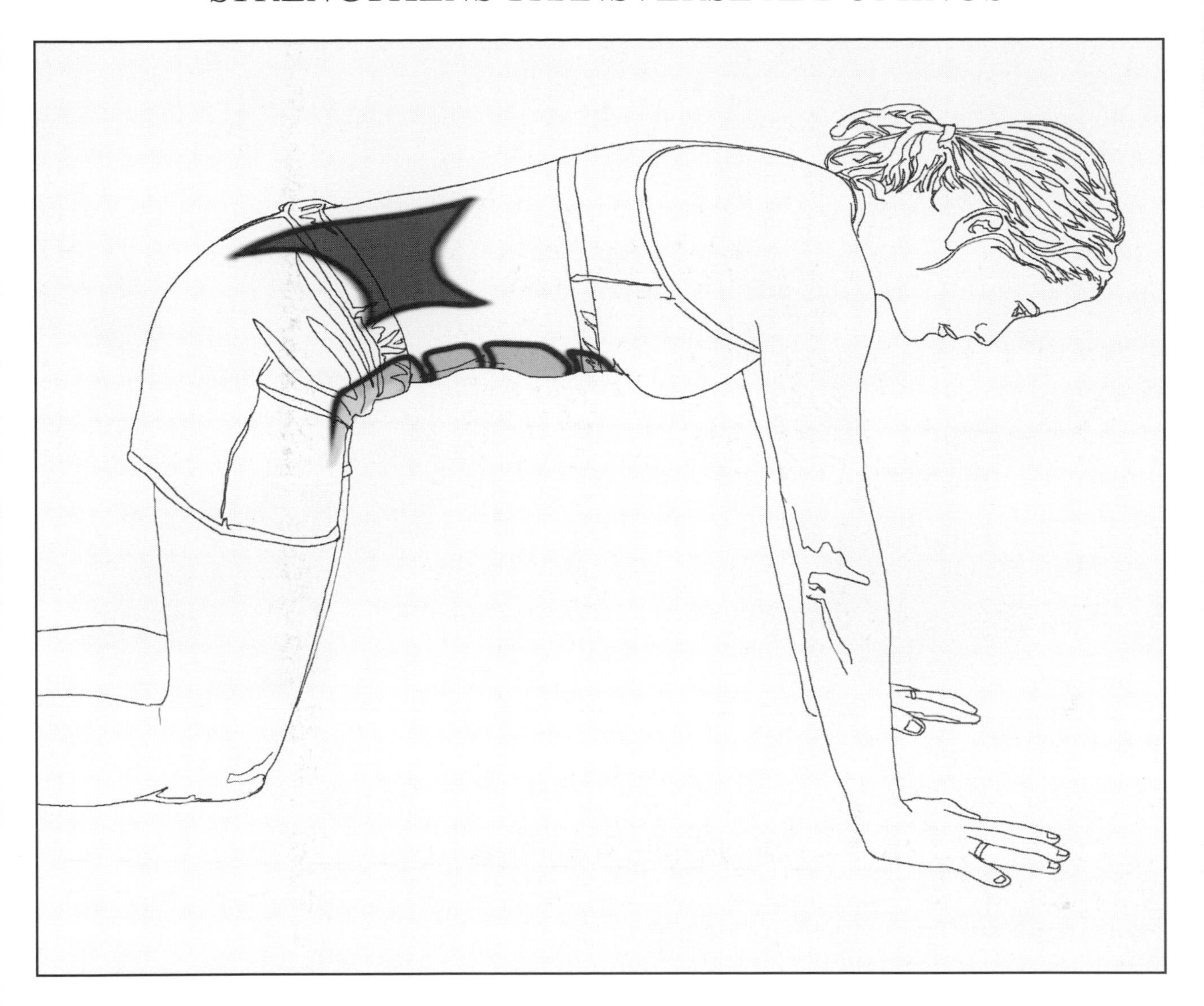

FITSKIING MUSCLES AT WORK

The transverse abdominal hold improves strength in your deep pelvic floor muscles. These are the same muscles that help you go to the bathroom. By strengthening these muscles, you will reduce your risk of injury. These muscles rarely get worked; however, they provide a tremendous amount of stability to the rest of the body.

BOSU BALL ABDOMINAL STABILITY

STRENGTHENS RECTUS ABDOMINUS AND STABILIZERS

Exercise Description

1. Place the Bosu Ball so the ball side is faceup.
2. Sit on the Bosu Ball and get comfortable with your balance. Extend your feet upward while at the same time extending your arms. Your body should resemble a V.
3. While keeping your abdominals contracted make sure to maintain your balance.
4. Hold for the suggested number of repetitions.

WARNING!

Remember to get your balance before beginning this exercise. This will help prevent possible injury, and enable you to use proper form. If you have lower back problems, this exercise should not be performed.

EQUIPMENT EXPENSE

$125

BOSU BALL ABDOMINAL STABILITY

STRENGTHENS RECTUS ABDOMINUS AND STABILIZERS

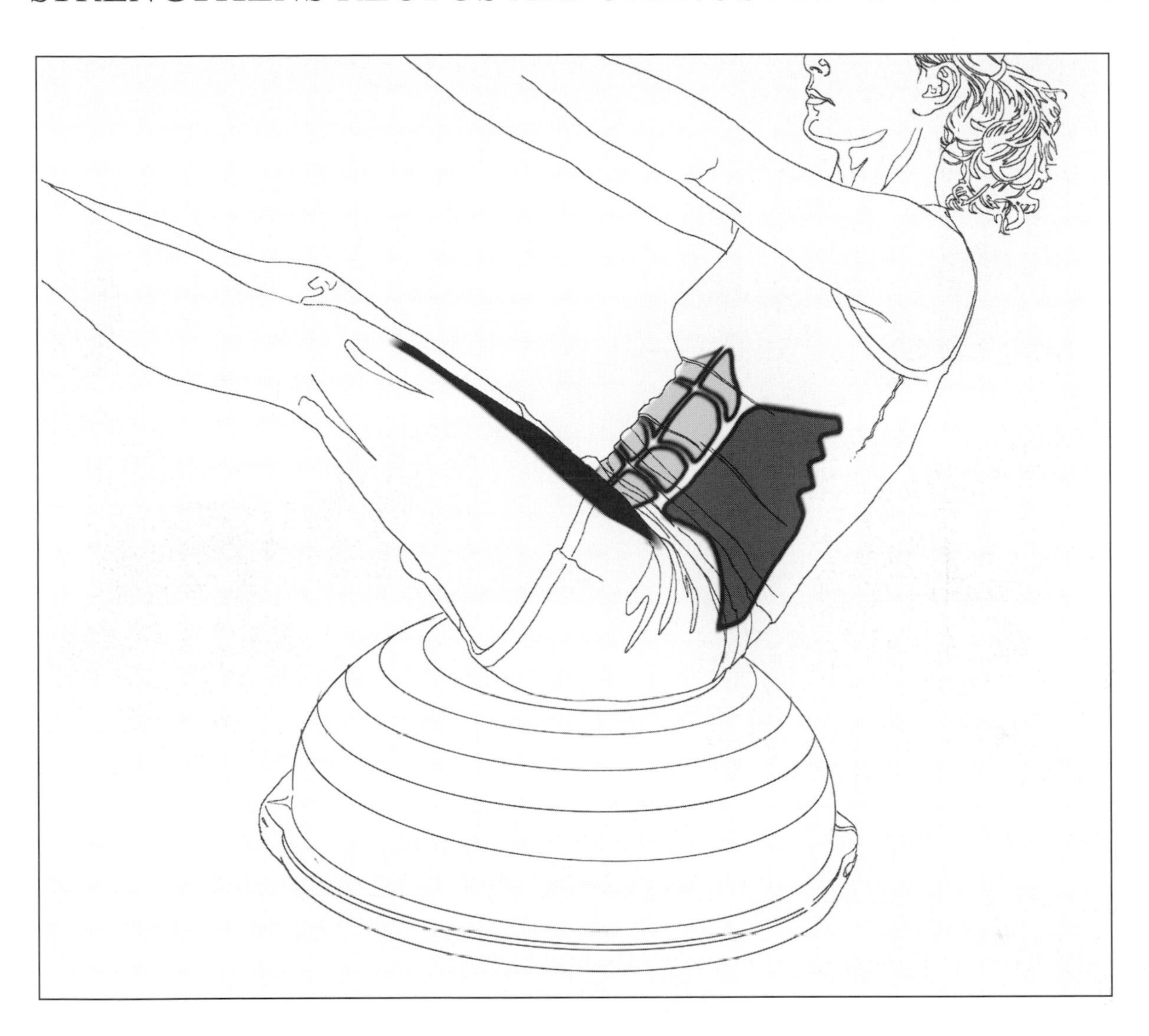

FITSKIING MUSCLES AT WORK

This is a static exercise that improves muscular endurance in the abdominal region as well as the front part of the thigh. The Bosu Ball abdominal stability exercise assist in improving stability with in the core area. This transfers over to your skiing by improving muscular endurance, strength and stability.

SIDE PLANK

STRENGTHENS OBLIQUES AND RECTUS ABDOMINUS

Exercise Description

1. Lie on your side with your legs straight.
2. Contract your abdominal muscles to support your spine.
3. While maintaining flexed abdominal muscles, hold the position for 5 to 10 seconds.
4. While your abdominal muscles are still flexed lower your body to the floor.
5. Repeat for the suggested number of sets and repetitions.

WARNING!

Although this is primarily an exercise to strengthen the oblique muscles, the shoulders are important for stabilization. If you have an injured shoulder, this exercise is not recommended.

TARGET TRAINING TIP

Remember to always focus on the muscles you are working. In the side plank, be sure to focus on stabilizing from the hips and oblique muscles.

SIDE PLANK

STRENGTHENS OBLIQUES AND RECTUS ABDOMINUS

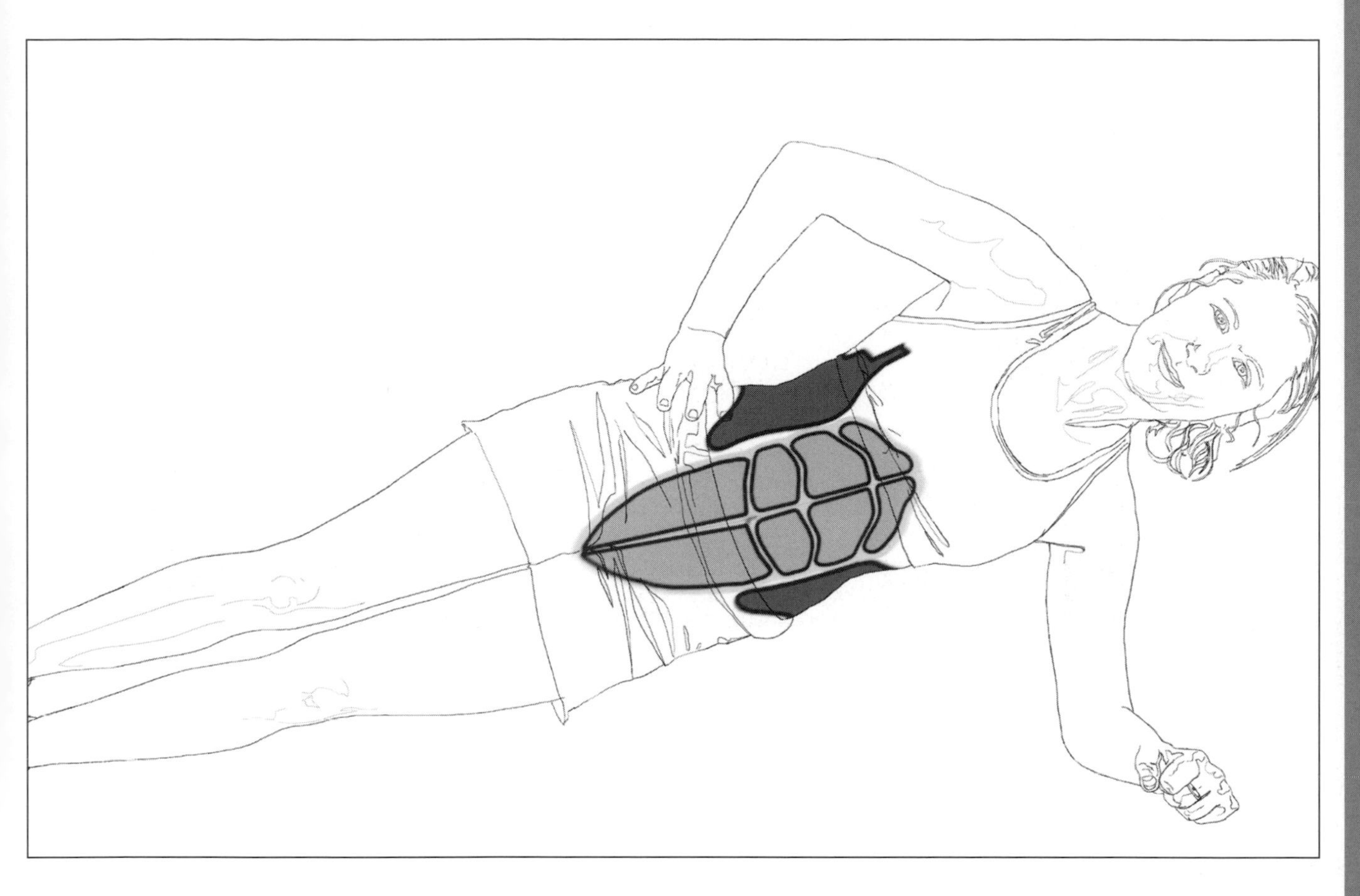

FITSKIING MUSCLES AT WORK

The oblique muscles are the strongest stabilizers of the midsection. As part of the core, they assist the skier in providing stability and maintaining balance.

By developing a strong midsection, especially the oblique muscles, you will be at less risk of injury, particularly to the lower back. These muscles are commonly neglected as many people focus on the rectus abdominus, or six-pack muscles.

If you have strong hip and oblique muscles, you will have an easier time regaining your stability if you catch an edge or lose your balance. You also might find them extremely helpful in supporting your body when your legs begin to fatigue.

DECLINE SIT-UP

STRENGTHENS RECTUS ABDOMINUS AND LOWER BACK

Exercise Description

1. Begin by lying on a decline bench. Cross your arms across your chest. Hook your feet under the safety pads.
2. Slowly lower your body until your lower back is just above the bench.
3. While keeping your abdominals contracted, bring your body back to the upright position. Do not release tension from your abdominals.
4. Repeat for the suggested number of repetitions.

WARNING!

This exercise is not recommended for individuals with back problems. Don't strain your neck when performing the exercise.

TARGET TRAINING TIP

Focus on your abdominal muscles to help ensure proper form and emphasis on the muscles being worked. To make the exercise more difficult add a 10 to 25 pound plate to your chest.

DECLINE SIT-UP

STRENGTHENS RECTUS ABDOMINUS AND LOWER BACK

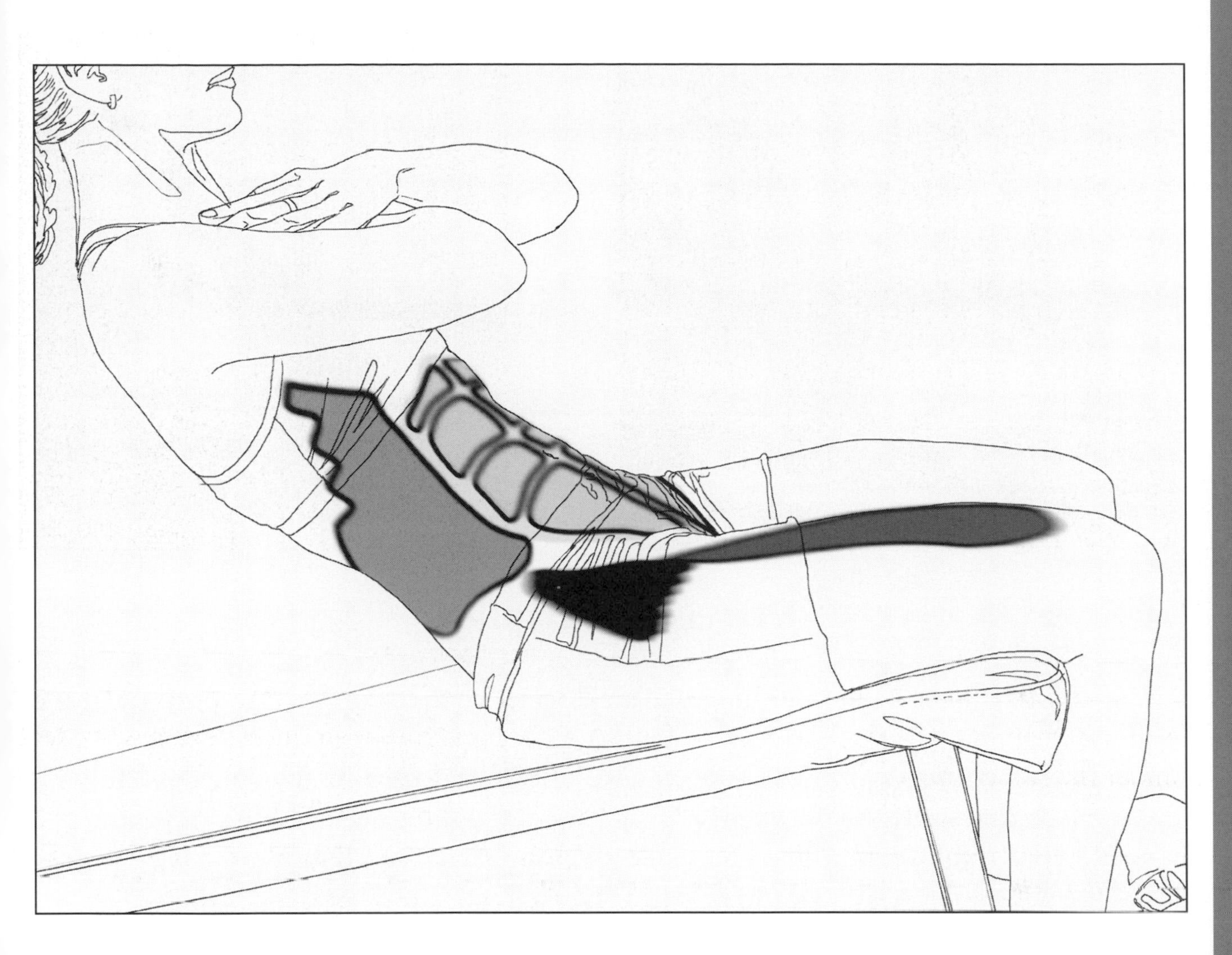

FITSKIING MUSCLES AT WORK

The decline sit-up is an old exercise that still is used today because it works. Some doctors and physical therapists don't recommend it because it can put more stress on the lower back. If you have a weak lower back start with the crunch or reverse crunch. When your health permits it, this is a great exercise to add weight to. Because the muscles in many of the abdominal areas are made up of fast-twitch fibers they respond better to more intensity and less volume. In other words; more weight and fewer repetitions. Remember to always focus your attention on the muscles you are working.

FIT BALL ROTATION

STRENGTHENS HIPS AND OBLIQUES

Exercise Description

1. Place a fit ball between your ankles. Make sure your lower back is pressed to the floor.
2. Rotate your trunk/torso to one side. Pause briefly and then return your legs so they make a 90 degree angle at your trunk.
3. Rotate your trunk/torso to the other side. Pause briefly and return your legs so they make a 90 degree angle at your trunk.
4. Repeat for suggested number of repetitions.

EQUIPMENT EXPENSE

$25 to $40

TARGET TRAINING TIP

Remember to always focus on the muscles you are working. In the fit ball rotation remember to focus attention on your rectus abdominus and oblique muscles. Keep your back flat against the floor during the exercise.

FIT BALL ROTATION

STRENGTHENS HIPS AND OBLIQUES

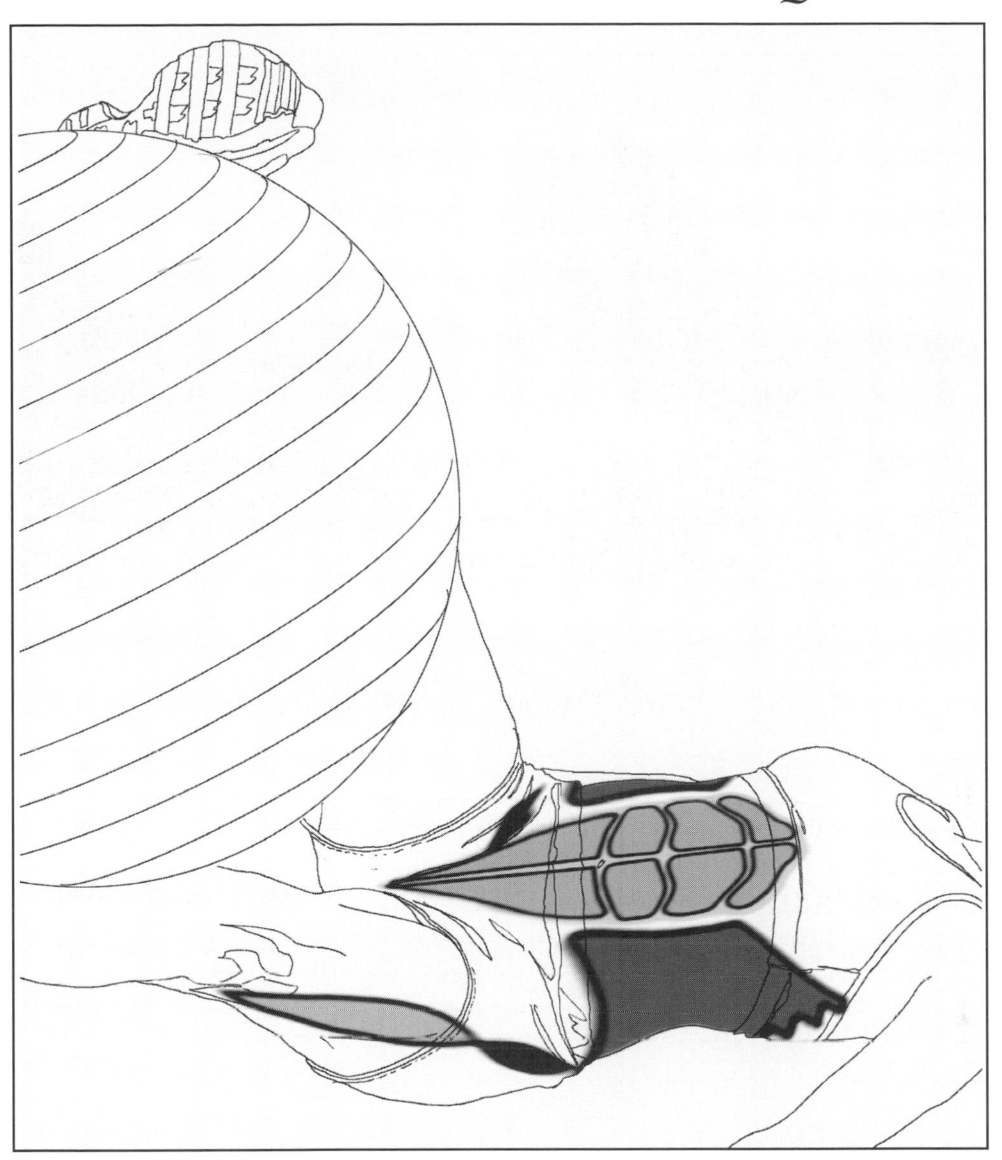

FITSKIING MUSCLES AT WORK

Skiing requires a lot of core strength. The fit ball rotation works the rectus abdominus, oblique, and abductor muscles. All these muscles are important in skiing becasue they provide more strength, stability, and power. If you are a freestyle skier, this is a great exercise to strengthen your rotation-related movements.

MEDICINE BALL CRUNCH

STRENGTHENS RECTUS ABDOMINUS

Exercise Description

1. Grab the medicine ball with your hands.
2. Keep your eyes focused on a point above you.
3. Crunch up, by flexing your torso.
4. Slowly lower your shoulders back to the floor.
5. Complete for suggested number of repetitions.

WARNING!

This exercise is not recommended for beginners or those who have back problems. Remember not to strain your neck while performing the exercise.

EQUIPMENT EXPENSE

$20 to $50

MEDICINE BALL CRUNCH

STRENGTHENS RECTUS ABDOMINUS

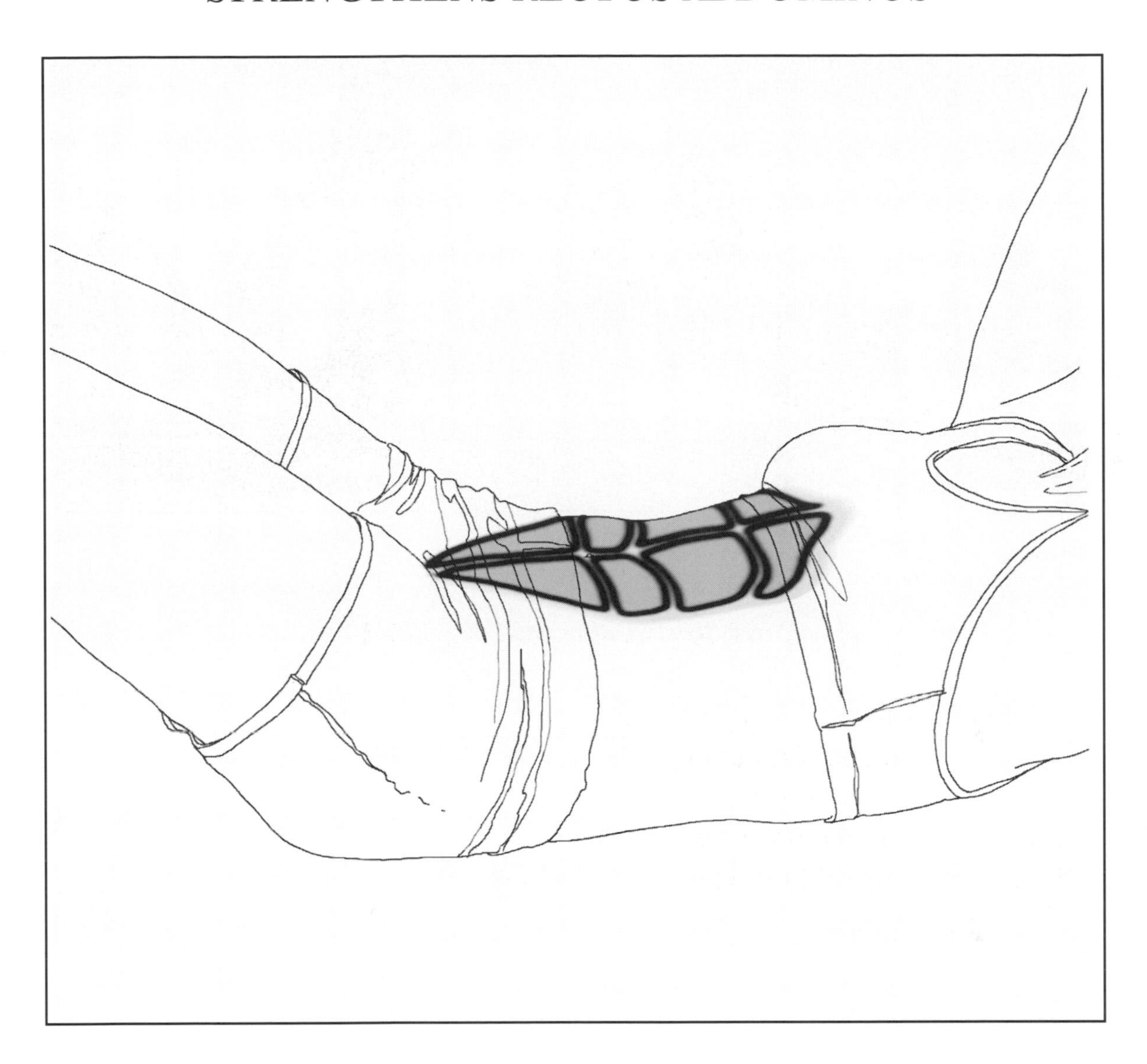

FITSKIING MUSCLES AT WORK

Similar to the crunch, the medicine ball crunch adds extra stress to the rectus abdominus muscles. By keeping your arms overhead, you also work the arm muscles that help you keep your poles in front of your body.

PLANK

STRENGTHENS SHOULDERS AND RECTUS ABDOMINUS

Exercise Description

1. Begin by placing your elbows and feet on the floor. Your elbows should be lined up below your shoulders. Your body should be about 2 feet off the floor.
2. Contract your abdominal muscles to support your body. Keep the focus on your mid-section, not your shoulders.
3. Maintain a flat body position, so that a perfectly straight line could be drawn across the top of your body.
4. Hold for the recommended number of seconds.
5. Repeat for the suggested number of sets.

TARGET TRAINING TIP

Remember to always focus on the muscles) you are working. In the plank be sure to focus on stabilizing from the hips and abdominal muscles.

WARNING!

Although this is primarily an abdominal exercise the shoulders are involved for stability. If you have a shoulder injury or back problems this exercise is not recommended.

PLANK

STRENGTHENS SHOULDERS, AND RECTUS ABDOMINUS

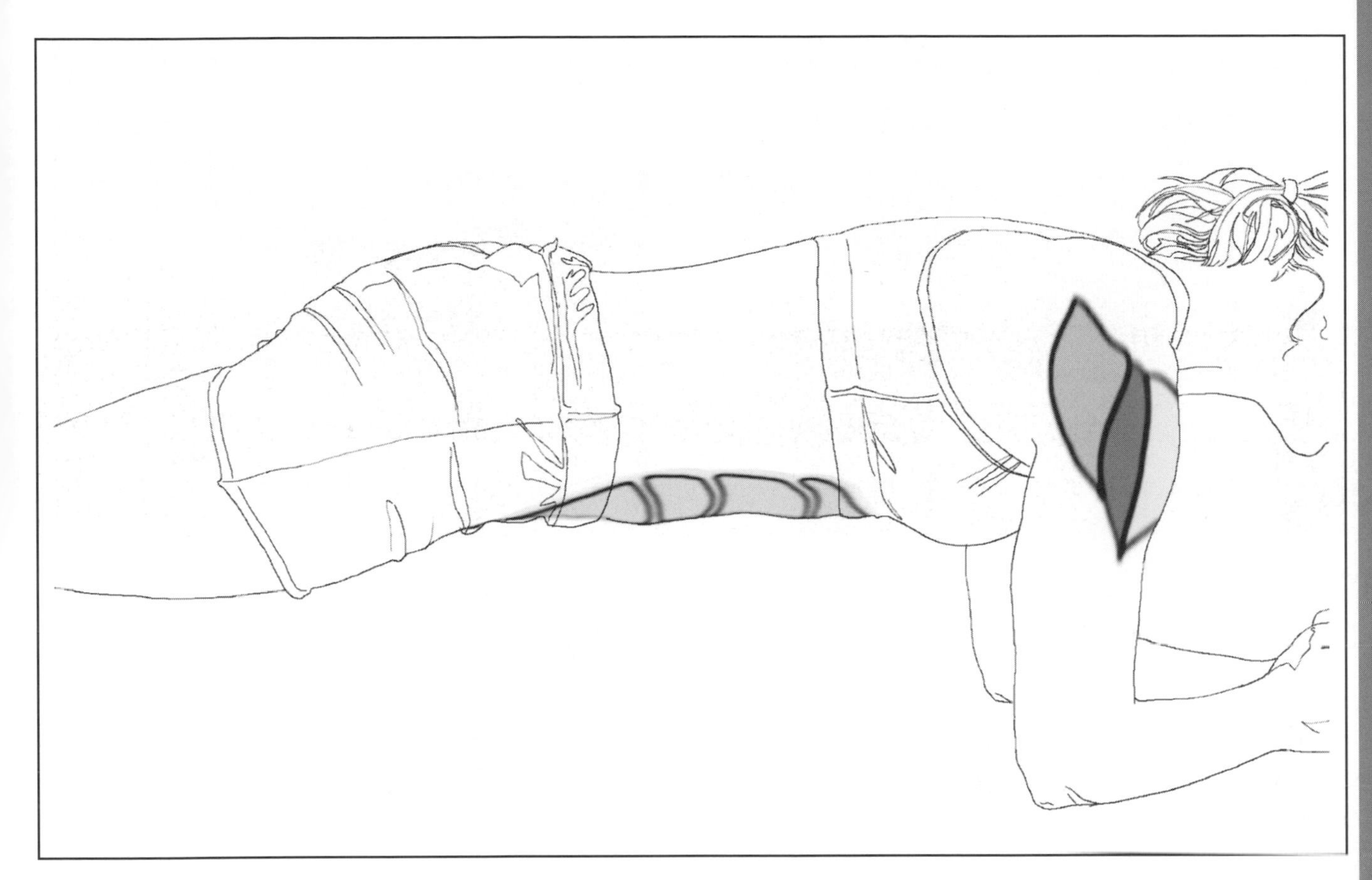

FITSKIING MUSCLES AT WORK

The plank is a favorite of skiers getting ready for the slopes. It strengthens the rectus abdominus muscles as well as the deltoid muscles. By improving muscular endurance in these areas, you will increase the amount of time you can ski as well as lessen your risk of injury. When your legs begin to fatigue, your abdominals provide extra stability to get you down the mountain.

ROPE CRUNCH

STRENGTHENS
RECTUS ABDOMINUS AND SERATUS ANTERIOR

Exercise Description

1. Begin by selecting an appropriate weight on the machine.
2. Grab the rope with both hands and kneel down on the floor.
3. Looking down at the floor, slowly flex or bend at the torso until your forehead almost touches the floor.
4. Remember to keep constant focus on the abdominal muscles. At the bottom of the movement, pause briefly and then slowly raise yourself to the starting position. Repeat for the recommended number of repetitions.

WARNING!

Remember not to strain your neck while performing the exercise. Don't use so much weight that you can't feel the abdominals working.

TARGET TRAINING TIP

Remember to pull with your midsection and keep constant focus on the abdominal muscles. For variation, try using a straight bar. This might help keep your focus on the abdominal muscles.

ROPE CRUNCH

STRENGTHENS
RECTUS ABDOMINUS AND SERATUS ANTERIOR

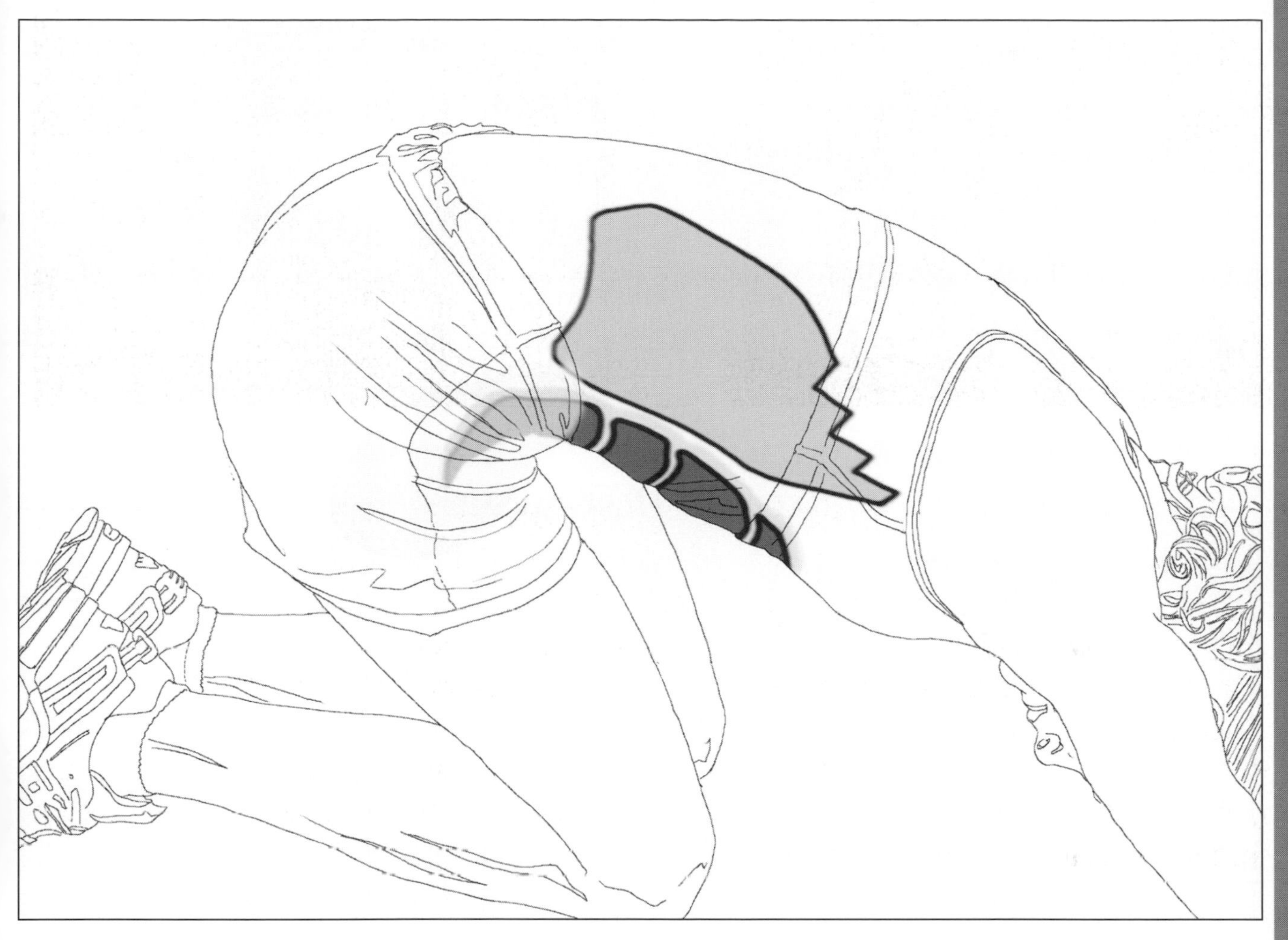

FITSKIING MUSCLES AT WORK

Rope crunches apply a crunching motion similar to what occurs when you are compressing your body through the bumps. By completing this exercise, you will have more stability in the bumps and on groomed runs.

FIT BALL SKI CRUNCH

STRENGTHENS HIP FLEXORS AND MID ABDOMEN

Exercise Description

1. Begin by placing a fit ball under your stomach. Roll forward until your shins are on the fit ball and your hands are on the floor.
2. Slowly bring your knees toward your abdominals in a crunching motion.
3. Pause briefly and then slowly return to the starting position. Remember to keep a constant focus on your abdominals.
4. Repeat for the recommended number of repetitions.

WARNING!

Although this is primarily an exercise to strengthen the abdominal muscles, the shoulders are important for stabilization. If you have an injured shoulder, this exercise is not recommended.

EQUIPMENT EXPENSE

$25 to $40

FIT BALL SKI CRUNCH

STRENGTHENS HIP FLEXORS AND MID ABDOMEN

FITSKIING MUSCLES AT WORK

One of the most ski-specific exercises you can perform, the fit ball ski crunch provides a motion similar to skiing. Your abdominal muscles go through a motion that is common when skiing bumps or steep terrain. This exercise also improves muscular endurance in the shoulders and triceps, which will assist you in pushing through cat tracks or the lift line.

WOOD CHOP

STRENGTHENS SERATUS ANTERIOR, HIPS, AND OBLIQUES

Exercise Description

1. Select an appropriate weight to begin the exercise. Grab the rope with both hands like you would a baseball bat or the upper portion of a golf swing.
2. Contract the abdominals and rotate your body downward as though you are chopping a piece of wood.
3. Drive through your opposing hip while focusing on the oblique muscles.
4. Keep your head forward while performing the exercise. Repeat for the suggested number of repetitions.

WARNING!

Remember not to overload the weight stack to the point where you can't feel your abdominals and obliques working.

TARGET TRAINING TIP

Drive through your hips and abdominal muscles. Try to use your arms as little as possible. Keep the attention on your midsection.

WOOD CHOP

STRENGTHENS SERATUS ANTERIOR, HIPS, AND OBLIQUES

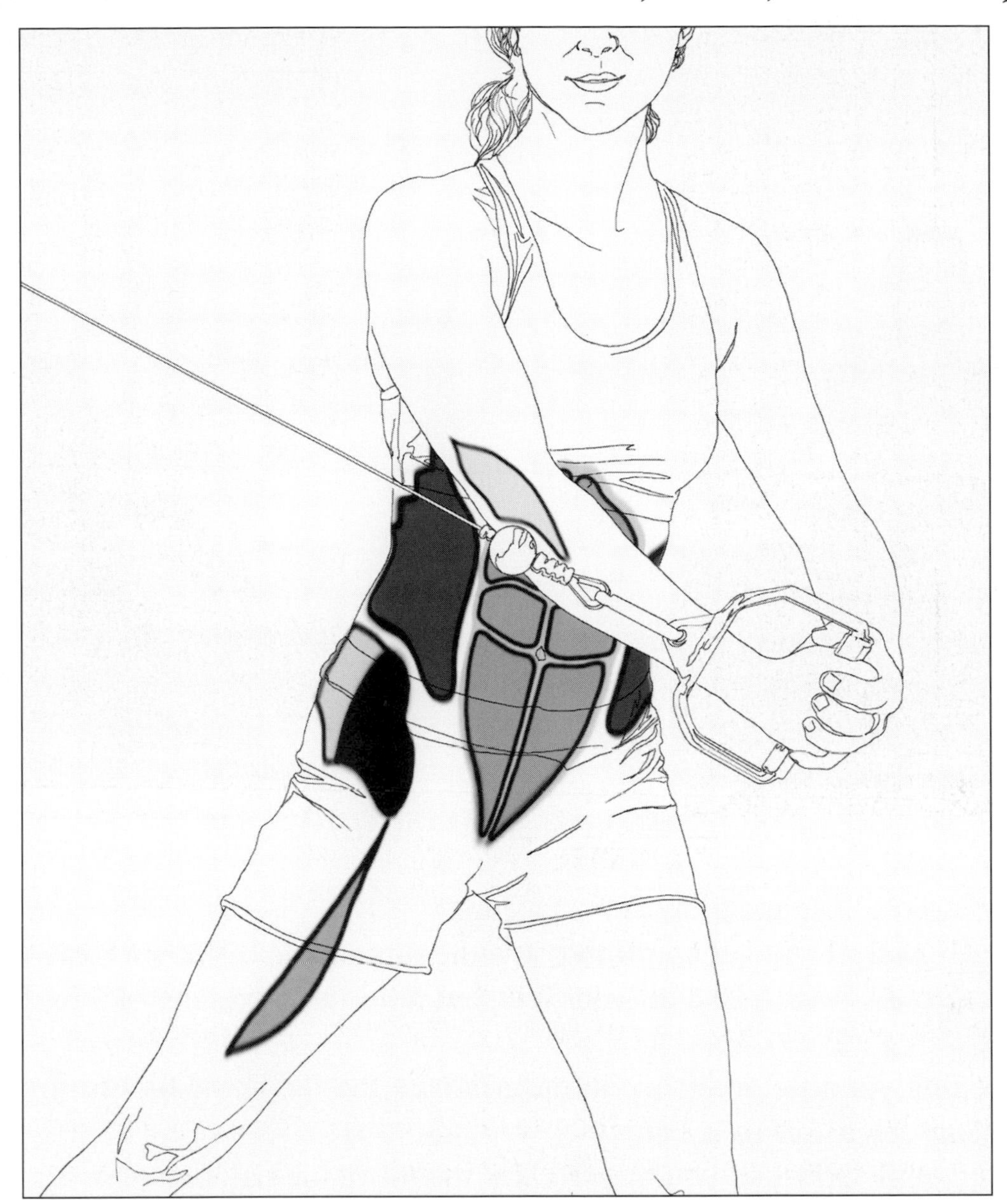

FITSKIING MUSCLES AT WORK

This is a great, overall upper body and core exercise. It teaches many of the core muscles to work together in one powerful motion. The wood chop also improves rotation strength, which will help provide stability between turns. If you play golf, it also can improve the power of your swing and might improve your drive. Remember to focus on one smooth, powerful motion and think about the muscles you are working.

MEDICINE BALL ROTATION

STRENGTHENS

BALANCE, OBLIQUES, MID ABDOMEN AND HIP FLEXORS

Exercise Description

1. Place the Bosu Ball so the ball side is faceup.
2. Sit on the Bosu Ball and get comfortable with your balance. Grab a medicine ball that you feel comfortable with. Extend your feet and hold the medicine ball in front of your body.
3. While keeping your abdominals contracted rotate the medicine ball from side to side, keeping constant focus on your core.
4. One rep is completed when you have rotated the medicine ball to both sides of the body. Repeat for the recommended number of repletions.

WARNING!

Remember to find your balance before beginning the exercise. This exercise is not intended for beginners.

EQUIPMENT EXPENSE

$25 to $125

1. Four Square Plyometric
2. Single Leg Lateral Hop
3. Hill Bounding
4. Jump Lunge
5. Medicine Ball Side Toss
6. Medicine Ball Sit-Up and Toss
7. Medicine Ball Overhead Toss
8. Stair Jumps

What Are Plyometrics?

You may have heard this word at one time or another in the gym or even on the slopes and wondered what foreign language someone was speaking. In some ways, exercise terminology can be a foreign language. I know I felt that way when working on my degree in kinesiology.

Plyometrics basically is a fancy way of saying that the stretch-shortening cycle between muscle contractions is reduced. That probably didn't help much either. A practical definition is "a quick, powerful movement while prestreching the muscle." In other words, you are trying to get as much range of motion as possible to create more power and recruit more fast-twitch muscle fibers as quickly as possible.

In contrast to a regular strength-training exercise, such as a bench press or biceps curl, the plyometric exercise is performed quickly and ballistically as opposed to slowly and controlled. Although you still want to feel your muscles work, the most important component is moving the weight and moving it quickly through a full range of motion.

Technically speaking elastic energy in your muscles and tendons is increased with a rapid stretch and is then stored. When immediately followed by a contraction of the muscles (concentric action), the stored energy is released. What is the difference between doing a squat at normal speed and doing one rapidly? If you wait too long between the stretching (lowering of the weight) of the muscle and the contraction of the muscles (upward portion), then the muscles lose the stored energy as heat. This is why plyometric exercises are done quickly and powerfully. If you are interested in the neurophysiology of the plyometric exercise, log on to www.fitskiing.com and go to the appropriate link.

FOUR SQUARE PLYOMETRIC

STRENGTHENS
COORDINATION, AGILITY AND CALVES

Exercise Description

1. Tape two strips of masking tape in a cross on the floor so it creates four sections, or use two resistance bands and do the same.
2. Stand on one foot to begin and jump in a clockwise fashion into each section. Begin slowly and get comfortable with the exercise. After you feel confident with the exercise speed up the exercise quickly bounding from section to section.
3. Repeat with the opposite leg. After both legs have completed one clockwise set, repeat counterclockwise with both legs. Each clockwise and counterclockwise motion is considered one repetition.
4. Complete the suggested number of repetitions and sets.

TARGET TRAINING TIP

Remember to start out slowly (about half of your maximal speed) to get comfortable with the exercise. When you feel comfortable pick up the speed and try to move quickly from section to section.

IMPROVES BALANCE

By moving quickly from section to section you will improve balance and stability. This will translate to more balance on each individual leg. By contracting your abdominal muscles, they will learn to work in conjunction with the rest of your body and create even more stability.

SINGLE LEG LATERAL HOP

STRENGTHENS STABILITY, POWER, AND CALVES

Exercise Description

1. This exercise can be done inside or outside. Just make sure you have about 4 feet of open space on both sides. Begin by placing a piece of masking tape lengthwise on the ground. It should measure about 4 or 5 feet in length.
2. Stand on one foot and get comfortable with your balance. Bound over the tape, pole or stick slowly on one foot. As you feel more comfortable with the exercise, increase your speed to about 80 percent of what you feel you could maximally perform. One rep is completed when you bound over both sides of the tape.
3. Repeat with the other leg.
4. Complete the suggested number of repetitions and sets

TARGET TRAINING TIP

Move explosively from side to side, driving from the outer hip of the leg being used. Remember to keep your abdominals tight for good support and balance.

WARNING!

If you have knee-related problems, this execise is not recommended. Remember to start slowly (about half of your maximal speed) and get a feel for the exercise.

HILL BOUNDING

STRENGTHENS POWER, CORE, QUADRICEPS AND CALVES

Exercise Description

1. Begin this exercise outside on a hill with a 10 percent to 20 percent grade. That is simila to the maximal grade on most gym-quality treadmills.
2. To get used to the exercise, jog about 40 meters up the hill. After a couple of short jogs do one sprint of the same distance. Rest, and then begin to bound from side to side slowly up the hill. Bounding is basically done by jumping forward on one foot and then immediat driving off of that foot forward in to the next step.
3. When you feel comfortable with the exercise, increase your speed focusing on powerin through your hips and thighs. You should perform this exercise at maximal effort whil maintaining good form.
4. Complete suggested number of repetitions and sets.

TARGET TRAINING TIP

Explode off of each foot. Try to keep as little time on the ground as possible. This will enable your muscles to react more quickly when you are on the slopes.

WARNING!

If you have knee-related problems this exercise is not recommended. This exercise is not meant for beginners. Advanced individuals should start out slowly and gradually getting more explosive as you feel comfortable.

JUMP LUNGE

STRENGTHENS POWER, CORE, AND LEGS

Exercise Description

1. This exercise can be done inside or outside. Begin in a lunge position. Your hands should be at your sides.
2. Jump as high as you can while thrusting your arms forward. Contract your abdominals upon leaving the ground.
3. Land on both feet and maintain your stability by keeping your core muscles tight. Squat into the lunge position and repeat.
4. Complete the suggested number of repetitions and sets, and then switch the back leg to the front and the front leg to the back.

TARGET TRAINING TIP

Explode off of your feet as much as possible. Try to keep ground contact to a minimum because this will improve your reaction time on the slopes. Remember to keep your abdominals tight throughout the movement to help maintain stability.

WARNING!

If you have lower back or knee-related problems, do not perform this exercise. This exercise is not intended for beginners. Advanced individuals should begin slowly at about half your normal explosiveness and speed.

MEDICINE BALL SIDE TOSS

STRENGTHENS CORE POWER

Exercise Description

1. This exercise can either be done inside or outside. Begin in a lunge position, with a partner standing about 10 to 20 feet (depending on your height) directly across from you. Stand sideways to your partner and position the medicine ball on the side of your body, away from your partner. Your arms should be in line with your torso.
2. Step forward with the leg facing your partner and toss the ball across your body, focusing on using your core to toss the ball.
3. Your partner should be standing straight to catch the ball. After your partner has a good grip on the ball, he or she should turn sideways and repeat the above. This is a power exercise that should be done explosively and quickly.
4. Complete the suggested number of repetitions and sets.

TARGET TRAINING TIP

Use your oblique muscles to toss the medicine ball in one powerful motion. Focusing on these muscles will help you perform the exercise properly.

EQUIPMENT EXPENSE

$20 to $40

MEDICINE BALL SIT-UP AND TOSS

STRENGTHENS CORE POWER AND HIP FLEXORS

Exercise Description

1. This exercise can be done inside or outside. Begin by sitting on the floor or ground. Grab a medicine ball with a weight you feel comfortable with. Lie flat on your back with your legs slightly bent or fully extended. Fully extend makes the abdominals work harder.
2. Extend the arms all the way behind the head and explode upward in one powerful sit-up motion. About midway through the movement, release the ball to your partner.
3. Your partner will catch the ball and then repeat the same motion.
4. Complete the suggested number of repetitions and sets.

TARGET TRAINING TIP

To make this exercise easier, begin with your legs bent. This will take some of the stress off of the lower back and midsection. To make it more difficult, keep the legs straight.

WARNING!

Start out slowly (about half of your normal explosiveness and speed) to get comfortable with the exercise. If you have lower back problems, this exercise is not recommended.

MEDICINE BALL OVERHEAD TOSS

STRENGTHENS BACK AND CORE POWER

Exercise Description

1. This exercise should be done outside with a partner. Begin by grabbing an appropriate-weight medicine ball. Stand about 10 to 20 feet (depending on height) directly across from your partner.
2. Bring your arms behind your head with a slight bend to the elbow. Powerfully toss the ball to your partner, releasing it just as your hands come above your head. Remember to use your core to help in the exercise.
3. Make sure you extend your arms all the way down to your sides after you release the ball. This will help activate your latisimus (back) muscles.
4. Your partner should repeat the same motion. Repeat for the suggested number of repetitions and sets.

TARGET TRAINING TIP

Remember to follow through with your arms. This will create more upper body power and work your lat muscles. When releasing the ball use your abs. This will recruit more fast-twitch fibers and enable you to be more responsive on the slopes.

EQUIPMENT EXPENSE

$20 to $50

STAIR JUMPS

STRENGTHENS LOWER BODY POWER AND CORE POWER

Exercise Description

1. This exercise can be done inside or outside. However, make sure you have enough space between stairs to do the exercise properly if you are inside. Each stair should be about 5 feet from the next stair. If not, you might need to skip a few stairs.
2. Begin by flexing slightly at the knee. Bring the arms behind you slightly. Take a deep breath and bound upward while contracting your abdominal muscles. Make sure you thrust your arms forward.
3. Land with knees bent at about 90 degrees. Relax and reset yourself.
4. Repeat for desired number of repetitions and sets.

TARGET TRAINING TIP

Be explosive! Don't simply jump to the next stair. Get as high as you can in the air and really focus on thrusting your body forward. This will help in becoming more responsive on the slopes. It also will help improve reaction times and stability while skiing moguls.

WARNING!

Remember to find a solid, surface to perform this exercise. If you have knee-related problems this exercise is not recommended. Remember to begin slowly to get comfortable with the exercise.

DOWNWARD DOG

IMPROVES
OVERALL FLEXIBILITY AND CIRCULATION

Exercise Description

1. This exercise is great to do before a long day of skiing. It relaxes the shoulders and back. It also stretches the hamstrings and calves.
2. Begin by kneeling on the floor and stretching your hands in front of your head. Push yourself up, extending the legs until your body resembles a reverse V shape.
3. Extend the arms so they are in line with your head; at the same time, extend the legs. Try to press your heels to the floor. If you can't, don't strain your calves trying to. Relax and let it happen over a period of time.
4. Hold for 30 seconds to 1 minute and then repeat. Continue for the suggested number of sets.

1. Downward Dog
2. Calf Stretch
3. Chest Stretch
4. Hamstring Stretch
5 Piriformis Stretch
6. Lower Back/Hip Stretch
7. Latisimus Stretch
8. Lower Back Stretch
9. Quadriceps Stretch
10. Triceps Stretch
11. Overhead Stretch

Why Stretch?

1. Stretching improves flexibility thereby assisting in preventing injuries.

2. When you stretch after working out, you remove some of the lactic-acid that has built up during your training session. Lactic acid is that nasty by-product that leads to fatiguing muscles and the soreness you get about 48 hours after your workout.

3. By increasing your range of motion through stretching, you will be able to increase the range that the muscles can work. This creates more power and leads to more explosiveness on the slopes or any other sport you may participate in.

4. Stretching feels good.

CALF STRETCH

IMPROVES
CALF FLEXIBILITY

Exercise Description

1. This stretch can be done in a number of ways; however, for this book I have chosen the quickest way in case you feel the need to stretch immediately following a day on the slopes. Recall that in Chapter 7, I recommend stretching after a long day of skiing.
2. Begin by standing with one leg in front of the other. You should have about 2 feet to 3 feet between your legs. Extend the back leg to the point where your knee is locked or almost locked.
3. Press the heel of the rear leg to the floor as far as it will go. Remember not to go to a painful range, only to moderate discomfort.
4. Hold for 30 seconds to 1 minute and then repeat with the opposite leg. Continue for the suggested number of sets.

CHEST STRETCH

IMPROVES
SHOULDER AND CHEST FLEXIBILITY

Exercise Description

1. The chest is one of the hardest muscles to stretch on your own. The stretch illustrated here is most effective when it is done properly. Begin by finding a doorway or post to place your arm against.
2. Bend the elbow to a 90 degree angle and place one foot in front of the other. Lean forward until you feel a stretch in the chest area.
3. You may feel the stretch in the shoulder at first. If this happens, make sure you focus on the chest muscles. This will help keep the attention on the correct muscles. After the initial stretch, take a deep breath and lean forward while exhaling.
4. Hold for 30 seconds to 1 minute and then repeat with the opposite arm. Continue for the suggested number of sets and repetitions.

HAMSTRING STRETCH

IMPROVES
HAMSTRING FLEXIBILITY

Exercise Description

1. This stretch can be done in a number of ways; however, for this book I have chosen the quickest way in case you feel the need to stretch immediately following a day on the slopes. Recall in Chapter 7, I recommend stretching after a long day of skiing.
2. Begin by standing with one leg in front of the other. Extend the front leg until the knee is slightly bent or locked. Reach forward with your arm and extend it toward your front foot.
3. You should feel a slight stretch in your hamstrings. Take a deep breath and stretch a little further while exhaling.
4. Hold for 30 seconds to 1 minute and then repeat with the opposite leg. Continue for the suggested number of sets.

PIRIFORMIS STRETCH

STRENGTHENS
HIP AND PIRIFORMIS FLEXIBILITY

Exercise Description

1. Your piriformis muscles are deep to your glutial muscles and are positioned near the sciatic nerve. Many times the piriformis muscles can become tight and wrap around the nerve, causing a painful problem called sciatica. By stretching this area, you can help prevent this problem while keeping your hips and lower back more flexible.
2. Begin by lying on the floor, with one leg bent and your foot on the ground. With your spine pressed to the floor grab the ankle of your other leg with one arm and your foot with the other. Pull until you feel a slight stretch around your hips and lower back. Take a deep breath in and pull your leg toward you a little more while exhaling.
3. Remember not to go to a painful range, only to moderate discomfort.
4. Hold for 30 seconds to 1 minute and then repeat with the opposite leg. Continue for the suggested number of sets.

LOWER BACK/HIP STRETCH

IMPROVES
LOWER BACK AND HIP FLEXIBILITY

Exercise Description

1. This stretch works the lower back and hip muscles. By increasing flexibility in your lower back, you can help prevent injuring those muscles.
2. Begin by lying down on your back with your legs extended. Extend one arm straight out to the side. Bring one leg across the body and grab the knee with the opposite arm.
3. Make sure to keep your back on the ground. Remember not to go to a painful range, only to moderate discomfort.
4. Hold for 30 seconds to 1 minute and then repeat with the opposite leg. Continue for the suggested number of sets.

LATISIMUS STRETCH

IMPROVES
LATISIMUS FLEXIBILITY

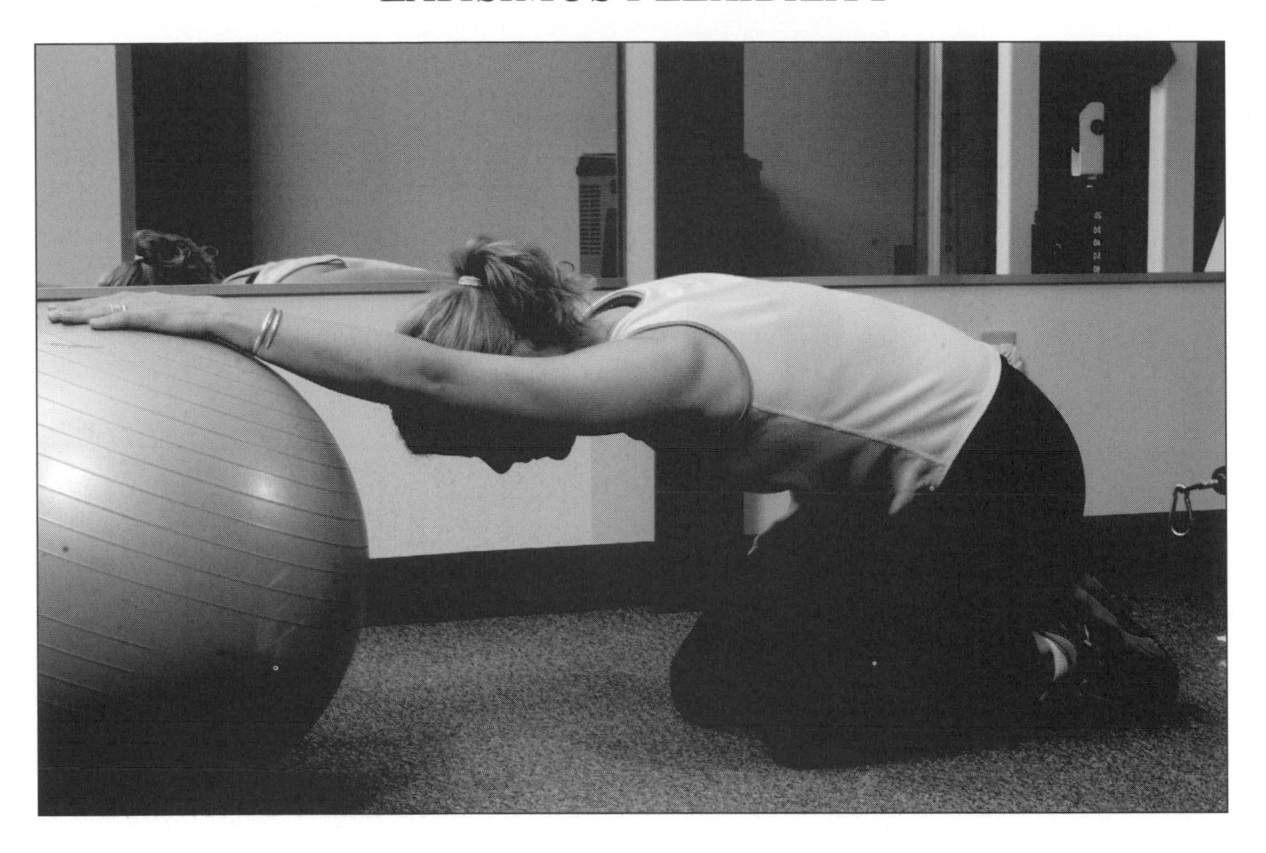

Exercise Description

1. This stretch can be done in a number of ways, but I have found that using a fit ball is the most efficient.
2. Kneel on the ground and place one arm on the fit ball. Slowly bend down and pull back at the same time.
3. You should feel a slight stretch. Take a deep breath and lean down and back a little more while exhaling.
4. Hold for 30 seconds to 1 minute and then repeat with the opposite arm. Continue for the suggested number of sets.

LOWER BACK STRETCH

IMPROVES
LOWER BACK FLEXIBILITY

Exercise Description

1. This is a great stretch for relaxing at the end of a long day of skiing.
2. Begin by lying on your back with your knees slightly bent. With both arms, grab your legs and bring them toward the chest. Take a deep breath and pull your legs toward your chest a little more while exhaling.
3. Make sure to relax your spine and your neck while performing this exercise. Remember not to go to a painful range, only to moderate discomfort.
4. Hold for 30 seconds to 1 minute and then repeat. Continue for the suggested number of sets.

QUADRICEPS STRETCH

IMPROVES
HIP FLEXOR AND QUADRICEPS FLEXIBILITY

Exercise Description

1. After a long day on the slopes, this stretch is a must. It can be done in a number of ways, but this is probably the quickest and most efficient.
2. Begin by standing on both legs with your arms at your sides. Flex one leg back until you can grab the top of your foot with your arm behind you. Pull until you feel a slight stretch on the front part of your leg (quadriceps).
3. Take a deep breath and pull your leg up and back a little further while exhaling.
4. Hold for 30 seconds to 1 minute and then repeat. Continue for the suggested number of sets.

TRICEPS STRETCH

IMPROVES TRICEPS FLEXIBILITY

Exercise Description

1. This exercise provides a good stretch for the triceps and the lat muscles.
2. Begin by standing on both feet and bringing one arm over your head. One arm should be bent at a 90 degree angle. Grab your elbow with the other arm and pull until you feel a slight stretch.
3. Take a deep breath and pull the elbow down a little more while exhaling. You should feel a stretch in your back (lats) as well as the back of your arms (triceps).
4. Hold for 30 seconds to 1 minute and then repeat with the other arm. Continue for the suggested number of sets.

OVERHEAD STRETCH

IMPROVES OVERALL UPPER-BODY FLEXIBILITY

Exercise Description

1. This exercise is a great overall stretch for the upper body. It should be done before and after upper-body workouts and your day on the slopes.
2. Begin by standing on both feet with your arms at your sides. Take a deep breath and raise your arms overhead. While exhaling cross your arms overhead and reach up as far as you can.
3. Remember to stretch only to moderate discomfort, not pain. If you start to feel pain, then relax and wait for a minute or so before you try again.
4. Hold for 30 seconds to 1 minute. Continue for the suggested number of sets.

SCOTT

CHAPTER NINE

FITSKIING FOR KIDS

A Word of Caution

Although FitSkiing has provided some useful insight into the world of training children, it is not a replacement for having your children work with a good trainer. Remember to use your best judgement when having your children perform any of the information provided in this chapter. FitSkiing takes no responsibility for the way you train your children. It is the recommendation of this book that you and your children work with a highly qualified trainer certified by the American College of Sports Medicine or the National Strength and Conditioning Association.

Always remember to provide adequate supervision and spotting when working with children. To find a qualified trainer in your area visit www.FitSkiing.com for more information.

According to the 1996 surgeon general's *Report on Physical Activity and Health,* close to one half of children ages 12 to 21 are not involved in vigorous activity on a regular basis. Fifteen percent of children are considered sedentary.

This is only one factor that should motivate you to get your children skiing! What child doesn't enjoy playing in the snow with siblings or other kids? Skiing is a good way to get your children to exercise without the stigma of "exercise" attached to it. It is also a good way to help them develop their motor skills so they will be better prepared for other activities that come their way. The following are just a few reasons to get your children on the slopes skiing:

• Gets them active and helps them learn that exercise can be fun.

• Improves motor development.

• Increases their confidence level.

• Gets the family active together.

• Leads to making new friends.

• Provides a life-long activity that will help keep them fit.

Those are just a few of the reasons you should get your children skiing. Although children can strap on a pair of skis just as an adult can, you should be aware of some important differences before you hit the slopes with your children. In this chapter, you will learn the four basic guidelines to prepare your children for skiing.

• *You will learn which strength and conditioning activities will help improve your children's abilities on the slopes.*

• *You will learn what limitations your children have regarding strength training.*

• *You will learn how to work with your children to build their confidence so they are more comfortable when they begin skiing.*

• *You will be provided with a sample workout and training program for your children.*

Strength and Conditioning for Children

Sometimes in our busy schedules we lose sight of the fact that children are not adults. Whether they are 5 or 15 years old, children have different training needs and precautions to take than adults. They should participate in fitness programs that increase aerobic fitness, flexibility, muscular endurance, and strength and that improve overall body composition. They should not focus on developing specific sports skills. The following are some things to keep in mind when you are training with your children.

• A child, no matter how big or strong is still growing and enjoying new activities for the first time.

• The focus on resistance training programs for children should be on learning new skills, building friendships, and experiencing success, not on competition.

• Encourage your children to try skiing but don't force them.

• Adult training guidelines are different than those for children and should not be applied to children.

A well-rounded ski fitness program for children includes aerobic fitness training, stretching, and strength-training exercises. Some of the benefits of a strength and conditioning program include:

• Increased strength in the muscles.
• Increased endurance in the muscles.
• Improved sports performance.
• Less risk of injury.
• Increased self-confidence.
• Improved overall health and well-being

Many times I am asked when children can start training. As with many things in the field of exercise, you probably will get a different answer from anyone you ask. Some will tell you not to have your children involved in any strength training until they reach 15 years of age. Others will tell you that children can start as young as five. I base training children more on their maturity level than on their age, although I don't recommend strength training for children under the age of 6. If a child has the emotional maturity to follow and accept directions, then they are probably capable of participating in a strength-training program. For some, that might mean they start as early as age 6. For others, it might be 10 years of age or older. Children of any age require close attention when they are resistance training.

A common misconception associated with strength training and children is that it will damage the bones. Injuries to bones at this age are a serious concern, but this type of injury can be avoided if proper instruction is given and exercises are performed correctly. Strength training can increase the strength of bones and may be be a benefit to girls who are at risk of developing osteoporosis (bone deterioration).

Although weight training is typically safe for children if they are surpervised properly they need to be aware that if proper training is not followed, they risk injury. Children should never be unsupervised when they are training. Using a certified strength coach by the National Strength and Conditioning Association is a good way to make sure your children are being trained properly. Go to www.nsca-lift.org

to find a trainer in your area. The following are some guidelines you should follow when designing and implementing a strength program for children.

• All workouts must be surpervised closely by a competent adult.
• A medical exam should precede any training program to make sure the child is healthy.
• Every child should be mature enough to follow and adhere to instructions.
• A safe, hazard-free environment should be provided.
• A warm-up of 5 minutes should be completed before beginning a strength training session.
• Children should be encouraged to ask questions and be praised for participating.

FitSkiing for Kids Training Guidelines

Children are different than adults when it comes to implementing a program to improve skiing. The following are general guidelines for the FitSkiing for kids program. The program is 6 weeks in length and can be repeated after a 2-to-4 week break of other types of activity such as soccer, baseball, or skiing. As with adults, children need variable stimulation to keep them interested. Taking a month to enjoy other activities is a good way to keep your children motivated. *The following program should be repeated no more than four times per year for children under the age of 15.*

FitSkiing for Kids
Stage Instructions
• 1 warm up set (50% of work set)
• 2 work sets
• 12-15 repetitions each set
• Increase weight by 2-5 pounds when you can complete the fifteenth repetition in the second set
• Weight training RPE: 7
• Rest 1-2 minutes between sets
• 10-30 minutes of aerobic activity per week
• Begin with 10 minutes the first week and add five minutes per week until 30 minutes are reached
• Aerobic RPE: 6-7

Remember this program should be done for 6 weeks and then a break of 2 to 4 weeks should follow. The following section provides specific exercises to perform for each workout. Your children will be performing two workouts per week with 72 hours between each workout. Try completing the workout with your children or having a group workout with other kids to make it more fun. Adult supervision is a must at all times. Get other parents involved to make sure they feel comfortable with the workout facility and instruction. Also, have your children perform a 5-minute warm-up before they begin.

FitSkiing for Kids
Weight Training Workout One
Dumbbell Squat
Lat Pull-down
Dumbbell Bench Press
Dumbbell Shoulder Press
Dumbbell Curl
Triceps Press-down
Crunches
Downward Dog
Chest Stretch
Hamstring Stretch
Quadriceps Stretch

FitSkiing for Kids
Weight Training Workout Two
Single Leg Curl
Lat Pull-down
Dumbbell Bench Press
Lateral Raise
Biceps Curl with Band
Triceps Press-down
Crunches
Overhead Stretch
Hip Stretch
Low Back/Hip Stretch
Latisimus Stretch

To improve your children's aerobic system, they should find an activity they enjoy doing 3 days per week such as running, biking, hiking, and so on. Children enjoy doing things outdoors, so try to provide them with cardiovascular opportunities outside. Sometimes setting up an obstacle course that includes jumping, running and similar activities, is a good idea because it provides varying stimuli to keep children interested. Obstacle courses also can improve your children's balance and proprioceptive abilities, which will help improve their performance on the slopes. Children should increase their aerobic training from 5 minutes to 30 minutes or more over the course of the 6-week program.

Training Safety

The following is a list of guidelines to follow to keep a safe training environment for your children.

- An adult should always be present when children are training.
- Improper form should always be corrected by a trainer or an adult.
- Start slowly with exercises and then progress.

• Strength training should be appropriate for the ability level of each child.
• Children should not perform maximal lifts.
• When pressing weights overhead, be careful.
• Children should not hold their breath when lifting.
• A spotter should always be present when a child is lifting a weight overhead.
• Remember to emphasize lifting with the legs and not the back when children pick up weights from the floor.
• The training area should be well lit and have a nonskid surface to exercise on.
• Warm up and cool down before and after exercising.
• Children like to explore, so remove any potential hazards from the exercise area.
• Remember to have your children drink plenty of water before, during, and after weight training or any other strenuous activity.

Motivation for Children

How do you motivate your children to train before they hit the slopes? Next, you will find a list of motivational techniques you can apply.
• Above all else, make sure your children are having fun and enjoying the strength-training program.
• Set realistic goals.
• Remind your children that it takes time to get in shape and learn a new exercise.
• Encourage questions and listen to your children's concerns.
• Exercise with your children or have other children exercise with them.
• Be enthusiastic and show support for strength-training efforts.

Starting Early

Childhood is probably the most important time for kids to develop healthy eating and exercise habits. If your children are active in skiing, soccer, football, or any other activity that involves vigorous exercise, they will be more likely to continue to exercise as adults. The great thing about skiing is that you don't need a team like football or soccer, and it can be performed late into your seventies or eighties. Although this book is about getting in shape for skiing, it is important for children to get involved in many different activities that provide success and develop skills, and make them feel good about themselves.

The surgeon general's *Report on Physical Activity and Health* says that children ages 6 years and older should participate in activities that enhance muscular strength and endurance. This is just one more reason for children to start training early. Now, get your children skiing!

bollé

A Word of Caution

Although FitSkiing has provided some useful insight into the world of ski-related injuries, this chapter is not a replacement for working with a good orthopedic specialist and physical therapist. Always use your best judgement when reading or performing any of the information provided in this chapter.

In addition, always consult a doctor before you treat any injury or begin any exercise or rehabilitation program. Enjoy the slopes, but remember to ski at your level, not someone else's.

According to the *Sports Medicine Bible*, the best way to avoid and prevent ski-related injuries is threefold.

- •Experience
- •Ability
- •Attitude

One should invest in proper skiing instruction with a certified instructor. You also might consider receiving strength and conditioning instruction from a certified trainer. Well-conditioned skiers are less likely to sustain injuries than skiers who fatigue significantly during a day on the slopes. Awareness of your strength and weaknesses is also important. If you are a beginner, you shouldn't venture into the

		TYPES OF TREATMENT	
Treatment Type	**When To Use**	**Intensity/Duration**	**What It Does**
Rest	Anytime	With knees slightly bent lye flat on back/20 to 30 minutes, 4-5 times per week	Relaxes muscles/alleviates stress
Ice	Immediately after injury or for post exercise swelling	20 Minutes per session/use towel to protect skin from burning	Decreases inflammation and pain
Hot packs	See a health professional/never use post injury or exercise	20 Minutes per session/use towel to protect skin from burning	Relaxes muscles prior to other treatments
Electrical stimu-lation	See a health professional	May promote muscle contractions. Apply with heat or cold for 20 minutes	Increases blood flow/circulation by using electrical impulses. Decreases spasms
Ultrasound	See a health professional	Gel applied first/10 minutes	Improves blood flow and tissue temperature by transmitting pulsed sound waves
Tens	Typically for chronic back pain	Intensity varies/20 minutes to a whole day	Increases functional use, decreases pain and assists in pain tolerance through nerve stimulation
Traction	See a health care professional	Usually 10-20 minutes/done by clinical specialist	Reduces pressure and assists in muscle relaxation. Pulling and relaxing pattern
Bracing	Adjunctive treatment suggested by health care professional	Provides protection without promoting dependence and disuse	Alleviates muscle spasms, increases joint stability

back country and try to ski expert terrain. Finally, attitude is also important in skier safety. Just because your friends might have the ability and experience to jump off a 20-foot cliff doesn't mean you should do the same.

Unfortunately, injuries are a part of any sport, including skiing. Last year alone, an average of two to four injuries occurred per 1,000 days skied. The most common were knee related, with shoulder and back injuries not far behind. Although other injuries occur in skiing, this chapter will focus primarily on the prevention and treatment of knee, shoulder and back injuries related to skiing. This book will cover different types of treatments for injuries.

Rehabilitation

Any rehabilitation program should utilize a team approach. Your rehabilitation program should return you to the highest possible level of activity while minimizing your risk of injury.

Anytime you visit a physical therapist or rehab specialist he or she should develop a program based on the demands of your daily living activities. In other words, if the program that the specialist designs for you takes 4 hours per day and you work 8 hours and have two kids, then it doesn't necessarily provide you with a workable program.

Your group or team should consist of four individuals: you, your doctor, a physical therapist, and a strength coach. You should work toward a common goal. Your doctor, physical therapist, and strength coach should converse regularly and be on the same page regarding your rehabilitation program.

The effects of immobilizing a joint or limb can be minimized by including range of motion (ROM) work, strength training, and stabilization of the injured area. Your injury should never be overstressed during the first stage of treatment. Make sure your program is progressive (changes continually according to your progress), and systematic (there must be a reason for the exercise and treatment sequence), and it maintains functionality for your life (allows for normal daily living and schedule).

Regarding functional progression, a periodized, stage-related program should be implemented. Not unlike organizing a research paper, marketing report, or anything else that requires a predetermined outcome, a rehabilitation program needs to be implemented with a guide to ensure appropriate progression. Most importantly, each phase should reduce pain and stress, while increasing mobility and strength. It also should improve posture, balance, and aerobic fitness. Each type of injury might require a different type of periodization and stage-related program.

The Knee

Knee Basics

The knee is considered one of the largest and most complex joints in the body. It is involved in almost every ski movement you perform. The knee joint provides tremendous stability and mobility in many of your everyday movements. Unfortunately, the knee joint is highly susceptible to injury. Up to 40 percent of all ski injuries are related to the knee; this is the highest percentage of all injuries that occur while on skis. How does one prevent an injury to the knee? Follow the prevention protocol that follows and you will have a better chance of staving off a trip to the doctor's office.

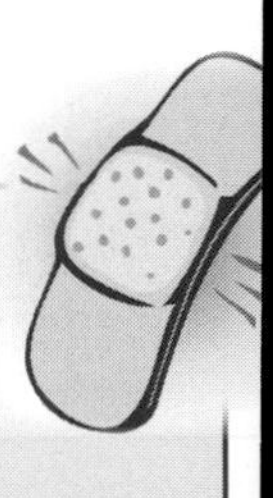

MOST COMMON SKI RELATED KNEE INJURIES

1. ACL
2. MCL
3. LCL
4. MENISCUS TEAR
5. PATELLA INJURY

Functionality

The structure of the human body greatly

Preventing ACL Injuries

1. Don't straighten your legs when you fall. Try to keep your knees slightly bent
2. Until you've stopped sliding don't attempt to stand.
3. Maintain an upward position of the arms and don't land on your hand
4. Unless you have checked the terrain below, don't jump. If you do jump, land on both skis and keep your legs bent to absorb the impact.

According to the ACL Awareness Program developed by Carl Ettinger, 62% of ACL injuries can be reduced by adhering to the above chart

depends on the knee joint because of its mobility. Some of the general movements the knee joint allows are:
Flexion and Extension
Rotation of Tibia

In full knee extension, the tibia cannot rotate, therefore making it a prime candidate for a ski injury.

Common Ski Injuries

Although the knee can handle and produce large forces, it is still susceptible to injury. The following is a detailed description of each mechanism of injury.

1. Anterior Cruciate Ligament (ACL)
   Hyperextension (locking out the knee); applying an accelerated force while laterally rotating your leg or decelerating suddenly while laterally rotating your leg; for example, skiing steep terrain, catching an edge, and twisting the leg to the side.
2. Medial Collateral or Lateral Collateral Ligaments (MCL, LCL)
   Applying outside forces from the medial or lateral portion of the knee (i.e., being hit by a skier or snowboarder from the side).
3. Medial or Lateral Meniscus
   Hyperextension; rotation of the leg laterally or medially while compressive forces are applied; for example, skiing bumps, catching an edge, and twisting the leg to the inside or outside.
4. Patellar Fracture
   Sustaining a blow or falling on the pattellafemoral joint while your knee is flexed; for example, landing on your knee while falling on hard-packed snow or ice.

Treatment

Type of Treatment	When to Use	What it Does	Intensity/Duration
Rest	Anytime	Relaxes muscles and alleviates stress	Until area of pain dissipates/ up to 72 hours
Ice	When inflammation occurs/ Immediately after injury	Decreases Pain and Inflamma-tion	Post Exercise/Wrap in towel for 15-20 minutes per session/4-5 times daily
Compression	For minor swelling or a temporary brace	Provides support to injured portion/Assists in decreasing swelling when combined with Rest and Ice	Until swelling decreases
Elevation	If swelling and discoloration are present	Allows blood to flow away from inured area decreasing swelling	At rest

Rehabilitation

Most injuries typically heal in three separate stages: inflammatory, reparation, and the remodeling stage. You should be aware of four major types of ski-related knee injuries: ACL, MCL/LCL, meniscus tears, and pattelofemoral-related injuries. In this chapter you will find charts for the rehabilitation of each of these types of injuries. They are divided into three levels of intensity, as well. Level 1 usually concerns itself with the first 3 days. This level can last up to 2 weeks. The ultimate goal of this level is to control pain, swelling, and possible damage to the injured area. Level 2 refers to weeks 2 through 12 post surgery or after the injury has occurred. The outcome of this level should be to control pain, protect the area while it is healing, and restore normal movement. Finally, level 3 typically occurs from week 5 and up to 12 months, depending on the severity of the injury or the type of surgery. During this level, you should expect to prepare the injured area to adapt to normal loads and minimize the chance for reinjury.

INFLAMMATORY STAGE/LEVEL 1

INJURY TYPE	LENGTH OF TIME	SPECIFIC GOAL	ACTIVITY
ACL	0-6 WEEKS POST SURGERY OR INJURY	PREVENT ATROPHY/CONTROL STRESSES ON INJURED AREA/ REDUCE PAIN AND SWELLING	NON WEIGHT BEARING MOVEMENTS/ CRUCHES/ CONTROLLED WALKING FOR 1-2 WEEKS/USE OF BRACE MAY BE NEEDED
MCL/LCL	0-2 WEEKS POST INJURY/ SURGERY	MAINTAIN NORMAL PATELLO-FEMORAL MOVEMENT/CONTROL STRESSES APPLIED TO INJURY/ DECREASE SWELLING	PARTIAL WEIGHT BEARING FOR 1-2 WEEKS, PROGRESSING TO FULL WEIGHT BEARING/CONTROLLED WALKING
MENISCUS TEAR	0-3 WEEKS POST SURGERY	SAME AS ABOVE	REDUCE PAIN AND CONTROLLED TOE TOUCH WEIGHT BEARING
PATELLAR INJURY JOINT DYSFUNCTION	0-2 WEEKS POST SURGERY	REDUCE PAIN AND SWELLING/ RESTORE NORMAL PATELLAR MOVEMENT	RANGE OF MOTION (ROM) EXER-CISES PERFORMED WITH PAIN FREE TOLLERANCE/STRETCHING

REPARATION STAGE/LEVEL 2

INJURY TYPE	LENGTH OF TIME	SPECIFIC GOAL	ACTIVITY
ACL	7-12 WEEKS POST SURGERY OR INJURY	PAIN FREE ROM OF KNEE FLEXION/DECREASE USE OF CRUTCHES/IMPROVE HAM-STRING AND CALF FUNCTION	PROPRIOCEPTIVE WORK AND BAL-ANCE TRAINING/SWIMMING, WALKING, CYCLING/CONTINUED OVERALL BODY CONDITIONING
MCL/LCL	2-6 WEEKS POST INJURY/ SURGERY	PAIN FREE ROM DURING KNEE FLEXION	SAME AS ABOVE FOR ACL
MENISCUS TEAR	4-8 WEEKS POST SURGERY	SAME AS ABOVE//FULL WIGHT BEARING WITH ASSISTANCE OF DEVICE AS APPROPRIATE/FULL KNEE EXTENSION	SAME AS ABOVE/50-100% WEIGHT BEAR-ING BY WEEK 8
PATELLAR INJURY JOINT DYSFUNCTION	3-4 WEEKS POST SURGERY	PAIN FREE ROM OF KNEE FLEXION/ELIMINATE NEED FOR TAPING	PROPRIOCEPTIVE AND BALANCE RE-LATED TRAINING/SWIMMING, WALKING, CYCLING/CONTINUED OVERALL BODY CONDITIONING

RECONSTRUCTION STAGE/LEVEL 3

INJURY TYPE	LENGTH OF TIME	SPECIFIC GOAL	ACTIVITY
ACL	13-16 WEEKS POST SURGERY OR INJURY	IMPROVE QUADRICEPS FUNC-TION AND PERFORMANCE/FULL ROM	CONTROLLED PROGRESSIONS OF WEIGHT LOADING TO MAXIMAL CAPACITY/WORK ON INTENSITY, VOL-UME AND REST TO PREPARE AREA TO MEET REHAB GOALS
MCL/LCL	6-10 WEEKS POST INJURY/ SURGERY	SAME AS ABOVE	SAME AS ABOVE
MENISCUS TEAR	9-20 WEEKS POST SURGERY	SAME AS ABOVE	SAME AS ABOVE
PATELLAR INJURY JOINT DYSFUNCTION	5-6 WEEKS POST SURGERY	SAME AS ABOVE	SAME AS ABOVE

Exercises for a Healthy Knee

The best way to treat a knee injury is to prevent it from getting injured in the first place. The following exercises will help strengthen the area around the knee so you will be less likely to injure it. The chart describes which exercises to perform with the recommended number of sets, repetitions, intensity level, and recovery between sets. It is important to note that although the exercises might be included in the FitSkiing workout, the repetitions, sets, and intensity have changed. Training to prevent injury is not necessarily the same as training to improve skiing power and strength. You might want to refer to Chapter 6 to refresh yourself with the aforementioned terminology.

EXERCISE	SETS	REPS	INTENSITY 1-5	RECOVERY BETWEEN SETS
Single Leg Bosu Ball Balance	2*	30 seconds to 1 minute	3	1 minute
Single Leg Press	2*	8-10	4	1.5 minutes
Lunge	2*	8-12	4	1.5 minutes
Leg Curl	2*	8-15	4	1 minute
Quadriceps Stretch	1	30 seconds to 1 minute	3	none
Hamstring Stretch	1	30 seconds to 1 minute	3	none

*Denotes that a warm-up set is not included and should be done prior to the actual work sets. Warm-up sets should be performed with 50 percent of the working set weight.

The Shoulder

Shoulder Basics

Shoulder injuries are common at almost every age and in every sport. They often occur in skiing because the skier braces the fall with an arm. Other times, the skier lands on the shoulder directly. The impact of the shoulder joint on hard-packed snow is painful. Shoulder injuries account for up to 25 percent of all skier-related injuries.

Shoulder injuries can happen acutely (for example, suddenly falling) or from repetitive strain. Two of the most common mechanisms leading to an injury to the shoulder are collisions and falls. Therefore, this section will deal with the acute injuries rather than the repetitive ones.

Functionality

The shoulder joint can produce great force and varied ranges of motions. Injuries typically create strength imbalances, weak muscles surrounding the joint, or a weak joint capsule. If any of these structural weaknesses are present, movements may be hampered. The shoulder performs the following five movements:

1. Flexion and Extension
2. Abduction and Adduction
3. External and Internal Rotation
4. Protraction and Retraction of the Scapula
5. Elevation and Depression of the Scapula

Common Shoulder Injuries

Although the shoulder can handle minor impacts such as landing directly on a hard surface like snow or ice, over time the potential for injury increases. Below you will find a brief description of some of the most common ski-related shoulder injuries.

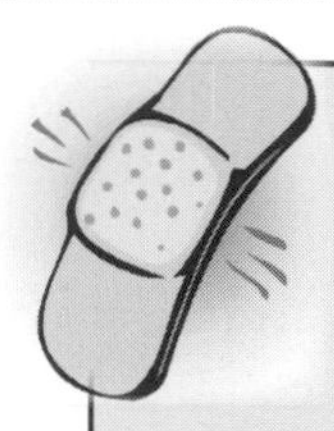

MOST COMMON SKI RELATED SHOULDER INJURIES

1. DISLOCATIONS
2. COLLAR BONE FRACTURES
3. AC JOINT SPRAINS
4. HUMERUS FRACTURES
5. ROTATOR CUFF INJURIES

1. Dislocations

Dislocating the shoulder can be painful. It normally occurs when one is skiing, loses balance, and outstretches the hand to brace the fall. The head of the humerus (top portion of the upper arm bone) is pulled out of its alignment (commonly said to be pulled out of the socket). This might require an x ray, but not always. You probably will be holding the shoulder so it does not move because if it does, it can be painful.

The sooner the shoulder is put back in place, the better. Many times the doctor can realign it right in the ski patrol office. Unfortunately, sometimes one has to go to the hospital and receive a general anesthetic. After you have dislocated your shoulder once, you are almost certain to dislocate it again. Unfortunately, the structural integrity of the joint is never as strong again. The only upside is that most of the time, it is not as painful the next time.

2. Collarbone Fractures

This is the most commonly fractured (broken) shoulder bone in the entire body. Collarbone fractures are caused by the transmission of force up the arm, which eventually is absorbed by the clavicle, resulting in a break of the bone. Typically, localized pain occurs in the area, as well as swelling. A fracture of the collarbone usually occurs between the middle and outer portion of the bone. This also happens to be the weakest area of the clavicle. The nice thing about a collarbone fracture (if there is one) is that it heals fairly quickly.

3. AC Joint Sprains

AC joint sprains normally occur during a fall that results in direct impact on the outside of the upper arm. The ligament that connects the clavicle and the shoulder blade typically is damaged and possibly tears, causing a distortion in the joint. As with any other sprain, there are three degrees of severity depending on the damage (see the following information).

4. Humerus Fractures

The humerus attaches the elbow to the shoulder. Three main types of fractures occur in skiing:

1. The upper portion of the bone breaks (affect the head and neck).
2. The middle or shaft of the bone fractres.
3. The portion near the elbow fractures.

The first two types of fractures typically happen due to direct impact to the humerus, such as a collision with a tree or a fall directly onto the bone itself. The final type of fracture typically occurs in children although it can happen to adults.

5. Rotator Cuff Injuries

I probably have seen more rotator cuff injuries in my line of work than any other type of shoulder injury. However, they are not as common in skier-related injuries. The rotator cuff basically refers to the soft tissue that holds the shoulder together and allows for the appropriate range of motion. The muscles that comprise the rotator cuff are small and basically support the shoulder joint. Therefore they are typically susceptible to injury. Many times, injuries to the rotator cuff requires aggressive physical therapy.

Below you will find treatment and rehabilitation information on shoulder injuries.

Treatment

INJURY TYPE	TREATMENT
Strain/sprain/ dislocation	Level 1. R.I.C.E. Level 2. Correct rehabilitation to prevent reoccurrence; exercises to improve strength/surgery possible Level 3. Immediate care/ putting the shoulder back in place (doctor)/ice to control possible internal bleeding and swelling/immobilization/surgery may be necessary/rehab asap
AC joint sprains	Ice Stabilization Physician referral Rehabilitation
Rotator cuff injuries	Level 1. Ice/antiinflamatories/exercise Level 2. Immobilization Level 3. Surgical repair/rehabilitation/strengthening program

Rehabilitation

Four levels of rehabilitation apply to shoulder injuries:

1. Immediate Motion
2. Mid-Level
3. Strength
4. Return to Activity

The following chart will assist you in progressing from injury back to normal daily activities. Always remember to consult your doctor before beginning any strength or rehabilitation program.

Immediate Motion

Goal	Treatment options	Progression
Establish non painful ROM/ prevent disuse atrophy/decrease pain/ decrease swelling/ eliminate muscle spasm/ improve core stability/improve balance	1. ROM: immediate motion is allowed in a protected non painful arc of motion/internal and external rotation exercises 2. Flexibility: pain free ROM 3. Strength: internal and external rotation, shoulder elevation (shrugs), scapular retraction. 4. Therapeutic modalities: used to control pain and inflammation	Non painful ROM/ minimal tenderness to the touch/ good strength of the rotator cuff and scapular muscles as determined by a physical therapist or orthopede.

Mid-Level

Goal	Treatment options	Progression
Return to full non-painful range of motion/eliminate swelling and pain/progress to full muscle control of the shoulder/correct muscle imbalances/improve overall functional movement and strength	1. Improve muscular strength and coordination 2. Resistance training may include physioband and physioball exercises. Shoulder flexion (front raise) and external rotation 3. Improve complex diagonal patterns (PNF) 4. Continue therapeutic modalities to manage pain and inflammation	75% Of strength return determined by physician or physical therapist/ no pain to the touch

Strengthening

Goal	Treatment Options	Progression
Improve muscular strength, power and neuromuscular control to normal levels/preperation for normal activity	1. Increase intensity of previously suggested exercises. 2. Lat pull-downs; seated rows (with cable tubing);bosu ball push up.	Full physical examination upon which doctor has no negative remarks regarding injury/ strength should be at 85% or greater

Return to Activity

Goal	Treatment Options	Progression
Increase levels of normal activities (i.e. skiing) progressively. Maintenance of muscular control, endurance, strength and power.	1. Patient should be placed on proper strengthening and conditioning program regarding their sport or daily activities, 2. Continually strengthen the rotator cuff muscles by performing external and internal rotation.	Return to normal activity.

Exercises for Healthy Shoulders

The best way to treat a shoulder injury is to prevent it from getting injured in the first place. The following exercises will help to strengthen the area around the shoulder so you will be less likely to injure it. The following chart describes which exercises to perform with the recommended number of sets, repetitions, intensity level, and recovery time between sets. It is important to note that although the exercises might be included in the FitSkiing workout, the repetitions, sets, and intensity have changed. Training to prevent injury is not necessarily the same as training to improve skiing power and strength. You might want to refer to Chapter 6 to refresh your memory with regard to the aforementioned terminology.

EXERCISE	SETS	REPS	INTENSITY 1-5	RECOVERY BETWEEN SETS
External Rotation	2	10-15	3	1 minute
Internal Rotation	2	10-15	3	1 minute
Front Raise w/tubing	2*	8-12	3	1 minute
Lateral Raise	2*	8-12	3	1 minute
Bosu Ball Push Up	2	10-12	3	1 minute
Overhead Stretch	1/each side	30 seconds to 1 minute	3	none

*Denotes that a warm-up set is not included and should be done prior to the actual work sets. Warm-up sets should be performed with 50 percent of the working set weight.

The Back

The spine has three purposes:

1. Maintain and support the trunk
2. Provide protection for the spinal cord and nervous system
3. Acts as a Shock Absorber

The spine is not unlike the supporting structures of a building. Although other factors that go into constructing a building, the beams and two-by-fours are what keep the house from falling. Similarly, your spine keeps your body from collapsing. Its main function is to support the head and the trunk. The spine or vertebral column is made up of individual bones called vertebrae. They are separated by soft, spongy intervertebral discs. The spinal cord has five disinct sections.

- Cervical: 7
- Thoracic: 12
- Lumbar: 5
- Sacral: 5; they are fused to form the sacrum
- Coccygeal: 4; the last 3 are fused together

The spinal cord runs through the middle of the vertebrae and carries nerves that transmit impulses that tell your muscles to contract and relax (among many other things). The more extensive the damage is to the spinal area, the higher the degree of injury is. If the spinal cord is damaged near the neck (cervical spine), it can affect function below this area. If the damage is extensive, one might become what is known as a quadriplegic. Damage to the lower portion of the back or spine might cause little functional loss. Generally speaking, the higher the injury is on the spinal cord, the more damage it will cause.

Ski-Related Back Injuries

The most user-friendly way to understand back injuries is to think of the spinal column as a series of blocks one on top of another, with a soft portion between each block (intervertebral discs). Picture a hole in the middle of each block where the cord passes. The spongelike discs allow the back or spine to flex forward, backward, and sideward. It also enables the body to rotate or twist from side to side. The strength of the blocks varies. The cervical vertebrae are weaker and small, so less force is needed

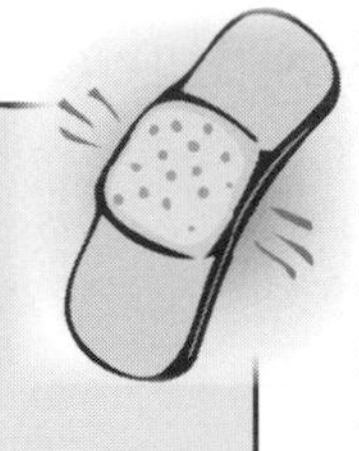

MOST COMMON SKI RELATED BACK INJURIES

1. HYPER EXTENSION (SIMILAR TO WHIPLASH)
2. COMPRESSION (BONES ARE PUSHED DOWN ONTO ONE ANOTHER)

for them to break. The lumbar vertebrae need to support more of the body and are therefore larger and stronger. A lot more force is needed to damage them. The middle of the spine, or the thoracic region, has two portions. The upper portion is easy to break; the lower portion is more difficult to injure.

When a skier falls, the forces push forward and backward causing damage to the spinal cord. Forces also can be applied downward, literally squashing the bones. This can result in a loss of height. Always ski to your own ability to mitigate any injuries.

Signs and Symptoms of Back Injuries

It is important to note that even if the injured person can move his or her limbs, it does not mean a spinal injury has not occurred. In most cases, I try to view the glass as half full, but in cases where skiers have endured high-impact forces (such as a fall), I always assume the worst. The following are common symptoms that a person will complain about if he or she has an injury to the spinal cord::

- Pain anywhere from the neck down.
- Loss of function (can't move arms or legs).
- Loss of sensation (for example, the skier might not feel pain when pinched).
- Loss of consciousness.

First Aid

The most advantageous way to learn first aid is to take a certified first aid course. The Red Cross or a local fire department are good places to contact to find out about these classes. In the text box, you will find a brief overview of what to do if a possible spinal injury has occured. This overview should not be mistaken for a certified class or viewed as a prescription to perform as a medical professional would.

FIRST AID FOR BACK INJURIES

1. Safety

The most immediate consideration in any situation involving an accident is to consider your own safety first.

2. Call 911! or Have Someone Find a Ski Patrol

Don't panic and allow the medical professionals to do there job once they arrive.

3. Keep it Basic

Keep the airway open and allow for proper breathing and circulation. Don't let a spinal injury get in the way of these two life threatening circumstances.

4. Keep the Patient Calm and Still

Do not allow the injured to move themselves unless it is a life threatening situation. The neck in particular most be kept absolutely still. The best way is to have one person hold each side of the head.

The Lower Back

The lower back is one of the most common areas that affects one's performance on skis and in everyday life. Eight out of ten adults experience lower back pain at some point in their life. Acute and chronic lower back pain accounts for more than 90 million lost production days annually. This costs businesses more than $100 billion annually.

Lower back pain can be caused by many things, including the following:

•Poor posture and body mechanics
•Stressful living
•Lack of flexibility and fitness

These are correctable and, once they are altered, will improve your odds of mitigating lower back injury and pain from reoccurring. This section discusses lower back injuries and provides strategies for strengthening this area.

Common Injuries

Acute Lower Back Pain

Occurs suddenly.
Happens when you are doing something you don't normally do.
Induces pain that normally lasts for short durations.

Chronic Lower Back Pain

Caused by any movement, typically from overdoing an activity.
Reoccurs throughout one's life.

The following chart defines common lower back injuries and ways to rehabilitate them. Always consult an orthopedic specialist before performing any of this information.

Common Injuries and Rehabilitation

Injury	Duration	Goal	Activity
Acute low back muscle strains and sprains/acute low back pain	0-4 Weeks	Protection of area injured/pain control	Ice and electric stimulation for muscle spasms
Chronic low back strains and sprains/ chronic low back pain	3-6 Months and possibly longer	Risk reduction of injury/improved biomechancs/ exercise adhereance/ maintenance of healthy body weight	Ice/heat/electrical stimulation/ultrasound
Spondylosis/ spondylolysis/ spondylolitesis	If symptomatic	Pain control/injured area protection	Ice/electrical stimulation to decrease muscle spasms
Disc bulge/disc herniation	0-12 Weeks	Injured area protection/increse mobility/mitigate pain and muscle spasms	Ice/traction/electrical stimulation

Lifestyle Changes

You can do two major things to prevent the risk of injuries to the lower back. First, educate yourself about injury prevention and when exercising or lifting, use correct body mechanics. Second, perform exercises to increase the strength of your supporting musculature. Doing the following will help you maintain proper body mechanics when lifting.

•Keep abdominals tight and avoid flexing forward at the waist with your head down.
•Lift with your legs.
•Get close to the object being lifted.
•Keep the object at waist level.

Exercises for a Healthy Back

The best way to treat a back injury is to prevent it from getting injured in the first place. The following exercises will help strengthen the area around the spine so you will be less likely to injure it. The following chart describes which exercises to perform and the recommended number of sets, repetitions, intensity level, and recovery time between sets. It is important to note that although the exercises might be included in the FitSkiing workout, the repetitions, sets, and intensity have changed. Training to prevent injury is not necessarily the same as training to improve skiing power and strength. You might want to refer to Chapter 6 to review the aforementioned terminology.

EXERCISE	SETS	REPS	INTENSITY 1-5	RECOVERY BETWEEN SETS
Opposing Arm/ Leg Extension	2	10-15	3	1 minute
Lying Back Extension	2	10-15	3	1 minute
Oblique Crunch	3	30 seconds to 1 minute	3	2 minutes
Lat Pull-down	2*	8-12	3	1 minute
Scapular Retraction	2	10-12	3	1 minute
Abdominal Crunch	3	30 seconds to 1 minute	3	1 minute

*Denotes that a warm-up set is not included and should be done prior to the actual work sets. Warm-up sets should be performed with 50 percent of the working set weight.

Now you have all of the information you could ever want about how to treat and prevent injuries right? It is hoped that FitSkiing has provided you with some valuable knowledge to assist you if you do get injured. Always remember to ski to your ability.

CHAPTER ELEVEN

BUILDING YOUR FITSKIING GYM

The original concept of the FitSkiing workout was that it could be used anywhere at any time. Although many of the exercises described throughout this book were performed in a gym, FitSkiing has provided an alternative to each exercise so it can be performed anywhere. In this chapter, you will learn:

- Whether you are a candidate for a home gym.
- How to build a FitSkiing gym for less than $100 and up.
- Where to buy the equipment for your home gym.
- The FitSkiing home workout.

Are You a Candidate for a Home Gym?

Exercising from home is a good alternative for those who are short on time, can't afford a membership to a health club, or can't seem to get motivated to the gym. Many might be interested in building a home gym but are intimidated or overwhelmed by the thought of it. Before you invest your hard-earned money or time building your gym, consider your exercise needs, available space, and budget.

Exercise Needs

If you need the social atmosphere of a health club to motivate yourself to work out, then a home gym is probably not for you. On the other hand, if want the most efficient workout and are not concerned with the juice bar crowed then a home gym might be for you. If you need lots of equipment because you like variety then a home gym probably isn't for you unless you have lots of space and money. If, however you are happy with a couple of pieces of space-saving equipment then a home gym is a great addition to your floor plan. The final thing you might want to consider is the number of people who will be using the equipment. If you have four or more people using the equipment in your home, you might want to consider a membership to a gym because it could be difficult to schedule everyone's workout. On the other hand, if it is just you and one other person, a home gym is a perfect way to get in shape for skiing in a short amount of time.

Budget

Strength and cardiovascular training equipment can be expensive. However, if you know what to look for, it can be cost-effective. Later in this chapter, you will find the perfect equipment to fit your budget. Whether you have $100 or $10,000, you can outfit a gym for your FitSkiing workouts.

Space

This is a big issue in deciding whether you are a candidate for a home gym. If you live in a closet in New York City, you are probably better off going to the gym or investing in the Base FitSkiing Gym. If you have unlimited space, then your options are numerous. Most of us are somewhere between the two. The following section offers a simple guide to help you determine how much space you will need for each piece of equipment.

Building Your Gym

Constructing your own workout space might not be as difficult as you think. Imagine having just three or four pieces of equipment that are space efficient and cost less than $1,000. The following section describes three separate home gyms in three different price categories. The Bronze Gym is a bare, bones workout center designed to get you in FitSkiing shape. The Silver Gym is an intermediate-level gym that includes more free weights. The Gold Gym includes a multi purpose machine and cardiovascular equipment. Choose the one that best fits your budget, space, and needs.

How Much Space Do You Need?

Treadmill: 30 Square Feet
Free Weights: 20-50 Square Feet
Rowing Machine: 20 Square Feet
Stair Climber: 20 Square Feet
Ski Machine: 25 Square Feet
Multi Station Machine: 100-200 Square Feet
Bosu Ball: 10 Square Feet
Jump Rope: 10 Square Feet
Fit Ball: 10-20 Square Feet

The Bronze Gym (The FitSkiing Gym): Less than $100
Fit Ball: $25
Resistance Band Set: $20 to $35
Yoga Mat: $20
Total: $65 to $80
*See the FitSkiing Home Gym Workout

The Silver Gym: Less Than $500
Bosu Ball: $100
Set of Selecterized Dumbbells (5 to 45 pounds.): $250
Fit Ball: $25
Yoga Mat: $20
Resistance Band Set: $20 to $35
Total: $415 to $430

The Gold Gym: Less Than $7000
Multi Purpose Machine: $1,000 to $,3500
Elliptical Machine: $1,000 to $2,500
Bosu Ball: $100
Fit Ball: $25
Set of Selecterized Dumbbells (5 to 85 pounds.): $750
Resistance Band Set: $20 to $35
Yoga Mat: $20
Total: $2,915 to $6,930

Where to Buy Equipment

A local equipment dealer can help you find the equipment best suited for you. If you don't have a dealer close by or you simply don't have the time, the Web sites below will help you find what you need. You also can visit www.fitskiing.com for more information.
www.bodytrends.com
www.performbetter.com

The FitSkiing Home Workout

The FitSkiing workout at home includes exercises that can be found in Chapter 8. Even though this is a different workout than those in Chapter 7 you should still find your FitSkiing baseline fitness level in Chapter 2. Where your baseline fitness level ranks on the scale will determine the duration and intensity of your workouts. Follow the general phase guidelines in Chapter 7 for the Basic or Advanced workout. The following are the exercises you should perform in the FitSkiing home workout. Follow the "Improve Overall Strength and Condition" stage of the Basic or Advanced program for 6 weeks instead of 4 weeks. Repeat it once. After 12 weeks, you should be ready for the slopes.

Home Program
Weight Training Workout One/Three
Transverse Abdominal Hold*
Lunge
Lateral Lunge
Fit Ball Leg Curl
Step Up
Reverse Calf Raise (manual resistance)
Crunch*
Back Extension*
Downward Dog
Hip Stretch
Quadriceps Stretch
Hamstring Stretch
**Perform as many repetitions as possible*

Home Program
Weight Training Workout Two
Transverse Abdominal Hold*
Push Up (Bosu Ball Optional)
Straight Arm Pull-down (Bosu Ball Optional)
Biceps Curl with Resistance Bands
Triceps Press-down with Resistance Bands
Front Raise with Resistance Bands
Lateral Raise with Resistance Bands
Fit Ball Reverse Crunch*
Opposing Arm/Leg Extension*
Downward Dog
Overhead Stretch
Lat Stretch
Chest Stretch
**Perform as many repetitions as possible*

That is the FitSkiing Home Gym workout. Now start training; the snow will be falling soon!

"KNOWLEDGE SPEAKS BUT WISDOM LISTENS."

-JIMMY HENDRIX

CHAPTER TWELVE

FREQUENTLY ASKED QUESTIONS

Q. I'm confused about how to determine which FitSkiing program I should be performing. How do I know if I should be using the Basic or Advanced workout?

A. In Chapter 2, where you determine your FitSkiing baseline fitness level, you will find a system to help you decide which program you should be performing. If you still have trouble figuring out which program to complete, start with the Basic program. If it is not challenging enough, move to the Advanced program. You should always start with something a little easier and then progress to the more advanced training.

Q. My motivation just doesn't seem to be there. What can I do to help motivate me to train?

A. This is probably one of the most difficult aspects of anything you do. Whether it is getting into shape for the ski season or going to work, motivation can be the key to success. Reread Chapter 3 on defining your goals. This should help you develop a program to reach your goals. If you are still having trouble with your motivation, subscribe to magazines such as *Ski* or *Skiing*. The different articles and pictures might help motivate you to start training. I like to post different photos or pictures from different magazines on my refrigerator to get me excited about the season. I also watch old Warren Miller films to motivate me to train.

Q. I am having trouble sticking to the diet outlined in Chapter 5. What sorts of things will help keep me on track?

A. Another tough area for many people to tackle is revamping their eating habits. First, don't think of eating as a diet. Many people find that cheating once or twice a week with something they enjoy helps them stay on track. On the other hand, some people find that if they cheat once, then they continue cheating. Try to find foods that are recommended in Chapter 5 that you enjoy eating. After a while, eating healthy will become a habit just like anything else. When you are out for a day on the slopes, you can diverge from your normal eating habits because you are burning so many more calories. This is not a platinum card to drink a case of beer, however. Like anything worthwhile, eating to get in the best shape of your life might be somewhat challenging at first.

Q. Do I have to stick with the exact exercises in the FitSkiing workout? I really like power cleans and the bench press.

A. By all means, perform exercises that you enjoy doing. The FitSkiing workout is designed for skiers and, therefore, all the exercises will benefit your skiing. However, if you want to throw on a power clean instead of another exercise once in a while, that is perfectly okay. The bench press is a great exercise for developing overall upper body power. The dumbbell bench press, which is included in the FitSkiing workout, is more ski specific because you are using independent arm action or unilateral movement. However, the barbell bench press can be used instead on occasion if you like. It is probably best suited for stage 3, improving power endurance, speed, and balance.

Q. I am training with the Basic FitSkiing program and want to try some of the advanced plyometric exercises. Is that ok?

A. It is fine to try some of the advanced plyometric exercises; however, you should find a certified strength and conditioning specialist to help guide you through them. Remember to start out slowly until you feel comfortable with the exercise, and progressively increase the speed and intensity.

Q. My FitSkiing baseline fitness level put me in the advanced category, but it is a little tough to complete. Should I switch to the Basic program?

A. It is always best to start out with a slightly easier program and then progress to the more intense training. If you jump into something too quickly and it is too difficult, then you risk injury and overtraining. Start with the Basic program for stage 1, and then progress to the Advanced program for stages 2 and 3.

Q. How do I know if I am overtraining?

A. Overtraining is common, especially with athletes and those who want results quickly. The following are some common symptoms of overtraining. If you notice any of these, stop your training for a couple of days and then begin your workouts again. If you still feel the symptoms, you might not be eating enough or something more serious might be the cause. Consult your doctor if any of the following symptoms persist for more than a week.

Excessive fatigue
Lack of appetite
Depression
Lack of mental focus
Muscle soreness for more than a week in a specific body part
Nausea
Decrease in strength or overall performance
Fatiguing too quickly

Q. The exercises and descriptions in Chapter 8 are great, but I want something easier to carry for recording my workouts when I am training. Is a FitSkiing workout log available?

A. It will be available soon. The FitSkiing workout log will be available in December 2003, and will provide all the exercises and quick reference guides that the book includes. It also will have a workout log where you can record your results.

Q. I am a little concerned about my children training with weights. Is weight training safe for children?

A. Being concerned is a good sign that you will take the time and energy to monitor your children's workouts properly. Although many regard weight training for children as unsafe because their growth plates might close too early and the could damage their bones, new studies have shown that children who train with weights are more likely to stave off injury and have more confidence when they are playing sports. On the other hand, it is important that children have proper weight-training instruction in a safe environment. It is also important that children not try to lift weights too heavy for them, because they are more susceptible to injury than adults are.

Q. Should I have parents sign a release of liability if I have other children training at my house or gym?

A. Yes. You always should be aware that you are responsible for the children you are supervising. To be totally risk free, hire a trainer who specializes in working with youth athletes. Find an ACSM or NSCA, certified strength and conditioning specialist to ensure proper training and instruction.

Q. I am thinking of hiring a personal trainer. How do I know if he or she is qualified?

A. Hiring a personal trainer or strength coach is a great idea, especially when you first start training. A good trainer will have at least a bachelor's degree in an exercise-related filed, 2 or more years of experience as a trainer, and a certificate from a reputable certification institution. The American College of Sports Medicine, National Strength and Conditioning Association, American Council on Exercises or International Sports Sciences Association are good certifying companies. You also should look for someone who meshes well with your personality. If you have a hard time getting motivated, you don't want a trainer who is quiet and reserved. If you have a somewhat dominating personalitty, find a trainer who is more easygoing yet secure and who can take a few punches.

Q. How much should I spend on a trainer?

A. That is a tough question to answer. It depends on the area and their credentials. If you are in parts of the Midwest for example, the going rate for a trainer with only a fitness-related certification is about $35 per session. In parts of California the same trainer might charge about $50 per session. If your trainer has a degree in nutrition and is an RD or nutritionist, expect to pay about $100 or more per session. If you are working with a strength coach who has a master's degree or Ph.D., then expect to pay about $100 or more per session. Like anything else, you should pay a trainer what he or she is worth. If your trainer stands around just counting repetitions and has little education or experiece with training then you shouldn't pay more than about $20 per session. If, on the other hand the trainer designs a new program for you every month and helps you with your nutrition and motivation, then pay them accordingly. I have worked with trainers who charge $50 per session and I end up tipping them an extra $20 because they are worth it.

Q. The chapter on Preventing and Treating Injuries provides some great information. Is there another resource you can recommend for more in depth information?

A. In the Appendices you will find an Further Reading section, that recommends other resources for more information. Many colleges and universities also offer great continuing education programs in athletic training.

Q. Will there be an updated version of FitSkiing in the future?

A. As long as people find FitSkiing helpful and useful, a new version will be updated every 2 to 5 years. Until then, you can log on to www.fitskiing.com for updated information and new articles every month.

FITSKIING MEAL PLANNER MENU TRACKER Day 1	
Meal Number	**Food**
1	
2	
3	
4	
5	
6	

FITSKIING MEAL PLANNER MENU TRACKER Day 2	
Meal Number	**Food**
1	
2	
3	
4	
5	
6	

FITSKIING MEAL PLANNER MENU TRACKER Day 3	
Meal Number	**Food**
1	
2	
3	
4	
5	
6	

FITSKIING MEAL PLANNER MENU TRACKER Day 4	
Meal Number	**Food**
1	
2	
3	
4	
5	
6	

FITSKIING MEAL PLANNER
MENU TRACKER
Day 5

Meal Number	Food
1	
2	
3	
4	
5	
6	

FITSKIING MEAL PLANNER MENU TRACKER Day 6	
Meal Number	**Food**
1	
2	
3	
4	
5	
6	

FITSKIING MEAL PLANNER
MENU TRACKER
Day 7

Meal Number	Food
1	
2	
3	
4	
5	
6	

Workout 1
Weight Training

Exercise	Seat Adjustment	Week 1 Weight/Reps	Week 2 Weight/Reps	Week 3 Weight/Reps	Week 4 Weight/Reps

Workout 2

Weight Training

Exercise	**Seat Adjustment**	**Week 1** Weight/Reps	**Week 2** Weight/Reps	**Week 3** Weight/Reps	**Week 4** Weight/Reps

Workout 3
Weight Training

Exercise	Seat Adjustment	Week 1 Weight/Reps	Week 2 Weight/Reps	Week 3 Weight/Reps	Week 4 Weight/Reps

Interval Training				
Interval Number	Week 1 Time	Week 2 Time	Week 3 Time	Week 4 Time
Example	**120 Seconds**	**120 seconds**	**110 seconds**	**120 seconds**
1				
2				
3				
4				
5				
6				
7				
8				
9				
10				

Speed Training Workout 1					
Week	1	2	3	4	**Example**
Number of Intervals					**5**
RPE					**8 to 9**
Rest Between Intervals					**2 Minutes**

Speed Training Workout 2					
Week	1	2	3	4	**Example**
Number of Intervals					**10**
RPE					**9**
Rest Between Intervals					**2 Minutes**

Speed Training Workout 3					
Week	1	2	3	4	**Example**
Number of Intervals					**15**
RPE					**9 to 10**
Rest Between Intervals					**2 Minutes**

APPENDIX C
RECOMMENDED READING

1. The Athletic Skier
2. Nutrition for Dummies
3. Strength Training Anatomy
4. Optimum Sports Nutrition
5. Self Matters
6. Jumping Into Plyometrics
7. Breakthrough On the New Skis
8. Ski the Whole Mountain
9. Body for Life
10. Complete Idiots Guide to Strength Training

APPENDIX D

FORTHCOMING BOOKS FROM ACTIVE MEDIA

2004

FitWork©: *Your Guide to Peak Performance; Before, During and After Work*
Available Fall 2004

FitKids©: *Your Comprehensive Guide to Health and Fitness for Kids*
Available Winter 2004

2005

FitGolf©: *Your Guide to Peak Golf Performance*
Available Spring 2005

FitSkin©: *Your Guide to Healthy and Vibrant Skin*
Available Summer 2005

FitRunning©: *Your Guide to Peak Running Performance*
Available Fall 2005

www.actvmedia.com